The Reverie

JASON SHPRINTZ

Corner Store Press, LLC
Philadelphia

Corner Store Press, LLC
Philadelphia, PA
www.cornerstorepress.com

This book is a work of fiction. Names, characters, places, and incidents either are products of the author's imagination or are used fictitiously. Any resemblance to actual events or locales or persons, living or dead, is entirely coincidental.

Cover designed by Dominic Davi
www.dominicdavi.com

For more information about author Jason Shprintz visit
www.jasonshprintz.com

ISBN 978-0-9903803-1-3 (pbk)

To Mom, Dad, and Jen

PART ONE

ONE

5:44 p.m. – Roulette Table 22

After a steady decline over the span of several hours, Martin shuffled the eighty dollars' worth of chips in front of him as the dealer spun the wheel. He asked the man sitting across the table the score of the Lakers game.

"Lakers still up twenty-seven. How many times you gonna ask me that?"

"Every minute till the game's over."

Martin grabbed a stack of baby-blue chips and moved them around the board. He almost always played the same numbers: six, sixteen, twenty-six, and thirty-six. When he felt frisky, he'd split the zeroes or go hard on a random number, looking for a quick hit.

"How much you got riding on it?" the man asked him.

"A lot," answered Martin.

"How much is a lot?"

"Enough to make me wanna ask the score every minute till the game's over."

Martin wasn't trying to be rude to the man, despite his smartass remark. Once a bet was in play, he made a point to never talk about it until it was done—a gambler's superstition that he played very close to the chest.

"No more bets," the dealer said, waving his hand over the board for the eye-in-the-sky.

Martin watched as the ball dropped and bounced off the spinning wheel. It looked for a moment as if it might land on twenty-six, but then it hopped out in the final seconds and rested on thirty.

"Thirty, red," the dealer said, placing his marker on the number and clearing the rest of the board with one swipe of his left arm, picking up another hundred or so for the casino.

Martin leaned back in his chair and tried to catch a glimpse of the game on the television across the room, but the angle wouldn't allow it. He bent over the table to ask the same man as before, "What's the Lakers score now?"

"Tell ya what, buddy. You tell me what you want the score to be, and I'll tell you when it gets there." He was a younger man in his late twenties, with dark, tousled hair and dressed in a striped blazer with a starched, lime-green shirt under it. His growing annoyance with Martin was about as noticeable as his sharp clothing.

"Place your bets, gentlemen," the dealer said.

Martin grabbed another twenty baby-blue chips and scattered them in stacks of five on the sixes, then stood up to check the score himself. The Lakers were up by twenty-six now, with just under two minutes left. The spread was a substantial twenty-two points, and Martin had bet that the Lakers would beat it. He needed them to beat the spread. Everything in his world depended on the Lakers beating that spread.

He made his way back to the table just in time to hear the dealer say, "No more bets."

The ball bounced around, again almost finding a home on twenty-six before ricocheting out and landing on zero.

"Zero," announced the dealer.

Just like that, the young man in the blazer had won a little over fifty dollars.

Martin sneered. "The one time I don't split the zeroes," he mumbled to himself. "Of course it hits now."

"So are you a big Lakers fan?" the blazer man asked as he collected his yellow chips, leaving several behind as a tip for the dealer.

"Only when they beat the spread," Martin retorted.

"Who are they against? Detroit? Damn. That musta been one hell of a spread, pal. What was it, like twenty or something?"

"Twenty-two," Martin replied, annoyed that he was breaking his own gambler's code by even mentioning it.

"And they're up by what? Ugh! Twenty-six?"

Martin nodded his head as he moved his twenty baby-blue chips around: six, sixteen, twenty-six, thirty-six. The dealer spun.

"Relax. You're looking pretty good. They're in the final two minutes. Name's Dan, by the way. Nice to meet ya." Dan extended his hand.

Martin shook it without much energy or grip. He was a little embarrassed about how sweaty his palms were, yet still very uninterested in making a good impression. His attentions were elsewhere.

"No more bets," announced the dealer, waving his hand.

"And you are?" Dan asked after a drawn-out pause.

"Martin. It's nice to meet you," Martin replied more out of reflex than anything. His fingers shuffled his remaining twenty dollars' worth of chips. His eyes were so focused on his hands that he never bothered to look up and see the ball land.

"Seventeen, black," announced the dealer.

Martin moved the final stack around: six, sixteen, twenty-six, thirty-six. He then walked over to watch the game as a Pistons player stole the ball from the Lakers center and slammed it through the hoop in a crowd-pleasing dunk. Meanwhile, the rest of his team struggled, down by twenty-six points.

"What are you doing?" Martin asked the Detroit Pistons player through the television. "You're down by twenty-six. Just fucking lose already!" He dragged himself back to the roulette table in time to see the dealer swiping all of his chips off the board.

Dan hit his zero again and was all smiles about it.

Martin mumbled math under his breath: "Down 300, plus another two at craps. Seven-to-six odds. It was worth it…worth it."

He walked back over in time to see the game go to a commercial.

"Hey, Martin, how far ahead are the Lakers?" shouted Dan from across the floor.

"Twenty-six!" Martin shouted back. He then headed toward the ATM, still talking to himself. "I can collect on Wednesday, get paid on Friday. The money'll hold over. I can collect on Wednesday, pay Jenny on Thursday, get paid on Friday…" He swiped Jenny's card, punched in her PIN, and accepted the $5 surcharge before withdrawing the remaining $200 cash balance and heading back to the roulette table. As Martin approached, the dealer waved his hand, signaling no more bets.

"Let's hope for twenty-six, huh, Marty?"

Martin looked up and saw that Dan had put ten dollars on twenty-six. He gripped his hands into fists as the ball dropped, rebounded off the wheel, and continued to jump around the numbers until it fell in a casual manner on twenty-six.

"Twenty-six, black," announced the dealer.

"Hell yeah!" Dan cheered, pumping his fists in the air around him. "Now that's a come-up! What are the Lakers now?"

Martin shook his head in disgust.

"Nickels please," he told the dealer, pushing the ten fresh twenties across the board.

"Nickels inside," the dealer repeated, pushing two stacks of red back over to him.

Martin placed his bets on the four sixes before walking back to the game. There was less than a minute left, and the Lakers were up twenty-four points with possession of the ball.

"C'mon, Marty! How much they up?" Dan asked from across the room.

"Twenty-four!" Martin shouted. He watched as Dan dropped ten dollars down on twenty-four, and the wheel spun.

A Lakers player lined up at the foul line, but he missed the first shot almost in time with Dan hitting again, this time on twenty-four. Dan's uproarious cheer from the table made Martin sick. He walked back over and placed his chips on the four sixes, this time doubling his normal bet, placing ten dollars on each six for a total bet of forty dollars. Dan smiled in his direction, but Martin did not reciprocate, at least not until he walked back over to the television in time to watch the player make his second free throw attempt, putting the Lakers up twenty-five.

"What's the good word, Marty? Where they at?" Dan asked again.

"Up twenty-five!" Martin shouted back. His phone vibrated, and Jenny's name appeared on the screen. After a deep, cautious breath, he answered, "Hey, baby."

"Hey. Where are you? Are we still going out for dinner?"

"Umm…damn, I forgot all about that. I'm downstairs on a hot streak right now."

Silence.

"What's wrong, baby?"

"Martin, honey, you shouldn't be gambling. We talked about this."

"No, you don't understand. I'm about to win big on the Lakers."

"I knew we shouldn't have come here. We shoulda just gone on that cruise like my Mom suggested."

"Baby, did you hear me? I'm about to win big on the Lakers!"

"Twenty-five! Son of a bitch! Unbelievable!" Dan's voice could be heard from across the room.

Martin squinted and saw the illuminated board stationed above the roulette table light up with twenty-five.

"Wait a minute. Goddamn it, Martin! Did you take your boss's deposit money?"

Silence

"Goddamn it! Martin, that's over $5,000! You're gonna lose your job! I'm coming down. Don't move…and please stop gambling!"

"No, it's okay. Really. I'm winning. We're winning. We're gonna win big, baby!"

"Don't move!" Jenny shouted through the phone.

Martin looked toward the game. The Lakers were up by twenty-three with the ball and the shot clock unplugged. The Pistons had no chance to win, but Martin still had a chance to lose. In order for it to happen, Detroit would have to force a foul, get the ball back after a missed foul shot from the Lakers, and score. The likelihood of Detroit even bothering to force a foul while down twenty-three was so slim that when it happened, it made Martin's stomach twitch.

"Twenty-six again! Hell yeah!" Dan shouted, high-fiving anyone and everyone within arm's reach.

Martin ran back to the table. His $140 (or rather Jenny's) was still sitting uninvolved on the sidelines. He cursed himself for forgetting to bet and tripled up this time to make up for it. He then put the remaining eighty on black and ran over to the television, where a small crowd was forming.

"What's going on here?" he asked a young man in the center of the group.

"Detroit just forced a foul on LA, down by twenty-three! You believe that shit?"

The young man laughed and motioned to his friend beside him. "Yo, Phil, what was the spread on this game?"

"Twenty-one or twenty-two, I think."

"Damn, some poor son of a bitch is sweatin' this one, huh?"

Martin heard them, but he wasn't listening. His immediate focus was on the game. The Lakers player had two free throws, and even if he missed both of them, Detroit would only have six seconds to score. It still looked good for Martin, but it should have already been over.

The player shot and made his first free throw. Martin smiled and tapped his knee in approval. He caught a glimpse of Jenny walking out of the elevator doors and flagged her over to watch.

The same Lakers player lined up again on the second throw and took a shot. The ball ricocheted off the rim and bounced into the hands of a Pistons point guard.

Jenny made her way up the ramp, shaking her head in disappointment.

With six seconds left, the player maneuvered up the court.

"Seriously, Martin, no more gambling. We talked about this!"

Four seconds left…

"Five, red," announced the dealer as he dragged Martin's $140 bet toward the casino side of the table.

The player stepped over the three-point line and into the paint.

Three seconds left…

"I'll be right back," Jenny said, fumbling through her purse. "I'm gonna withdraw some money for dinner. When I get back, we're leaving! No arguments."

Two seconds left…

The Pistons player fired the ball back to his teammate, who was behind the three-point line.

One second left…

His teammate shot the ball toward the net. The buzzer went off, the light on the backboard illuminated, and the ball went in for the three, never touching the rim. The ticker at the bottom of the screen read: "Final score: Lakers - 110 | Pistons – 89."

"Hey, do you have my debit card?" Jenny asked as she searched through her purse. She looked up at Martin, who hadn't taken his eyes off the screen. "Wow, you were really right about those Lakers," she said. "Just to be on the safe side, though, I wanna carry the rest of our money. Honestly, I don't know what I would have done if you had lost that five grand."

TWO

5:44 p.m. – Blackjack Table 7

Alex, Sean, and Tim all dressed up for Alex's bachelor party the only way white, twenty-something American males knew how: by wearing blazers with button-up shirts underneath and matching slacks. Tim's was as plain as his personality, a wrinkled tan blazer and a pale, canary yellow striped shirt tucked into his waistband. Alex was a little more adventurous, dressed in a black blazer with a crisp, royal purple shirt. Sean was the dark horse of the trio; his blazer matched Alex's, but he coupled it with a starched gray shirt underneath. He left one less button fastened than Tim or Alex and had splashed himself with a fair amount of cologne as well. The three were the best-dressed men in the casino; the other occupants consisted mostly of senior citizens in sweatpants and fanny packs. They sat at a blackjack table in the Hotel Reverie and conversed as they waited for two more to join their group.

"Place your bets, gentlemen."

"So, Alex, are you excited about the wedding?" Tim asked, dropping a ten-dollar bet on the marker in front of him.

"Man, ya know, truthfully I am, but at the same time, I'm looking forward to it being over with."

"What do you mean?"

"Well, there's just so much planning and work involved. Her parents want a religious wedding, and my parents expect some big production. It makes for a lot of…tough financial compromises."

"Seriously, you must be killing your bank account on this thing," Sean said. "Hit me, dealer." He tapped his hand on the felt next to his thirteen, and the dealer drew a jack, busting Sean at twenty-three.

"Her folks are helpin' out a lot," Alex said, "and mine are too, really. It's just tough, and I'm looking forward to settling down after it's all said and done."

"You two wanna have kids?" Tim asked.

Sean chuckled. "Really, Tim?" he asked, placing another twenty-dollar bet on the table. "You're gonna ask this poor son of a bitch about kids?"

"Why not? He's getting married."

"Why not just cut his balls off right now?"

"Hey, man! There's nothin' bad about wanting to start a family with the woman you love," Tim said, more so to Alex than to Sean.

"Alex, listen to me, man." Sean placed his arm around Alex, drawing his buddy close. "Seriously, you know I love ya, man…and you know I think Melissa is the hottest thing on the East Coast—definitely the hottest chick you're ever gonna get in your lifetime—"

"Thank you."

"You're welcome, but the point is that you've only known her what, a year?"

"Three."

"Three years? Whatever. You're only twenty-eight, man. You've got your whole life ahead of you, plenty of time to fuck it up by having kids."

"Twenty-eight is the perfect time to start thinking about having kids," Tim said, tapping his finger next to his thirteen.

The dealer flipped over a seven.

"I think we're gonna wait till we know whether or not she's getting the job in Ohio anyway," said Alex. "We don't want to move around too much once we have kids, and we won't know about the job for a year or so."

The dealer flipped over fifteen, then hit for a six to make twenty-one, outdoing everyone else at the table. "Place your bets, gentlemen."

"Damn it, man," Sean said, shaking his head at Alex. "Marriage, kids…when the hell did you grow up?"

"Shit, I haven't grown up at all. I still have my old beer bong."

"But do you *use* it?" Sean asked. "Nope. You don't even chug beer anymore. You just sit at the house drinking chardonnay and munching on almonds, catching up on episodes of *American Idol* while Melissa complains about her day."

"Don't forget the part where I rub her feet."

"Oh, brother. Say it ain't so."

"Well actually, she's more into *The Voice* than *American Idol*."

The three men laughed until the dealer surprised them with twenty-one again.

"Damn, man," Sean said. "Keep this up, and I'm gonna be down 100 bucks in just ten minutes." His hand shuffled through his remaining chips as he portioned a stack to bet.

"I wonder how Dan is doing right now," Alex said, placing a fifteen-dollar bet in front of him.

"Right. Where is that weed-smoking son of a bitch anyway?" Sean asked Alex, matching his fifteen-dollar bet and then adding five more.

"He's playing roulette right now. He told me to text him when Joey gets here. Do you think he's up or down?"

"Probably down more than the three of us combined," Sean said. "Dan's always been a gambler, but he isn't much of a winner."

"Yeah, he's been gambling for so long you'd think he'd be better by now," Alex joked.

The three men laughed again as the dealer dealt Alex blackjack.

"Whoa! There it is! And I was about to accuse the system of being rigged!"

"It *is* rigged, buddy," Sean said. "They don't have all this fancy shit for giving away money."

Tim leaned over to the other two men, feeling left out of the conversation. "So when did you realize Melissa's the girl for you?" he asked Alex.

"Jesus Christ!" Sean said, jerking his head back and throwing his arms in the air. "This is meant to be a fucking bachelor party. We're not even supposed to mention her name."

"You said it first," Tim corrected.

"Did I?"

"Actually, Tim's right," Alex said.

"Well, I'll be damned. I guess I fucked it up then, but no more from here on out. Seriously, what we need is a blonde with big titties. Wait…is she-who-will-not-be-mentioned a brunette?"

Alex shrugged. "More of a very dirty blonde."

"In that case, we need a platinum blonde with big titties, a great ass, and three beers. Where do you think we can find one of those, Fred?"

The dealer smiled as he collected the losing bets off the table. "I'm pretty sure if you look around this hotel hard enough, you'll find what you're looking for," he said.

"See? That's just what I wanna hear. Thanks, Fred. This one's for you." Sean flicked a five-dollar chip Fred's way.

"Thank you very much, sir. Place your bets, gentlemen."

"So what we need to do," Sean continued, "is hit that Irish bar next to the lobby. You guys see the tail in there?"

"I didn't see any," Tim mumbled, placing his ten-dollar bet down in front of him.

"What's your plan?" Alex asked.

"I say we find a group of girls traveling, on vacation or whatever. We buy 'em a bunch of drinks, take 'em upstairs, and get 'em naked. Earlier today, you said you didn't want any strippers, but you never said anything about normal girls stripping."

Alex laughed. "Solid argument," he said, patting Sean on the back. "I can't say I approve, but I'd love to watch you try."

"Well, you'll get your wish, because as soon as Joey's finished checking us in, that's where we're going."

"No way, man," Tim argued. "I'm starving. We gotta eat something."

"Tim, it's a bar. Get some fucking hot wings or something."

"I don't want any fucking hot wings. I want a real dinner."

"What is this, a date? Want me to take you to a movie and give you a goodnight kiss too?"

"Fellas!" Alex held his arms up between them to signify peace. "We'll go to dinner first, then go to the bar. It's better if they're already kind of drunk when you start anyway, right?" he asked Sean.

Sean let out a small chuckle and nodded his head.

"Fair enough," he said with a smirk. "All right, buddy. It's your night. Dinner, then pussy. Have it your way."

"So I take it you don't ever plan on getting married?" Tim asked Sean.

"Nope," Sean snapped without hesitation. "Truthfully, I find the whole thing outdated and absurd. Men were once the breadwinners and women were the caregivers. That system worked. Now women are empowered. They follow careers and strive to achieve independence. I'm not looking for that in a chick."

"You'd prefer them to be dependent on you?" asked Alex.

"Meh, I guess not totally, but I still don't think the marriage formula really works anymore. Too many of those empowered women end up divorcing their deadbeat, foot-rubbing, *Voice*-watching, piece-of-shit husbands…no offense."

"None taken."

"Then they leave because they can. Women like you so much more when they think they can't have you. The minute they have you, they don't want you anymore."

"I'm pretty sure many of the women you've been with could say the same thing about you," Tim said.

"I'm sure they could, but it's not gonna be me on the other end. I've got no problems picking up strange girls in bars and fulfilling all my sick, twisted, sexual desires with them for one or two encounters. Shit, I bet a year from now, Melissa won't even suck your dick anymore."

"Hey! You're not supposed to say her name," Fred chimed in.

The trio erupted in laughter, and each tipped Fred an extra five.

"Fuck," Sean continued. "All right, maybe we should just get off the subject of women."

"Right. Let's talk about…love," Tim said, perking his head up as he did.

Sean rolled his eyes and feigned extreme pain. "Are you serious right now?" he asked Tim in exaggerated disbelief.

"You have a very interesting view on marriage," Tim said. "I noticed love doesn't seem to have anything to do with it."

"Thanks, Dr. Phil. I have plenty of love in my life. Like right now, I'd *love* a nine to hit." Sean tapped his hand.

Fred turned over a seven, making nineteen.

"Now I'd *love* for that to be good enough."

"What's up, faggots?" Joey announced as he walked up to the table. In strong contrast to the rest of the group, Joey was dressed in an extra large red sweater to accommodate his husky build. His tan khakis were held up by the last link on his brown leather belt.

"Thank God you're here, Joey," Sean said. He jumped off the stool to shake Joey's hand. "Tim was about to share a poem on the joys of getting butt fucked by the woman you love."

"Alex, is this true?" Joey asked.

"I think Tim's poem is sweet," Alex said, "and somewhat disturbingly graphic."

"Fuck all you assholes," Tim said, turning his head away in embarrassment. "Show me something pretty, Fred." He tapped his hand on the felt.

Fred flipped over an eight, making a very pretty twenty-one. Fred then flipped over his own cards to reveal a twenty.

"Thank you, Fred," Tim said, leaving an extra five for a tip.

"Anytime, sir."

Joey passed out the room keys and went on and on about the amazing suite.

When he asked what they were going to do next, Alex said, "I'll text Dan to tell him you're here. Then let's get some dinner."

THREE

6:52 p.m. – Deluxe

Deluxe was nestled on the second floor of the hotel. The dining room was enclosed by glass walls on three sides, providing an excellent view for diners, though there was little to see other than the lobby. Adjacent to the lobby was McKilligen's Pub, and outside the building was a barren highway and desert for miles. Deluxe was intended to be a four-star restaurant, but any serious critic wouldn't have given it more than two. The place looked nice enough on the outside, but the inside was a reminder that books shouldn't be judged by their covers: torn tablecloths, worn-out booths, fingerprinted glassware, and folded paper napkins stuffed under the table legs to keep them from tilting.

Obeying the "Please Seat Yourself" sign, Joey, Tim, Sean, and Alex made their way to a table in the center of the dining room. Similarly to the casino, Alex, Sean, and Tim were the sharpest-looking people there. However, the restaurant was much less crowded than the casino—only two other tables were occupied.

"Swanky place, Joey," Alex said as he pulled his chair out from under the table.

"Yeah, well, the brochure said it's a four-star restaurant," Joey answered. "Only the best for the bachelor."

"*This* place gets four stars?" Tim asked in disbelief.

"Yeah, man. Don't you recognize class when you see it?" Joey responded. He laid his napkin out over his potbelly and opened the menu.

Tim gave Alex a look of skepticism before gazing back at his own menu.

"So…anybody wanna call Dan?" asked Sean.

"I tried, but he didn't answer," Alex said, checking his phone for confirmation. "That means one of two things. Either he's on a hot streak and doesn't want to leave, or else he's on a cold streak…and doesn't wanna leave."

The four men exchanged glances before agreeing that Dan was on a cold streak.

At that precise moment, a pale waitress with chestnut hair walked over to greet them. "Hello, gentlemen. My name's Janice. What can I start you fellas off with?"

"Four shots of Jameson!" Joey announced without looking up from his menu.

"I don't do shots," Tim said, so soft-spoken that nobody had heard him.

"I'll take a Guinness as well," said Alex.

"Make that two," Joey added.

"I'll have two of whatever you drink," said Sean.

"Whatever *I* drink?" Janice asked.

"Yeah—one for me and one for you."

"Uh, that's very nice of you, mister…"

"Sean. My name's Sean."

"Sean, that's very nice of you, but they don't let me drink while I work."

"Well, what time do you get off work?" Sean asked.

Janice let out a little laugh. "I see you boys are gonna give me a lot of trouble."

"Nah, only this one," said Alex, pointing his thumb in Sean's direction.

"Mm-hmm," Janice replied.

"Well, maybe this one too," he said, now pointing at Joey. "You may need to bring in backup."

"I might just do that. But in the meantime, I'll be right back with your drinks." She walked toward the bar, and then turned to talk to another waitress who was already standing there.

"Jesus, man. The fucking waitress?" Tim asked, arching an eyebrow at Sean.

"Are you serious? She's hot, man," Sean said, gawking at her.

"She is pretty hot," confirmed Alex.

Joey concurred, nodding in silent agreement as his eyes read every detail of every dish.

Tim squirmed in his seat. "Why didn't you just hit one of those two old-ass broads downstairs at the blackjack table?" he scoffed, embarrassed that he was the only one who felt it was inappropriate

"Because neither one of them had an ass like that," said Sean, drawing his eyes to the curvature of Janice's bottom half.

"Watch it now, buddy. You're staring," Alex said.

"It's okay. She likes it."

Dan emerged from the doorway and stepped into the dining room with his arms outstretched. "We're about to get this party started!" he shouted, spotting Alex and the gang in the center.

"There he is," said Alex as he stood up to greet Dan. "How much did you lose? Five hundred?"

"Now, now, my good buddy—my poor, disillusioned, matrimonial inmate. All you gotta do to keep from losing is make sure you don't pick the wrong numbers."

"Get the fuck outta here! You're up?" Sean asked, not moving from his chair.

"Man, you shoulda seen it. The ball was hot—damn hot, I tell you! This poor son of a bitch, Marty…the fucking guy couldn't hit a number to save his life, but I was hittin' his left and right! Fuckin' amazing. The fucking Lakers shit on him something fierce, but in the meantime, I was raking it in."

"Nobody asked for your life story," Joey said from his seat. "How much are you up?"

"Let's just say dinner's on me tonight, boys."

The table erupted in cheers as everybody congratulated Dan on his unexpected come-up.

Dan grabbed a chair from another table as Janice returned with the drinks.

"Here you are, fellas," Janice said. "I brought over an extra shot of Jameson when I saw your friend coming in."

"Aren't you the greatest?" Sean said, glancing at Janice's ass before moving his eyes up to her face.

"And I didn't forget about you either. One raspberry cosmopolitan." She set the neon pink drink down in front of Sean with a casual superiority.

"What the hell is this?" he asked.

"It's what you ordered," she said. "What I drink. Enjoy."

Joey began laughing at the pink martini. "What's your name, sweetheart?" he asked as he struggled for air.

"Janice."

"Janice," Joey said. "You just earned yourself an extra couple bucks on the tip with that one."

"Yeah, you're only saying that because Dan said he's gonna pay," added Alex.

"When you're right, you're right."

"All right, boys, settle down," the no-nonsense waitress said, waving her hands over the table. "Are y'all ready to order?"

Everybody ordered a New York strip: Dan and Sean medium rare, Alex and Joey medium, and Tim well-done.

"You know you're killing the steak ordering it like that, don't you?" Sean asked Tim after the order was placed.

"Yeah," Tim snapped, "but that's kind of the point. I want the cow to be dead before I eat it."

"All right, all right. Enough," Joey interrupted. "As the best man, I'd like to make a toast." He raised his shot glass in the air. "To

Alex, a man who will soon be able to look at only one pair of tits for the rest of his life."

"Here, here!" the group chanted.

"To Alex," added Sean, "whose best blow jobs are long behind him."

"Here, here!"

"To Alex," Dan said, "who's now gonna need written permission to take a shit and at least verbal permission to fart."

"Here, here!"

"To Alex," Tim said, wanting to finish off the toast, "who was lucky enough to find the love of his life before any of us."

"BOOOO!" the rest of the men yelled, slapping Tim across the back of his head before Joey finished the toast.

"To Alex, my best wing man, my best bar buddy, my best pussy hunter, my best cunt licker, and my fifth best friend!"

"HERE, HERE!"

They clanged the shot glasses together, and then everyone but Tim pounded the Irish whiskey down their throats. Tim took a sip and placed it back on the table. Without asking, Joey grabbed Tim's remaining whiskey and slammed the rest. The five of them continued to joke and jab all throughout dinner, throwing lewd remarks and homophobic comments at one another. Once the bill came, Dan filled the book with three crisp hundred dollar bills he'd pulled from his pocket.

"Damn! You weren't kidding about that roulette," Alex said when he noticed Dan stuffing the black checkbook with the hundreds.

"I'm gonna go shoot some dice. Wanna join me, buddy?"

"Fuck no, he doesn't," Sean said. "We're going to that Irish bar downstairs, grab us some girls."

"I thought you were trying to hook up with the waitress," Tim said, casting Sean a questioning glare.

"Oh yeah!" Sean grabbed the checkbook stuffed with cash and carried it over to Janice, who was standing by the bar.

The rest of the men watched him work. Sean leaned against the bar and flirted with her, casually passing her the checkbook and saying something that made her smile, visible enough even for the peering eyes across the room to see. After a minute, Sean walked back over to the table wearing a grin that told the tale for him.

Tim looked disgusted, but the rest of the men seemed pleased.

"She's meeting us later," Sean said as he took his seat, "downstairs at the bar."

"Is she coming back with the change?" asked Dan.

"I told her not to worry about it."

"Goddamn it, you motherfucker!" Dan cursed at Sean. "The tab was 202 bucks; I put three bills in there!"

"Did you really expect me to ask for change while I was trying to coax her into meeting us downstairs?" Sean asked in an innocuous manner.

"You didn't *coax* her! You *bought* her…with *my* money!"

"I'll hit you back for it." Sean turned to Alex. "C'mon, man," he said. "Let's check out that bar."

"Fuck it," Alex said, standing up. "I'm ready for some more drinking."

"Well, I'm not leaving you alone with the love guru," Tim said, motioning over to Sean. "I'm with you. Let's do it."

"We don't have to babysit the guy," Sean answered. "He's a full-grown man, right?"

"It's a shame the same can't be said about you."

"Enough, children," Alex said as he mimed pushing Sean and Tim apart from across the table.

"Fuck that, man," Dan said, shaking his head. "You guys enjoy your bar. The craps table is calling my name. Besides, I gotta make some of that money back, since I just lost a hundred bucks to fucking Jane the waitress."

"It's Janice," corrected Tim.

"What-the-fuck-ever. You comin' or what, Joey?"

"Hell yeah," Joey said. "I haven't done any gambling yet, and drinks are free tableside. Why would I pay eight bucks for a beer when I can get it for free shooting dice?"

"Because it ends up costing you $300 for that so-called *free* beer," said Sean, laughing as he pushed his chair in.

"Only if you lose, asshole," Joey retorted.

"All right, gentlemen," Alex intervened. "Good luck at craps. We'll be in the bar getting toasty."

FOUR

6:52 p.m. – Casino Floor

Martin couldn't move after he confessed to Jenny what he had done. His core felt weightless; his arms were weak, and his legs stood erect, holding his lifeless shell of a body in place, poised and ready for the assault he was sure would come from Jenny, but that assault never came. Jenny heard the words from his mouth but provided none of her own. Instead, she nodded her head with slow, deliberate movements, and stared into his eyes as if the answer were embedded somewhere deep in his skull. Martin felt like a child confessing to breaking a neighbor's window, embarrassed and anxious as to what sort of punishment would be dealt, but Jenny's powerful eyes just gazed into his, displaying regret and disappointment, emotions he had thought her incapable of until he saw it for himself, standing frozen on that casino floor.

There was a short silence after he finished, just long enough for Jenny to accept what had happened and to process it. Once the absorption of Martin's guilty plea had fully taken effect, she turned her back on him and darted toward the lobby, eventually disappearing from sight entirely.

Martin didn't follow her, because he couldn't. He was still frozen, still paralyzed, and his body felt weak. He didn't move for almost twenty minutes, and when he did, it was only to sit down on a stained slot machine chair nearby.

Laughter and enthusiasm rained down upon him from the casino floor as he sat there feeling lonely, wallowing in regret. His body became warm, and his thoughts turned angry. *Why am I always the loser?* His brain churned out. *How come I can't ever win? How come the rest of the world gets to enjoy themselves, but I'm always stuck in last place? Why couldn't that goddamn point guard have missed that last fucking shot?*

He monitored the groups of strangers playing the games he agonized over at all the wretched tables that had tortured him for so long. He watched in jealous rage as people raked in chips as if the casino were giving them away, handing out money to everyone but him, the eternal loser. He rocked back and forth in his chair as the negative energy crept up and built inside of him.

A group of three attractive young girls tossed dice around on a craps table. They dropped randomly valued chips on arbitrary numbers that didn't offer the most optimal odds for a return on their investment. He grew furious at their inability to bet properly and continued to watch them with a menacing stare. They hung their purses off the handlebars on the lower side of the table, and he watched as one of the girls reached into her purple leather purse and pulled out a wad of cash, sorted and separated some of the bills in her hand, then put the bulge back into her bag. *What a bunch of dumb bitches,* he thought. *I deserve to have that money. I'm the one who knows how to play those games, how to bet properly. Those girls don't deserve to have that money. I do.*

Martin scratched the back of his neck, which started to tingle as he grew hotter. Every laugh and smile from those girls brought with it a crippling affliction, and his blood pressure and body temperature only shot higher, like mercury in a tropical sun. His core no longer felt weightless, his arms no longer weak. The noise inside his head grew louder, and he jumped out of his chair suddenly, feeling as if he knew how to make it all better. He slinked his way toward the group of girls, eyeing the purple leather purse he'd seen the girl pull the money out of. He hung momentarily off to the side as he envisioned the heist from start to finish. He imagined walking up to the table and bending down to tie his shoelace. He would then use his body as a shield to prevent anybody else in the room from seeing what he was doing, and he would reach his hand into the purse and grab the first thing that felt like money. He knew he'd have to be quick. *Yeah, they'll eventually look down. I've got, what? Maybe ten seconds…maybe less.*

He moved closer to the table, dropped down next to the purse, untied his left shoe, and slowly laced it back up again. He hunched over the purses and keenly looked around for peering eyes. After his shoelace was tied, he inched upward and gazed into the purple leather purse. The girls began celebrating another roll, giving Martin the perfect window of opportunity. His finger pried the side of the purse open and he spotted several bills sitting on top of some makeup containers and folded papers. He took another look around the floor, and then eased his left and middle index fingers into the purse in a scissor-like motion, attempting to grab some of the loose bills on top. On the lookout to make sure he wouldn't be caught, he failed to pay enough attention to what he was doing and knocked the purse off the handle, spilling some of its contents on the floor. He bumped his head on the table as he shot upward, and his hand moved to the back of his neck where he began rubbing the area to try to comfort himself.

"What are you doing?" the purse owner asked, bending over to pick up her bag and checking to make sure everything was still there.

"I-I was just tying my shoe, but I bumped my head on the table."

The three girls looked at Martin in almost the same menacing way he had stared at them from across the room just moments earlier.

"Come on, Stephanie," another girl from the group urged. "I'm bored. Let's get outta here."

Martin tried to explain himself as the three women cleared all of their chips off the table, but he had trouble making sense of his own words and they trotted away toward the elevator. The dealers all gave him skeptical looks when the girls left, and he hurried away in the opposite direction, feeling both ashamed and defeated.

After checking his pockets yet again for anything he might have missed before, he rediscovered that his only possessions were his driver's license, his cheap prepaid cell phone, and his room key. Dejected from the casino, and afraid that the pit boss was now monitoring him for his failed robbery attempt, he chose to go to his room. He hoped Jenny would be there so he'd have a chance to explain himself and apologize. She was all he had left after all.

He carried himself to the elevator and rode it to the third floor, where he and Jenny had rented a small, modestly priced efficiency room for the evening. He thought of how he was going to word his apology and visualized what he could possibly say to make the situation better. He held the door handle for a moment forming his admission in his mind. Confident that he would find the right words when the moment came, he slid the keycard into the slit. When the door clicked and the light turned green, he turned the handle and pushed the door open with authority. He marched into the dark room and flipped on the light switch. Jenny wasn't there, nor were any of her bags, her clothes, or anything else that would indicate she had ever been there at all.

FIVE

8:40 p.m. – McKilligen's Pub

"Excuse me, but do you mind if I ask you a question?"

"Uh…yeah, sure. Go ahead."

"Let's say, hypothetically of course, that you were hanging out with your friends at an Irish bar and you spotted a girl sitting all by herself. Now, this girl is something else, just gorgeous, dressed in tall black boots, sexy jeans, and with the most beautiful eyes. What would you say to this girl to get her attention?"

"I'd probably ask her if she was waiting for her boyfriend to show up."

"Really? You'd ask her that?"

"Yep, that's what I'd ask," said the girl in the tall black boots, sexy jeans, and with the most beautiful eyes. She then walked over to a man who had just entered the bar, swung her arms around his neck and gave him an extravagant kiss.

Sean returned to Tim and Alex, who were sitting at a high-top table in the corner.

"Man, Sean," Alex said. "Right before that bigger, more handsome dude walked in, you had that chick!" With that, he laughed and slapped his hand on Sean's back.

"Yeah, thanks, asshole," Sean said. "I was trying to get her for *you*, you son of a bitch."

"Me? Hell, I already have a girl. If anything, get her for Tim."

"Don't get her for me either," Tim chimed in. "I don't want any girl who'd fall for one of your corny lines."

"My lines are fantastic," Sean argued.

"Fantastically corny maybe."

"Yeah? Well, just think about my corny lines when I'm banging that waitress later," Sean said, rolling his eyes at Tim's insult. The three men then gulped their beer and surveyed the rest of the bar. It was a much larger place inside than out. The décor was primarily old polyurethaned wood with retro-style beer and whiskey advertisements plastering the walls. Most of the patrons were in their twenties or thirties, an even split of men and women, but there were more couples than singles. The lack of single women came as a surprise and a disappointment to Sean.

"So…any plans for the honeymoon?" Tim asked Alex.

"Jesus Christ," Sean muttered, shaking his head.

"What?" Tim asked, sounding innocent.

"We're going to Hawaii for a week," Alex said quickly. "It's not very original, but it is beautiful."

"Filled with beautiful women too," added Sean, "most of 'em in tiny bikinis and grass skirts. I hear it's real easy to get a lei there," he joked.

"I doubt he's gonna care about that, since he'll be with his wife," said Tim, rolling his eyes at Sean's cheesy attempt at double-entendre.

"Hey, man, in case the honeymoon turns sour…" Sean continued. "I'm just saying, if you pick up a rock in Hawaii and throw it in any direction, you're gonna hit a beautiful girl."

"Yeah, that's actually a sport there," Alex joked. "It's called 'chick hit.' Some of the best athletes in the world started their careers as chick hitters."

"Chick hitters!" Sean said, laughing and slapping his knee. "I bet I could be an all-star at that. Tim, you wouldn't even make the B-squad."

"I don't know about that. I'm pretty sure I could throw a rock at you pretty hard," Tim said to Sean before taking a sip of his beer.

"That's what I'm saying," Sean said. "You're too much of a dick hitter to be a good chick hitter. Chick hitting takes finesse and charm."

"Not to mention a good arm," added Alex.

"Yeah, that helps, but…oh shit! Look at her," Sean said, his eyes locked on the blonde woman who'd just entered the bar.

Her eyes were dark and clouded with smeared makeup—she had clearly been crying recently.

"Wow. She looks terrible," Tim said, shaking his head.

"What the fuck are you talking about?" Sean exclaimed in disbelief. "She's hot!"

"That's not what I mean," Tim said. "I mean she looks like she's had a terrible night."

"Tim's right," Alex said to Sean. "Her hair's a mess, her makeup's running, and her clothes are…well, just drab and wrinkled. She's not here to flirt."

"Good. That just means there'll be less competition," Sean said as he picked up his beer and walked over to her.

"Does that son of a bitch even have a conscience?" Tim asked Alex when Sean was out of earshot.

"I've known Sean for fifteen years. Believe it or not, he used to be a hopeless romantic like you."

"Really? What happened?"

"Couldn't tell ya," Alex said, taking a sip of his beer.

The disheveled blonde was by herself at the end of the bar, trying to flag the bartender.

Sean moved in from her right. "Excuse me. Do you mind if I ask you a question?" he asked her.

"What? Ugh…sorry. I-I'm a little busy, and—"

"Let's say you were a guy at an Irish bar with your friends, and you see this girl come in all by herself. She looks like she's had a terrible day—"

"Well, you're right there," she said with a hint of disdain.

"So what would you say to this girl to get her attention?" Sean asked, oblivious to her obvious display of contempt.

When the bartender finally walked up to them, she asked, "Can you tell me when the next bus to town leaves?" she asked.

"Not till tomorrow morning," the bartender replied. "I think around six or so."

"Damn it! Is there any other cheap way to get to town tonight? Miguel said you might know."

"Sorry. I'm not headed back tonight, or I'd drive you myself. Rough night at the casino?"

"You don't know the half of it." She turned around and scooted past Sean without even bothering to look up or say another word.

Sean walked back over to the table, his shoulders sagging and his eyes on the ground. "What a fucking bitch," he said, pulling his stool out from under the table.

"Dude, nothing about that girl said she was in the mood for flirting," said Alex.

"I guess it's just not my night."

"Janice will be down soon," said Tim, "and you've already got her on retainer."

"Huh? Janice?" Sean asked. "Who's that?"

"Really?" Tim asked.

Sean's eyes rose up and to the right as if to literally search his brain for an answer.

"Janice, the waitress from the restaurant earlier."

"Oh shit! Janice!" Sean said, laughing and slapping his knee. "Thanks, buddy. I almost forgot her name."

"Almost? You *did* forget her name," Tim said. "Hell, you forgot *her*."

"I didn't forget her," Sean snapped. "I just forgot her name, that's all. Maybe I've just had too much to drink. I'll remember now."

"So," Tim said to Sean with a little hesitation, "Alex mentioned that you used to be some kind of Romeo, a real hopeless romantic."

Alex and Sean exchanged looks.

"Oh? He said that, did he?" Sean asked.

"What happened, man? Why are you such a player now?"

"I grew up, that's what."

"C'mon, man," Tim said. "There must have been something specific that—"

"Nope. Sorry Tim, but there wasn't some monumental breakup or anything. When I was thirteen and didn't know anything about anything, yeah, I wrote poetry and shit."

"And you dropped a love letter into Ashley Sorprankis's locker on the last day of school," added Alex.

"Holy shit! I almost forgot about that," Sean said.

"A love letter?" Tim asked.

"Yeah, in like seventh grade or something," Alex said. "She thought it was from Billy Henderson."

"Yeah," Sean started to remember, "and Billy Henderson lied and took credit for it. That next year, she banged him. It shoulda been me. That bastard got the royalties on my writing."

"It would never have been you," said Alex, laughing. "Ashley wouldn't have had anything to do with you."

"What the fuck, man?"

"Buddy, do you remember Billy Henderson?" Alex asked Sean. "The guy was the tallest kid in our grade and was already starting to get definition in his arms. He had that chiseled fucking chin, not to mention the sports car his daddy bought him when he was sixteen."

"He didn't have the car when I wrote the letter though," Sean pointed out, his head sinking toward his beer.

"He didn't need it. He could have banged any girl he wanted to. In fact, he pretty much banged every girl we went to school with, anyone who was a nine or a ten."

"What's that old song? 'Some Guys Have All the Luck'?" Sean said, shaking his head.

"What's Billy doing now?" asked Tim.

Sean and Alex looked at each other for an answer before shrugging their shoulders.

"Who knows?" Alex said.

"I bet he's doing something with his dad's business," Sean said. "He's probably some douche bag CEO or some suit-and-tie bullshit."

"Dan would know," Alex said. "He used to sell the kid weed in high school. Billy was one of his best customers."

"That's right! Dan *would* know," Sean said in agreement.

"Wait…so the three of you knew each other in high school?" Tim asked.

"The *four* of us," Sean corrected. "Me, this fucking guy, Joey and Dan were the crew back in the day."

"Kind of," Alex said. "I was friends with all of them, but Dan and Joey never really got along. Actually, if memory serves, you and Joey didn't get along too well either," he said to Sean.

"Well, that's because Joey was always doing outrageous shit."

"Like what?" asked Tim.

"Like taking a shit in some random bastard's car after homecoming," said Alex.

"What!?"

"Goddamn it!" Sean shouted. His eyes widened, and a smile crept across his face. "I remember that!" He leaned back on his stool and gazed toward the ceiling. "All four of us were at the football game, but Dan left to get high with some of the players. Then me, you, and Joey walked to McDonald's with all that fucking blue face paint on—"

"Yup," Alex continued, "and we saw that beautiful red Camaro with the top down. Joey was convinced it belonged to somebody we knew."

"But it didn't," added Sean.

"No," Alex agreed, "but Joey was convinced, so the idiot jumped in, pulled down his pants, and took a big, steamy shit right on the driver's seat."

"Oh, man!" Tim said, shaking his head. "What happened?"

"You got really pissed off, but I forget why," Alex said, pointing to Sean.

"I got pissed because *your* boy Joey took a shit in somebody's car."

"No, it wasn't that," Alex said, "and he was your boy, too, even if you didn't like him. It had something to do with that Christine girl, the one you used to work with at the deli."

"You're right!" Sean said. "We were headed to McDonald's to meet up with Christine and her hot friends. She saw me across the parking lot and ran over to tell me something, but when she saw Joey taking a shit, she freaked out!"

"That was it!" Alex said, laughing and nodding his head. "You were so pissed at Joey for that."

"Pissed? Are you kidding me? I was fucking livid. I'd been trying for months to bang that girl, and in one fell swoop—or one fell poop, actually—Joey cock blocked me in the worst way. He was always doing shit like that, always cock blocking both of us."

"Yeah," replied Alex, still smiling. "Remember what he said to Christine?"

"Uh…" Sean furrowed his brow, trying to remember.

"'Just stay right there, honey,'" said Alex in his best Joey impression. "'I'll only be one more minute, and then she's all yours.'"

"That's right!" Sean said, pounding his fist on the table. "Then the jackass made a face like he was giving birth, and Christine ran away screaming."

"Yup. Good times," Alex said.

"Good times," Sean agreed. "I need another beer. How's everyone else looking?"

"I'm ready for another," Tim said.

"I'm all for another round," Alex added.

Sean walked to the bar and returned with three Guinnesses and three shots of Jameson.

"I told you, I don't drink whiskey," Tim said discouraged as Sean placed the shot down in front of him.

"Aw, c'mon, buddy," Alex said. "For me?"

"Yeah, for Alex," Sean said. "You're not gonna turn down a toast to Alex during his bachelor party, are you?"

"I guess I don't have a choice," Tim said, grabbing the shot glass with some hesitancy.

Sean raised his shot in the air and said, "To the old crew!" He clinked his glass on Alex's, then said, "And to the new crew," and clinked Tim's.

"Here, here!" they all exclaimed and pounded the shots back.

Sean slammed his glass down first, a half-second before Alex. Tim took a little longer and chased his drink with a healthy sip of water.

The three men joked for a while longer before a familiar voice called out to them: "I hope you boys aren't having too much fun without me."

None of them had noticed Janice walking into the bar, but once they realized she was there, it was difficult not to pay attention. She was wearing a sleek black dress with fishnet stockings and blood-red heels. Her small, red leather jacket matched the heels perfectly, and her dark hair cascaded down her shoulders in waves. For the first time since the guys had checked into the hotel, they were not the best-dressed people in the room.

"Damn, girl! Look at you," Sean said, standing up to give her his seat.

"Thank you, Sean. Such a gentleman."

"That's my middle name."

"I bet. Anyway, we haven't been formally introduced," Janice said, extending her hand toward Alex.

"Alex," he said, lightly squeezing her hand, "and this is Tim."

"Nice to meet you both."

"Nice to see you again Janice," Alex replied.

"What are you drinkin', milady?" Sean asked Janice.

"I'll have what I gave you earlier."

"Comin' right up!" Sean moved to the bar while simultaneously sending a text to Alex: "Fuck! WTF did she give me B4?"

"So, Janice, busy night tonight?" Tim asked.

Alex texted Sean back: "Rasp cosmo I think."

"Nah, just the normal weirdoes. Hey, Alex…"

"Yes, Janice?"

"Can you make sure Sean knows it's a raspberry cosmopolitan?"

Alex laughed and nodded his head. "Way ahead of you," he said, lifting his phone up as proof.

"Thanks," she said with a smile. "So, tell me, which one of you guys is the bachelor?" she asked.

"That'd be me," Alex said, setting his phone down on the table.

"Oh, the listener. What a lucky lady."

Just then, Sean came back with the drink. "Raspberry cosmopolitan," he said, placing it down in front of her, "just the way you like it."

"Phenomenal. Thanks for remembering."

"I always pay attention to detail," he said, pulling up a stool next to her.

"Clearly," Janice replied, nodding her head.

Tim and Alex snickered as Sean moved in closer.

"Look! The highlights of the Lakers game," Alex said, nodding toward the television. "I heard they killed it. C'mon Tim, let's go check it out."

Tim and Alex walked over to the bar, leaving Sean alone with Janice at the table.

"That should give him the space he needs," Alex said.

"Yeah, but will it give *her* the space she needs?"

"Good point," Alex said with a nod.

The two men sat in silence, watching the basketball highlights.

After a moment, Tim mustered up the courage to speak. "Hey, Alex…"

"What's up, buddy?"

"Do you think I'm a pussy?" Tim asked.

"C'mon, man! What the hell kind of question is that?"

"I'm just sayin'…you know, I had a much less exciting childhood than you guys, and I don't talk to girls like you do. I still get all…nervous and shit. Like, I could never pick up a waitress at a restaurant and meet her for drinks later."

"You could," Alex assured him. "If you liked the girl enough, you'd ask her out."

"Not if she was a total stranger, like Janice was to Sean."

"Sean's much deeper than he appears. Honestly, you guys aren't that much different from one another."

"I don't know about that," Tim said, shaking his head.

"I do. You asked me earlier what happened to Sean, why he's no longer a hopeless romantic."

"Yeah."

"He lied when he told you nothing happened. Freshman year, he fell in love with this girl. He did everything for her, even bought her flowers and wrote poetry and all that mushy shit."

"Because he wanted to bang her?" Tim said.

"Nope. Well, I'm sure part of him did, but he never talked about her like that. He just went on and on about how amazing and smart she was and all that stuff. He said she'd changed his life, and he even swore they were gonna get married."

"Really? So what happened?" Tim asked.

"He found out she'd been banging some other guy for a month," Alex said. "It was some older dude, a friend of her brother's. Sean lost it. I mean, he really lost it…in a very bad way."

"Damn."

"He went on this anti-girl kick for about six or seven months. Shit, that was one of the few times when he and Joey actually got along. During that time, they hung out a lot, drinking and causing trouble."

"What kind of trouble?"

"Just kid shit," Alex said. "Stealin' spray paint and tagging buildings and that kinda shit—nothing super serious."

"When did Sean go all girl crazy again, like he is now?"

"Eventually he met this other girl, Trina, a total fucking slut, and he lost his virginity to her. After that, he started hitting on slutty girls and stopped hanging out with Joey. He hasn't changed much since then."

"So…how is it you think we're anything alike?" Tim asked, staring into his beer.

"He put himself out there and got hurt, and he hasn't been the same since. If he hadn't changed who he was to overcompensate being hurt, the two of you would practically be the same guy…well, except that he drinks whiskey."

Tim let out a nervous laugh. "I guess it makes sense," he said, not wanting to disagree.

"Cheer up, buddy. He's most likely gonna bang that waitress tonight, but you'll have a bachelor party long before he will."

"Thanks, man."

"No worries," Alex said. He gulped down the remainder of his beer and then looked back at the table, only to find that Janice and Sean were already gone. "Looks like he's well on his way."

Tim turned around and saw the empty seats. "Damn. Doesn't she know he's a player?" Tim asked.

"Sure, but maybe she is too."

It didn't make sense to Tim that a pretty girl could be a player, but he would have felt stupid arguing the point, so he took another sip of beer instead.

"I'm gonna go find Dan and Joey," Alex said, placing the empty beer mug on the bar. "Maybe I'll sneak in some more gambling before I call it a night. Wanna come with?"

"Nah. I've done enough gambling today. I think I'll just sit here a while and nurse a beer or two more."

"All right, buddy. Just don't beat yourself up too bad."

"I won't," Tim lied as he finished the rest of his beer. "Excuse me? Bartender, I'll have one more."

SIX

11:21 p.m. – Casino Floor Men's Bathroom

Sean splashed water on his face, paused, and let it drip into the sink for a second or two, then patted his skin down with a brown paper towel. He arched his back and stretched, cracking the bones in his back while checking himself out in the mirror. He always enjoyed looking at himself after fucking. The way his chest popped made him feel more confident, proud. His eyes wandered toward the attendant's station, and he wondered where the man was. Cigarette packs, gum, mints, and cologne all sat unguarded. Feeling as confident as he did, Sean snatched an unopened pack of cigarettes, leaned against the back wall, and dropped a dollar or so in change into the tip jar.

He began to head back into McKilligen's but turned around immediately and made his way to Deluxe when he saw Tim still sitting at the bar. He didn't feel like being bothered by anyone, particularly Tim.

The restaurant was empty, with not a guest, server, or bartender in the joint. The lights were dim, and the chairs were already sitting on the tabletops, upside down. Despite the place being obviously closed, Sean still crept through the unlocked door and made his way toward the abandoned bar in the corner. Hiding in the shadows, he lit up a cigarette and inhaled deeply.

He felt a sense of self-satisfaction as the foreign vapor filled his lungs, and he thought about Janice. Something about her bothered him; there was something different about their interlude. It had all started innocently enough, right there in Deluxe several hours earlier. When she'd walked into McKilligen's, she'd had a sway about her, a confidence he admired and might have even been a bit intimidated about. There was poise in her stride, as if she knew what everyone in the room was thinking, him included.

Sean took another drag of his stolen cigarette and spun his head around, looking for any watching eyes. Convinced that he was alone, he jumped behind the bar in search of any alcohol they'd failed to lock up. He got lucky for the second time that night when he found a half-full bottle of Crown Royal sitting by itself above the sink. He twisted the cap off and deeply inhaled the aroma. He brought the bottle up to his lips, sloshed the whiskey around in his mouth, and then followed it with another drag from his smoke.

He remembered talking to Janice briefly at the bar. "So…how was work?" he asked her.

"Do you really care?"

"Not really, but aren't we supposed to make small talk here?"

"Small talk is for men who don't know what they want or don't know how to get it. Do you know what you want, Sean?"

"I think I do."

"Yeah? Do you know how to get it?"

"I'd like to think so."

"Prove it."

Sean smiled at the memory as he took another swig of the whiskey. His nostrils began to burn from the alcohol, and he turned his thoughts to taking Janice up to the suite. She had a way about her that he had never encountered in a woman before. The normal things like money, status, or even wit did clearly nothing to impress her. She forced him to work for her mind, even though she practically gave him her body.

The suite was empty when they walked in, which was convenient; if it hadn't been, things would have gotten awkward very fast. Ravished with one another in such close proximity, they began to disrobe. Sean tugged her black dress up above her waist and ran his fingers along her panties, which were already wet from her excitement. Then he reached his hand under her lacy panties and worked his fingers around her clit. She gripped the back of his shoulders, digging into his skin while leaning against the wall for leverage. He continued working her most sensitive area, more and more forcefully by the second, and Janice began to moan. They stumbled out of the hallway and chose the closest room, the first one on the right. They practically fell through the door, and Sean almost threw her on the bed; his dick was rock hard, and he didn't want to waste another second. Janice tossed her leather jacket on the floor and kicked off her heels. Sean moved in closer, but Janice pushed him away long enough for her to unzip her dress and let it fall down to her ankles. Sean's pants were already off, and his cock was raging, demanding attention. He circled around Janice like a hawk on the prowl.

Janice reached down and grabbed a condom from her dress pocket. "Put this on…and then fuck me silly."

Sean obliged. He strapped the rubber on and pulled her by her thighs toward him. When he slid into her, the wet walls of her pussy gripped around his shaft. His hips gyrated and he grabbed her hair with his right hand and twisted it around his wrist. He then gripped her thigh with his left hand and began pounding her as hard as he could. After fucking her, doggy style, for what Sean considered to be a while, he wanted to see her full body, so he tried to twist her around.

"No, don't stop. Keep going, baby," she begged.

Eager to please, he kept fucking her from behind, trying hard to make her have an orgasm. When she finally cried out in ecstasy, it pushed him over the edge. He moaned as he filled up the condom inside of her. The two of them laid there for a moment, panting, before each climbed out of their instinctual ecstasies and returned to their senses.

"Damn, girl. I think I need a cigarette. You want anything?" he asked, still breathing heavily.

"No, I'm okay."

"All right, baby. Just wait here. I'll be right back."

Sean smiled as he sat at the empty bar in Deluxe and reminisced. He pulled the bottle of Crown Royal back to his lips and took another swig. "Put this on…and then fuck me silly," he said to himself. "Wow. What a girl." As much as he hated to admit it, and as much as it went against his womanizing reputation, he was smitten. There was just something about Janice. The way she moved, talked, and fucked was unlike anyone else he'd ever met. Other girls waited to make a move, only willing to react to what Sean did, but Janice refused to wait for anything. She was in control, making him wait for her. It was new, different, exhilarating, and sexier than anything he'd ever experienced.

Sean took one more drag from his cigarette before snubbing it out on the bar. A little drunk and overly confident, he sneaked the Crown Royal bottle into his jacket before walking out of Deluxe. The bottle was too big and bulky to fit in his pocket, so he had to carry it with his left hand under the cover of his blazer. It looked absurd, but nobody seemed to be paying much attention to him. As he walked back toward the room, his mind was racing. He had no idea what he was going to say or do. Normally, he wouldn't have given two shits; most of the time, he'd just have to figure out what to say to get the girl to leave, usually something to the tune of, "So, uh…I just got out of a terrible relationship, and I'm in a strange place. I'll call you later this week." But something told him Janice wouldn't buy that, and he didn't want her to leave anyway. She'd fucked him unlike any other girl. Most of all, she acted unlike any other woman he'd known, and he couldn't let such a catch get away.

In the elevator, Sean started to think about what Tim had said earlier, his ideas about marriage and love. *Maybe he has a point.* Sean wasn't getting any younger and he knew it. He'd never really seen himself as being locked into a serious relationship as an adult, but he'd never met anyone like Janice either. He didn't know her all too well yet, but the parts he did know, he loved. Before the doors opened to let him out on the top floor, he decided that he'd treat Janice the way she deserved: differently. *Hell, I'll court her…maybe even pop the question someday.* Just thinking about it made him happy and warm, something Sean hadn't really felt about a woman for a long, long time.

He slid the keycard into S2 and opened the door. Immediately, his nostrils were assaulted from the earthy aroma of marijuana smoke. He expected to find his friends getting high, but he was surprised to find nobody there. More surprisingly, when he opened the door to his room, Janice was nowhere to be found. He searched high and low for any sign of her, but her sexy red heels were gone, along with her matching jacket. Sitting on the nightstand was a note, scribbled in a woman's neat handwriting on a Hotel Reverie notepad:

> Sean,
>
> Thank you for a great evening. I think we both needed this. I just got out of a God-awful relationship and am trying to get back on my feet. I'm sure you understand. Love you till the sun comes up…
>
> Janice

Sean read the letter three times before he truly understood that she wasn't coming back. He twisted the cap off the pilfered Crown Royal bottle and brought the whiskey to his lips. "What a fucking bitch," he said as the amber liquid dribbled from his mouth and onto the note. "'Love you till the sun comes up?' Fuck you, Janice."

SEVEN

4:55 p.m. – Deluxe

"Pre-shift in five minutes!"

Janice cursed several times under her breath while she attempted to rub a fingerprint off a wine glass. She pressed down on the napkin with her thumb, but the smear refused to vanish. The more time she spent on it, the more frustrated she got until the glass finally shattered in her hand. She stood, shaking, with shards of glass between her fingers, and hatred began to build inside her.

Mary came over with another glass. "Easy there, Hulk. We need these."

"Seriously Mare, if I have to listen to that little shit boss me around like he's—"

"Like he's you're boss?" Mary interrupted. "C'mon, girl. You're better than that."

"I hate this job."

"The job hates you, too, Janice."

Janice smiled and gave Mary a hug.

"C'mon. May as well get it over with," Mary said, looping her arm in Janice's.

"I'll be right there. I'm gonna have a smoke first."

"Janice—"

"I need it today, Mare—just one. I'll be right there."

Mary shook her head and made her way toward the kitchen.

Janice walked down the back stairwell. She took out a nearly full pack and lit one up, then thumbed through old texts on her phone. It was all a painful sort of déjà vu for her. She had been working at Deluxe for almost seven years, already six years longer than she'd planned to be there. Her so-called temporary employment now felt inescapable. She stared at the walls, looking at every detail, every scratch and dent and hole and mark. She wondered, as she choked down the rest of her cigarette, when she'd see those suffocating walls for the last time.

After she smoked her cigarette down to the filter, she pulled herself up and walked back toward the kitchen. Mary was already there, along with a couple of cooks who spoke a small amount of broken English, men whose names were only known to the chef. Chef Nobles, aka Chef No Balls to Janice, made his way toward the rest of the staff, basking in his unwarranted grandeur. He had a habit of making people feel inferior, and it was even evident in his prideful stride. Janice despised him for it; then again, she despised him for everything.

"All right, ladies," Nobles began, "I'm very busy tonight, so let's get through this quick. The hotel is at 50 percent occupancy, so you can expect a somewhat busy shift. The soup of the day is lobster bisque topped with crème fraîche. Fish of the day is gonna be Alaskan halibut, pan roasted with braised artichokes, fennel, and a shellfish nage."

"What the hell is that?" Janice blurted out.

"What the hell is what?"

"A shellfish nage?"

"It's a very thin cream sauce made from shellfish."

"Sounds tantalizing."

Chef Nobles couldn't discern whether or not Janice was patronizing him, so he just moved on. "For dessert, we have a flourless chocolate cake, gelato, sorbet, and crème brûlée."

"What are the gelato and sorbet flavors?" Mary asked, writing everything down as she always did; Janice, on the other hand, never wrote a thing down, and she rarely pushed the specials.

"Chocolate and vanilla gelato and pear and blueberry sorbet. And don't eat it! Sell it! Also we're eighty-sixing the roasted chicken, but we still have two orders of the chicken Florentine. I'll be in the office if you need me." With that, Chef Nobles walked away, and the two cooks babbled something in their native tongue and jumped behind the line.

Janice sneaked over to Mary. "So…are you having pear or blueberry sorbet?" she asked under her breath.

"Didn't you hear the chef? We're not allowed to—"

"C'mon, Mare! You know it sounds good."

Mary bit her lip and rolled her eyes. "Maybe later, after the shift. It'll be our reward…and our little secret."

"Whatever you have to tell yourself."

The two girls laughed as they moved into the dining room.

"So," Janice began, "any developments with you and Noah?"

"Developments?"

"You know…you think he's gonna ask or what?"

"I hope so," Mary said, looking away. "I think so. He's been extra jittery lately, so I know something's on his mind. Why? Did you hear something?"

"No."

"Janice, you have to tell me if you know something I don't."

"I didn't hear anything! I was just curious."

Mary stared Janice down, but Janice refused to give anything away, which was easy since she really didn't know anything.

"Well, I hope he does it soon," Mary said. "We're not gettin' any younger."

"You're telling me! Where's *my* knight in shining armor?"

"Maybe you'll meet him tonight," Mary said, smiling and bumping her hip with Janice's.

Janice let out a laugh. "I don't know, Mare," she said. "I'm not sure I'd want to date a guy who eats here. I'd hope he'd have better taste."

The two girls laughed again as two customers walked in and sat down in a booth to the left.

"I'll take it," Janice said, straightening her uniform.

"You sure?"

"Yeah. Who knows? Maybe one of these guys will be Mr. Right."

"Right!"

Janice walked over to the two men in the booth. Both were wearing dark turtlenecks and reeked of cigarettes. "Hello, gentlemen. My name is Janice. What can I start you fellas off with?"

The two men stared at her in silence for a full five or six seconds before proceeding to talk to each other in Russian.

Janice immediately rolled her eyes in disdain. As far as she was concerned, foreigners were the bane of the service industry. They required extra attention and tended to tip exponentially less. No more than ten seconds after she started trying to take their order, Janice already wished she'd given the table to Mary.

After a somewhat lengthy private conversation, one of the men asked, in broken English, "What you have for, say…vodka?"

"We have Grey Goose, Ketel One, Belvedere, Stoli, ABSOLUT—"

"You bring us bottle of Stolichnaya."

"I'm sorry, sir, but we actually don't do bottle service. I can serve it only by the drink or shot."

On that note, the other man began to argue in Russian with his comrade, which made Janice believe they both understood English better than they'd been pretending, and that made her even angrier.

"We'll have two of the tallest pours of Stolichnaya you can serve, neat," the original man said.

"Yes, sir."

"Uh, miss—"

"Janice."

"Yes, Janet, make sure they are warm. I don't want it cold."

"Yes, sir."

"No ice."

"Yes, sir," Janice replied. As she walked away, she began to curse under her breath. "I understand what fucking *neat* means, you foreign fuck. Go fuck yourself, prick."

She made the two drinks at the bar and returned to the table donning a professional smile. "Here you are, fellas. Are you all set to order?"

"You have fish, yes?" the same man asked.

"Actually, we have pan-roasted halibut with a shellfish nage."

The two men looked at each other in confusion.

"What is this shellfish nage?"

"A very thin cream sauce made from shellfish."

The two men once again looked at each other before turning back to Janice and nodding their heads in approval. They'd already finished their drinks in the two minutes it had taken for Janice to get the order.

"Another round, Janet."

"It's Janice…and yes, sir. Coming right up."

By the time Janice had punched in the order, Mary was talking to the diners at another table. Janice went behind the bar and poured three double Stoli neats, two for her table and one for herself. She shrank to the floor where no one could see her and poured the warm vodka down her throat.

"Janice!" Mary said as she stood back up.

"Don't worry, Mare. The table bought it for me." She motioned over toward the two Russians, who weren't paying any attention.

"Mm-hmm. I bet they did."

"How's your table?" Janice asked, trying to change the subject.

"A bunch of weirdoes, if you ask me—one with a very specific martini order."

"Oh geez. Are they cute? Maybe we could share a martini later?"

"Ew! Not happening."

Janice smiled as she carried the Stoli neats over to her table, glancing at Mary's table in the process. She deduced that neither of the men were cute enough to waste her time and collected the empty glasses off her own table in haste, then returned to Mary at the bar.

"Big spenders?" Mary asked.

"No, just big drinkers. Something tells me we're gonna be eighty-sixing Stoli by the end of the day with those two guzzling it all down."

"Heard that." Mary glanced behind Janice and tapped her on the arm. "Uh-oh," Mary said. "I think I just found four new contestants for your knight in shining armor."

"What on Earth are you talking about?"

"Look."

Janice looked toward the door and saw four men in their mid-twenties entering the restaurant. Three of them were slim and well dressed in blazers and button-down shirts, and the fourth was huskier and wearing a sweater.

"What's with the blazers?" asked Janice. "Where do they think they are?"

"They're cute…well, except for the fat one in the sweater."

"They're probably gay."

"Nope. Gay men have better fashion sense," Mary said, forcing Janice to laugh through her tough exterior.

"Very true," she said.

"Go get 'em, girl!"

Janice put on her professional smile and walked over to the four men in the center of the dining room. "Hello, gentlemen. My name is Janice. What can I start you fellas off with?"

"Four shots of Jameson!" the fat one shouted without even bothering to look up.

"I don't do shots," said the man in a yellow shirt, his soft-spoken proclamation an immediate turn-off for Janice.

"I'll take a Guinness as well," replied the cutest one. He had tan skin, a sharp purple shirt, and warm, comfortable eyes. Janice had to watch herself to keep from staring.

"Make that two," the fat one added.

"I'll have two of whatever you drink," said the fourth.

"Whatever *I* drink?" Janice asked.

"Yeah—one for me and one for you."

He wasn't as cute as Mr. Warm Eyes, but he did have a confidence about him that Janice found attractive. He also harbored the stink of a player, a stench Janice was all too familiar with.

"Uh, that's very nice of you, mister…"

"Sean. My name's Sean."

"Sean, that's very nice of you, but they don't let me drink while I work," Janice said, wondering if the smell of the vodka she'd just gulped down would make its way to Sean's nose.

"Well, what time do you get off work?"

Janice laughed at Sean's attempt to be smooth while secretly enjoying the attention. "I can see you boys are gonna give me a lot of trouble," she said.

"Nah, only this one," the cute one replied, nudging at Sean's arm.

"Mm-hmm," Janice said.

"Well, maybe this one too," he said now pointing at the fat one. "You may need to bring in backup."

"I might just do that. But in the meantime, I'll be right back with your drinks." With that, Janice turned around and walked toward the bar, where Mary was already standing.

"So? Any winners?" Mary asked.

"Well, Warm Eyes, the one in the purple shirt, is definitely in the lead. The creep at position four is, unfortunately, in second."

"Ew!" said Mary. "Number Four looks like a total ass-hat. Why does he have his shirt unbuttoned like that? I think the first guy should be ahead of him."

"No way. He's way too plain and quiet, and he doesn't even drink shots. Any arguments about purple shirt in position three?" Janice asked.

"No. Position three is definitely a hunk. Any rings?"

"Nope, not one."

"What are they drinking?"

"Beer and whiskey…and one raspberry cosmopolitan."

Mary twisted her body and cocked her head, trying to determine whether or not Janice was serious.

"The creep told me to get him whatever I drink, and that's what I drink."

Mary let out a laugh after Janice explained what had happened. "No way! He didn't really say *that*, did he?"

"Sure did."

"I don't think I've ever seen you drink a raspberry cosmopolitan in my life," Mary said, nudging Janice in the small of her back.

Janice smiled as she squeezed the lime and cranberry into the shaker. "Why, that's very observant of you, Mare."

"You're bad."

"Uh-oh. Looks like we have an add-on."

Mary and Janice watched as another man approached the table and sat down.

"And where does this one rank?" asked Mary.

"I'm not sure. Lemme go in for a closer look. Can you run my food for the two comrades over at Table Thirty-One?"

"Sure thing. Get 'em, girl."

Janice walked back over to the men at the table with the drinks carefully balanced on the tray. She set down the shots first, then the beers, and then she set the neon pink drink down in front of Sean with a mischievous pleasure over face.

"What the hell is this?" he asked.

"It's what you ordered, what I drink. Enjoy."

The fat one laughed a loud, obnoxious laugh before inquiring about her name. She gritted her teeth with anger, as she always did when she had to repeat her name to a table, but still felt satisfied that someone else thought that the neon pink drink was as funny as she thought it was.

The order was easy enough: steak all around. Janice began punching it in POS system as Mary walked over.

"Bad news, girl. The comrades want to talk to you."

"Shit. What about?"

"I don't know. They just keep asking for Janet."

"Goddamn it."

"Anything good with our boys?" Mary asked.

"Not really. They all ordered steak. At least none of them are pussy vegetarians."

Mary smiled and turned away at the sound of Janice saying "pussy."

"Well, I guess that's something," she said, trying to be positive.

"Let's see what the douche bags want," Janice said, switching back over to her professional smile as she walked over to the two Russians. "Is everything okay, gentlemen?" she asked.

The two men stared at their entrées, confused, as if they'd never eaten dinner before and didn't understand how to go about doing it.

"What is this?" the most talkative one asked.

"That is the halibut. It's what you ordered."

"Yes, this I know, but what is *this*?"

The man poked his fork at the sauce drizzled over the fish.

"That is the shellfish nage, remember? The thin cream sauce—"

"No, we don't want it. Just the fish."

Janice bit her bottom lip almost to the point of bleeding. She wanted to scream at them. She wanted to scream at them for ordering something they didn't want to eat. She wanted to scream at them for the hundreds of times she'd had to take something back because guests were idiots. Instead, calm, she grabbed each plate and said, "My apologies, gentlemen. I'll be right back."

Janice walked the plates into the kitchen, where the two cooks were already preparing the steaks for the other table. "Guys, I need these redone with no sauce!"

"*Que?*"

"No sauce! No sauce on the fish!"

The cooks looked at the stabbed tickets.

"I didn't write it down, because they didn't tell me no sauce. They just changed their minds."

"*Que?*"

"Goddamn it! Just make it again with NO SAUCE!"

"Aye! Alright, alright!"

One line cook began prepping two new plates while the other took the same fish filets and re-cooked them in a citrus sauce that masked the cream sauce.

After a couple minutes, Janice walked back out with the two "new" entrées. "Here you are, gentlemen. Can I bring you anything else?" she asked.

"More vodka, no ice, not cold."

Janice resisted the urge to roll her eyes and said, "Coming right up." She fetched them another round of drinks, then ignored them for the next half-hour. She saw the empty drinks and water glasses at their table, but decided they were no longer worth her attention. In the meantime, she talked with Mary at the bar. "So…you guys got any plans for tonight?"

"I don't know," Mary said. "He kind of ran out the door this morning. You don't think he's cheating on me, do you?"

"Noah? Mary, really? That boy wouldn't be able to cheat at Monopoly. He is *not* cheating on you."

"Good point," Mary said, smiling at the thought of the love of her life trying and failing to be unfaithful. "Uh-oh," she said. "Creep at six o'clock. You're up."

Janice turned around to find Sean walking up with the checkbook.

"Here you are, beautiful."

"I'll be right back with your change."

"No change necessary, but a drink would be nice."

"Want me to add it to your tab?"

"No, I plan on starting one downstairs. Why don't you join me when you're done? I'll make sure the guy makes an orange cosmopolitan, just the way you like it."

At first, Janice considered busting his balls for suggesting orange instead of raspberry, but after glancing at the enormous tip, she decided to let it slide. "I'll meet you when I get off, but I don't know when that will be."

"I'm not going anywhere."

"It was nice meeting you, Sean."

"See ya around, Janice."

Janice watched Sean walk back to the table. Not wanting to stand there by herself and seeing that Mary was talking to one of her other tables, Janice made her way over to the Russians, trying to look busy. "All finished, boys?"

"Yes. Bill please."

"Here you are," she said as she pulled a checkbook out of her apron. "I'll take it whenever you're ready." She cleared the plates and carried them into the kitchen, watching out of the corner of her eye as the two men stuffed some cash in the checkbook and walked away. She also waited for Sean and his friends to leave.

When Mary walked back over to the bar to punch in an order, Janice met her there with both checkbooks. "So, the blazer boys hooked it up a hundo," she said.

"Nice! Cash?"

"Yup."

"Nice job, girl. Are you going out with them?"

"I guess I kind of have to now. The creep wants me to meet him downstairs. Is it wrong for me to try to use him to get to the hunk?"

"No, I don't think so," Mary said. "He's just using you to get to the va-jay-jay."

"Good point. How'd the martini drinkers do?"

"Twenty percent. The comrades?"

Janice opened up the book. The total tab was $96.75, and they'd left $100. "About what I expected, a solid three-dollar tip."

"God, the nerve of some people," Mary said, shaking her head. "Everybody should be forced to work for tips at least one year of their lives."

"Wanna get into that sorbet before the next rush?" Janice asked, trying to forget about the insulting tip.

Mary gave her a look that said she had been waiting for this moment all night.

"Come on," she said. "Real quick, before Chef No Balls comes back."

EIGHT

10:49 p.m. – Casino Floor

"Fucking fags, all of 'em. Fucking unbelievable, the fucking faggots," Joey murmured as he stumbled around the casino floor, looking for the mysterious elevator that the posted signs advertised. "Fucking fags. Son of a…" He staggered about, drunk, as yet another sign pointed him in a new direction, another turn he had to make. The colors of the slot machines blurred together, and he was hot. "Dan's a fucking asshole, and that's that." He paused behind a *Wheel of Fortune* slot machine to finish off a miniature bottle of Ketel One. There wasn't as much remaining as he thought, so he patted his pockets down, trying to find something else to drink. The weight of the plastic bottles told Joey they were all empty. He hated plastic bottles. They felt so cheap.

"Sir, can I help you?" asked a voice coming from Joey's right side.

He turned his head to see the face of a young boy with shaggy blond hair. Obvious even to Joey's drunken eyes, the boy worked for the hotel; his cream shirt, red vest, and matching clip-on tie gave him away.

"Elevator!" Joey shouted. "Where the fuck is the elevator? I've been walking for miles!" Little droplets of spit spurted from

Joey's mouth with every word, and beads of sweat rolled down his neck.

"I can take you to the elevator, sir, if—"

"I'm in a fucking penthouse suite, bitch! Take me there right now!"

"Uh, sure, sir. I'd be happy to escort you to the elevator. Please follow me."

The boy started walking across the casino floor but had to slow his pace due to the severity of Joey's inebriated state. Joey had missed the elevator many times even though it was in the center of the circular room, and Joey needed the wall to help him stay on his feet.

Joey gripped the sides of chairs, leaning his weight into the cushions, and wobbled as he attempted to stay upright. The room was spinning too fast for him, and he couldn't maintain his balance. When he closed his eyes, his head began to spin, and his balance grew even worse.

After a short minute, the young boy found it to be too hard to watch. "Sir, please let me help you," he said. He flung Joey's arm over his neck and carried him toward the center of the room. It would have been a lot easier if Joey had had access to any of his motor skills, but at best, he was dead weight. Maneuvering a few twists and turns around the aisles, the bellhop managed to drag Joey to the front of the elusive elevator.

When Joey's eyes cleared and he saw the buttons and the sliding doors, he could barely contain his excitement. "You found it! You found the fucking elevator!"

"Yes, sir. It was no problem. Do you need anything else, Mr. Roznick?"

"Holy shit!" Joey backed up toward the elevator door, startled. He cocked his head to the side and peered at the bellhop. "How do you know my name?"

"Because, Mr. Roznick, we were introduced earlier…when you checked in."

Joey just stared at the boy, mesmerized and unable to comprehend this news.

"Noah, remember? I offered to carry your bags to the suite. You didn't have any but tipped me anyway. Miguel introduced us."

"Oh! Yeah, right. Miguel." The name pierced Joey's memory.

"Yeah, that's me. Will you be needing anything else, sir?" Noah asked.

"Ugh. No, I'll be fine."

"Very well, Mr. Roznick."

"God, man!" Joey cried out. "Just call me Joey, all right?" Joey reached in his pocket and pulled out a chip he'd won earlier in the evening. "Here ya go, kid."

"Thank you. mister…er, Joey. That's very kind of you."

"Hey, man, you found the elevator! It's the least I can do!"

The elevator doors opened, and Joey collapsed inside.

Noah reached in and pressed the floor for the suites, using his own card to gain access. "Enjoy the rest of your evening, Joey."

Joey thanked him with a half-wave, unable to get any words out before the doors closed. About seven seconds later, "You too, Noah" fell on deaf ears.

The doors opened on the top floor, and Joey stumbled out into the hallway. There were only two suites at the Hotel Reverie, S1 and S2. He tried his card in S1, but the little red light remained illuminated. Just for good measure, he tried again, only to get the same result. Then he turned around and tried S2. The little red light turned green, and the door clicked. He turned the handle and threw his body weight into the door to guarantee that it would open. He launched himself through the door and onto the floor inside the suite, smacking his head against the wall on the way down.

"Fucking shit," he complained, rubbing the sore spot on his head. He looked around and saw no one, then muttered, "Home at last."

After gathering himself off the floor, he managed to stumble into the living room, once again relying on the walls for support. The suite consisted of four bedrooms, a kitchen, a patio deck, and a spacious, swanky living room featuring only the most modern and trendiest furniture. It also held a fridge hidden inside a compartment on the couch, filled with miniature bottles of liquor, snacks, sodas, and wine.

Joey pried open the door to the mini-bar and grabbed three new bottles of Ketel One. He twisted off one of the caps and put the rim to his lips. "Fucking shit," he said before opening his throat and allowing the vodka to fall through. "Fucking plastic bottles!"

A woman's moan distracted him from his drunken rant, and he looked toward the direction of the noise. It was coming from one of the rooms in the suite, and even in Joey's inebriated and debilitated state he realized Sean was fucking some girl. He gulped until the bottle in his hand was dry, all the while staring at the door, listening to the two of them fuck on the other side. "Fucking shit, man." The words tumbled out of his mouth in slurs and a spray of spittle, and his temperature rose even further. Sweat droplets formed on his neck and soaked quickly into his sweater.

For a moment, he jumbled around in his pockets, the contents spilling out onto the floor: keys, loose change, and a small, neatly folded piece of paper. He already knew what the paper said, but he opened it to read it again anyway: "Room 401. Knock three times."

The animalistic grunts, groans, and moans coming from the other room soon became too much, and Joey couldn't take it any longer. He threw the paper on the floor and grabbed the remaining two miniature bottles of Ketel One. He then walked to the door as best he could, swaying back and forth as if he were on a boat, outstretching his arms for balance. He stumbled out the door, backtracked down the hallway, and descended down the elevator to the fourth floor. He fell out into the hallway when the doors opened and followed the first wall he could lean on, reading off the door numbers until he got to the very end. When he saw the gold "401" on the door, he knocked three times.

Shuffling sounds came from the other side, and the door opened.

NINE

10:49 p.m. – Casino Floor

"Hey, Dan! Yo, man, wait up!"

"Yo, Alex! What's up, man? Where're Tim and Sean?"

"Tim's still capping 'em off at the bar, and Sean's getting it on with that waitress, Janice."

"No shit? She actually showed?" Dan asked.

"Yep. Where's Joey?"

"Who the fuck knows, man. Dude, he went nuts after we left you guys."

"What? What the hell are you talking about?"

"I'll tell ya over a game of roulette."

"Wait," Alex said, pointing a finger at Dan. "Answer me honestly. Are you up or down?"

Dan rolled his eyes at the question, shrugging off Alex's stare. "I'm up, man," he lied, "but barely. I made a killing earlier at roulette and lost most of it on craps and dinner. I need to play with what works."

"All right, buddy. I'm with ya, but only for a little while, just to hear this story."

The two men walked up and down the aisles and alleyways until they found a table they liked, or rather one that Dan liked. It was a smoker's table, and while neither of them smoked, it seemed to be hitting Dan's favorite numbers, according to the screen positioned above it. They each exchanged for $100 in singles: green for Dan and purple for Alex, matching their shirts purely by coincidence.

"So? What happened?" Alex prodded as he organized the stacks of chips into miniature towers in front of him.

"Well, we walked over to the craps table, and I found out he has no clue how to play craps. I tried to teach him on the fly, but he was piss-ass drunk, so that didn't go well."

"Really? I don't remember him drinking that much at dinner."

"He didn't, at least not for Joey."

"Right," Alex said, "not for Joey."

Each man scattered his chips on different numbers. Dan bet heavy on single numbers, while Alex spread his bets around the board, and the wheel spun.

"First of all, when we left dinner, Joey went to the room first, and when he came back down I saw him drinking those little bottles you get from the mini bar."

"He's gonna pay for that shit," Alex said.

"Damn right he is."

The dealer cleared all the bets away after the ball danced around and landed on a lonely space. "Twenty, black. Place your bets, gentlemen."

"So yeah," Dan said, dropping more chips on the board, "he came back down, and it was obvious he was fucking blasted, but I figured what the hell? It's a bachelor party, right? So he jumped into the game for $200 and was standing right next to me and shit. Now, like I said, I was trying to help him learn the game, but basically he was acting like a dumb-ass child. I was doing the best I could, telling him where to put his money and whatever, but he was just pissing off everybody else at the table. Everyone started giving me dirty looks and shit, but what the fuck was I supposed to do, ya know? The dice were rollin', man, and I didn't want to leave the table."

The ball spun around and dropped on four before bouncing out and landing on six, where Alex had two bucks. "Six, black. Congratulations, sir."

"Yeah you'll be saying that a lot," Dan said to the dealer. "The guy says he doesn't play roulette, but it's all a hustle."

"I'm sure a two-dollar bet's not gonna break the house."

"Dude, times are tough for everybody."

"So what about Joey?" Alex asked as he collected his winnings and left two for the dealer.

"Like I said, he was pissing off the whole table, including me, with his drunken bullshit. Then he started dropping eff-bombs, a 'faggot' here and a 'fag' there, and some people nearby were getting really upset."

"Oh boy," Alex said. He rubbed the back of his neck with his left hand at the thought of an inebriated Joey upsetting a table of complete strangers.

"Oh boy is right," Dan continued. "They were ready to boot his ass out or kick it in the damn parking lot, and he actually looked at me like I was gonna have his back or whatever. But seriously, man, he was being an asshole. So I just told him to chill out. Well, when I said that, he flipped out on me and fucking stormed off. I tried calling him a few times, but it keeps going straight to voicemail."

"Did you check the room?"

"Nah, man. I didn't even leave the table till ten minutes ago."

The rolling ball rebounded against the spinning wheel and came to a halt on yet another lonely number. "Twenty-three, red," announced the dealer as he cleared all the bets off the table.

"Besides, man," said Dan, "he's all fucked up right now anyway. You don't hang out with Joey as much anymore, so maybe you don't know, but he gets wilder every day—like he's losing control or something."

"How often do you guys hang out?" Alex asked.

Dan shrugged. "Meh, once in a while. He'll buy weed off me every now and then, and that's all well and good, but then we'll go out drinking afterward, and he gets real ugly sometimes. He's in love with that 'faggot' word lately. He says it all the time, and people are turned off by it, and by him. Be careful, man. I mean, I know he's your best man and everything, and—"

Alex held up his hand to stop Dan from finishing. "Look, I've known Joey longer than any of you guys, and I know he gets outta control now and then, but I'm sure I can talk to him and help him mellow out."

"Yeah? Well, at least give him some time."

"Hell yeah I will," Alex said with a laugh. "How stupid do you think I am? I know Joey well enough not to go near him when he's drunk. I always make sure I see him during the day, like for the tux fitting. I can't keep up with him at night anymore. Hell, I can't keep up with any of you guys."

Dan slapped his hands together and doubled up on all his bets, putting forty dollars' worth of chips on the table. "All right, I'm feeling lucky," he said, his gaze fixated on the large numbered wheel in front of him.

"Whoa! Big spender."

"C'mon, man. Join me. If we hit, we'll hit strong. If we miss, we'll just roast this joint in my pocket. Can't beat those odds. It's a win-win situation."

Alex laughed. "I haven't smoked pot since high school, man."

"Don't say that. Now I kinda hope we lose."

"Fuck it." Alex topped off all his bets with the rest of his chips, twenty-six dollars more than Dan's.

The wheel spun.

"C'mon! Hit, hit, hit, hit, hit!" Dan begged the casino gods, tapping the side of the table.

The ball bounced around the edges, slid back and forth around the center of the wheel, then slowed down and dropped on a lonely number. "Thirteen, black. Sorry, fellas."

"No worries, Dealer. Here's a little something for you." Alex passed him a five-dollar chip from his pocket.

“Thank you very much, sir.” The dealer tapped the chip on a plastic block by his side, confirming it for the eye-in-the-sky, then dropped it into his tip bucket.

“Hey! Holdin’ out on me?” Dan asked Alex, standing up off his stool and pushing it aside.

“Nah. I just forgot I had it till the ball was in motion.”

“Liar. C’mon. Let’s roast this bone.”

“Let’s go to the room,” Alex said. “We’ll check to make sure Joey’s there. If he isn’t, we’ll smoke the joint and try to find him.”

“And if he is there?”

“We’ll smoke the joint and pretend he isn’t,” Alex said, laughing. “Then we’ll try to find his drunk ass.”

“I like the way you think,” Dan said, laughing along with Alex.

They continued to walk across the casino floor until Dan suddenly stopped in his tracks. “Hey, wait a minute. Is that Marty?”

“Who’s Marty?” Alex asked, trying to see who Dan was looking at.

“Hey! Yo, Marty! Hey, man! It’s me, Dan!”

TEN

9:22 p.m. – Room 302

The room was empty. Martin sat in the one forsaken chair, facing the empty room that just looked and felt depressing. Jenny's clothes were gone; they had taken up most of the space. Even his suitcase was nowhere to be found. The only things she didn't take belonged to the hotel. The plane tickets to get back home were gone. *It's probably for the better,* he thought. *There's nothing back home for me anyway.* He'd lived in Jenny's apartment, surrounded by Jenny's stuff.

His job was also gone, for all intents and purposes; he couldn't possibly face his boss after losing the deposit money. He had no valuables and nothing important. His soul ached deeply at that thought, for one of the worst parts about the whole thing was realizing he owned nothing he would miss if it were taken away. And there he was, sitting in a dimly lit room at the Hotel Reverie with no money, no clothes, no ticket home, no home to get a ticket for, no job, and no Jenny. *No Jenny. All just…gone.*

He tapped the side of his phone with his finger, debating about calling Jenny, but he had nothing to say. *Maybe it is for the better,* he thought again. Jenny was good, pure. She wanted a life and a future, and she deserved to have one. Martin knew he couldn't give her that. He knew she'd be much better off without him, but for his part, living without her was a troubling thought. She knew more about Martin than he knew about himself, and that was one of the reasons he'd fallen in love with her. He'd hoped he could count on her to save him from himself. He knew how much of a deadbeat gambling addict he had become, but Jenny saw past that. Jenny had seen a tired man trying to change his life, a heartfelt man with ideas and opinions and goals. Martin didn't see any of that, but he saw Jenny, and Jenny saw those good things in him.

But now that was all over. Now she was not there to see Martin for what he wanted to be, and he was forced to look at himself for what he truly was, for what he knew he'd always been: a weak little boy trying to become a man.

Martin stood up and walked around the room. He could really have used a drink, but he didn't have any money, and the shitty little room he and Jenny had rented didn't come with a mini bar. Instead, he looked around for anything he could sell, anything at all that might fetch him ten dollars for some well gin.

The managers of the Hotel Reverie were not fools; even the smallest-value items were bolted down or too heavy to move. Martin tried anyway, grabbing the edges and corners of desks and lamps, prying at them with his fingertips. He even went so far as to check the nuts and bolts, just in case a Phillips head screwdriver would do the trick, but everything was hidden or in an awkward spot. The desk was too heavy to move and too ugly to sell. The chair for the desk was in worse shape, so scratched up that no one in his or her right mind would have paid a dollar for it. Even the mirror on the wall was attached from all sides, but Martin tried anyway. He pried with his fingertips, wedging them between the mirror and the wall, and hoping the leverage would allow him to loosen the frame. The frame jiggled but held firm against the wall. Martin continued to try, digging his fingertips into the back of the frame. He pulled back with all of his force but his fingertips didn't have proper grip and he ended up stumbling backward. A sharp corner caught a hold of his ring finger on his right hand and sliced a half-inch cut just below the skin.

"Fuck!" he exclaimed, twisting his head and applying pressure. He glanced back toward the mirror, but instead of seeing behind it, he was now looking right into it. Looking back at him was a defeated man; a disgraced face with dark skin, dark eyes, and dark shadows; a pathetic human being, withered away by his own mistakes. That's when his reflection started talking to him.

"You know what you have to do, Martin."

"I loved Jenny. What have I done?"

"You know what you have to do, Martin."

Martin began to cry. He placed his hands over his eyes to push the tears back, but instead the saline mixed with the droplets of blood and created a pinkish stain over his palms and face.

"You know what you have to do, Martin."

Martin stood there, dumbfounded. He wanted to say something to the man in the mirror, but he couldn't conjure up the right words. The reflection was right: Martin did know exactly what he had to do. There was no way around it. The more he tried to come up with a reason, with an excuse not to go through with it, the more the signs told him he should. He stood there in silence, hoping something, someone would come to save him. He stood in silence as the seconds ticked away loudly, penetrating his eardrums and reminding him of his loneliness with every tick.

"You know what you have to do, Martin." The man in the mirror kept egging him on.

There's nothing left anyway. All the money's gone. Maybe if I had fucking ten bucks for a drink, I could talk myself out of this, but I don't even have that. All I've got is…well, nothing but a hotel room I can't pay for, a room with bolted-down desks and shitty, worthless chairs, and a mirror that talks.

"You know what you have to do, Martin."

"Yeah, I know! I know what I have to do, so just shut the hell up about it, would ya?"

Martin looked down at his hands, still stained pink. *I'll need something, something…sharp. A butcher's knife maybe. But where will I find one?* Then it hit him: *The restaurant! That's it! Deluxe will have butcher knives, steak knives, and anything else I need. Maybe I can even order a nice steak dinner with all the trimmings, my last meal, a little going-away present. Assuming, of course, that these greedy bastards will let me charge it to the room, which I won't be around to pay for. Yeah, that'll work just fine,* he convinced himself.

Martin tried to compose himself enough to put together some semblance of a plan. He knew he'd have to remain inconspicuous in order for it to work. If anybody suspected anything, they would thwart his attempt. *That can't happen. Everything has to go perfectly according to plan.*

He washed up in the bathroom as best he could, scrubbing his palms clean. He then patted his eyes dry with a washcloth and straightened his rumpled clothes, stretching out all the wrinkles so he wouldn't appear overly unkempt. Jenny had taken everything, so he literally only had the clothes on his back. After a little smoothing, pulling, and patting, he decided his attire was just fine.

The next step was to go down to the restaurant and order a steak: a rib-eye, rare, with a bottle of red wine.

"You know what you have to do, Martin."

"Yes," he replied. "I know what I have to do."

He walked out of the room and toward the elevator like a man on a mission. Deluxe was on the second floor, which made for a short elevator ride. The restaurant was empty, perfectly normal for the late hour. There was no hostess, so Martin strode over to two waitresses chatting at the bar. "I'd like a steak delivered to my room please," he said, barging into their conversation with little tact. "A rib-eye, rare. Mashed potatoes and a bottle of merlot as well."

"I'm sorry, sir," replied the blonde, "but we don't cook our steaks rare, and we don't serve rib-eye either. We only serve New York strip."

The brunette said nothing and just glared at Martin.

"Are you fuckin' kidding me?" Martin exclaimed, a little louder than he'd intended to.

The volume and harshness of his voice caught both of the girls by surprise, so much so that the brunette scurried away in haste.

Realizing he was drawing too much attention to himself, Martin shook his head and mumbled, "Fine. Medium rare, then, on the strip."

"What room are you in, sir?"

"Room 302. Just send it up and leave it in the room."

"And how would you like to pay?"

"Charge it to my room."

"Very good, sir. Have a nice day." Her reply was extra polite, and her pleasant personality was unexpected.

Martin suddenly felt terrible for having been so rude. "And, uh…put a twenty-dollar tip on there for yourself, miss…"

"My name's Mary…and thank you very much, sir. That's very kind of you."

"Yeah, don't mention it."

With that, Martin left, wondering whether or not the hotel would still give her the tip after they discovered that he wouldn't be paying the bill. He hoped they would.

He strolled around the casino floor, walking in a daze as the minutes ticked by, trying to give his steak enough time to cook. Occasionally, he would catch his reflection in a metal trashcan or shiny slot machine. His image was still taunting him so he aimed his gaze at the floor. He felt separated from the rest of the world. He had been through this before: broken down, a self-labeled outcast surrounded by the very thing that had taken his life from him.

The people who walked by, laughing and enjoying themselves, didn't even seem to notice him. Everyone was too busy having a good time, everyone except Martin. He had met Jenny during just such a disconnected moment in his life, right when he'd needed her most, while she was working as a cocktail waitress in Atlantic City. She had watched him go down a couple grand shooting dice at The Tropicana and felt terrible for him. She bought him a drink, and they started talking. Martin was vulnerable, ready to do anything for the woman who helped him through that rough time. Now, he could only seethe about how it had all turned out, how they'd ended up. "At least she's better off now," he said. "She doesn't have to worry about me anymore."

After a little while, he sneaked a cigarette out of an unattended pack on the edge of a roulette table and bummed a light from a nearby smoker. As he inhaled the tar and smoke, he watched people winning all around him. It was as if everyone in the casino was hitting their numbers. He grew angrier as the cigarette burned shorter and shorter, its orange glow turning the paper to ashes, almost mocking him somehow. His eyes frantically searched for a loser he could relate to, but the only loser in the room was him.

"Hey! Yo, Marty! Hey, man! It's me, Dan!"

Martin turned toward the familiar voice. *Just another winner to rub it in my face,* he thought. He flicked what little ash was left of his burned-out cigarette on the floor.

"Yo, Marty. What's goin' on, man?" Dan asked, energetic and smiling. "Yo, this is my buddy, Alex. We're here to celebrate his bachelorhood. What's going on?"

"What's going on?" Martin echoed, dead-eyed and barely moving. "Well, let's see. The only woman…no, the only person who ever meant anything to me just walked out of my life. I'm pathetic, a worthless, penniless nothing! I gambled away my job! I gambled away my future! And for what? For what? A couple hits on a roulette wheel? Now what have I got to show for it? Nothing! Fucking nothing! Hell, I don't even have anything left of this cigarette, which wasn't mine in the first damn place." Martin flicked the butt across the room toward some empty slot machines.

Alex and Dan stood frozen in shock. There was a short pause while all three tried to determine if anyone else in the room had noticed Martin's tirade. The laughter around them continued, making it apparent that Martin was, in fact, still very much alone.

Dan glanced over at Alex, and then looked back toward Martin. "Well…" he said, reaching into his jacket pocket and pulling out a fat joint. "Wanna get high?"

Martin stared at the joint just long enough to realize what it was before politely saying, "Yes. Yes, I do."

ELEVEN

9:45 p.m. – Deluxe

"Thank you, fellas. I'll be right back with your change."

"Nah, no change, sweetheart. That's all you."

"Well…thanks again."

Janice snatched the checkbook off the table and walked toward the bar. The rush had ended, and it was her last open table.

Mary was already at the computer when she walked over. "How'd table Forty-Three treat you?" she asked.

Janice opened the checkbook, and a sea of ones fell out on the bar. She counted them, doing the math in her head as she straightened the bills. There were seventy-five dollars altogether, and the total tab was seventy-three.

Mary could feel the heat coming off of Janice. "Sorry, but it happens, hon'," she said, trying to console her before she erupted.

"No, *I'm* sorry. Mare, I can't fuckin' take this anymore. This is the second shitty tip I got today. Fuck this."

"So what are you gonna do?" asked Mary, but it was too late.

Janice had already taken out the seventy-three to cover the tab, leaving the remaining two dollars, and walked back over to the table.

The three men were all standing, getting ready to leave.

Janice put the checkbook back in front of them. "Honestly, fellas, why don't you keep it? It's not that serious." She then made her exit, feeling a great amount of satisfaction for shoving the two-dollar tip back in their faces. She could hear them murmuring and arguing with each other as she walked away. Instead of turning around to face them, she smiled over at Mary, who was trying very much not to notice.

"Janice!" Mary said under her breath when Janice made it back to the bar. "You could get fired for that."

"Honestly, I hope I do. Maybe that'll be the swift kick in the ass I need."

"I can't believe you did that! Seriously!"

"Believe it, sister."

The two girls waited until the group of men left, wondering if they were going to say anything or call for the manager, but no one did.

"Well? What do ya think?" Janice asked. "You think since I called 'em out on their shitty tip that they reached down deep in their greedy little hearts and shallow pockets and decided a two-dollar tip was simply not enough?"

Mary didn't answer. Instead, she stood there shaking her head, wearing a cautious smile across her face.

"Let's find out."

Janice walked over and picked the discarded checkbook off the table. She walked back over to Mary and opened it in an obnoxious fashion in the air. A single dollar bill fell out and floated to the floor. "Holy hell! Those sons of bitches actually took a buck back!"

"Really?" Mary asked?

"I can't believe it! That just really made my night. I swear to God, Mare, the next asshat I see will get a lot more from me than just some nasty words. Furthermore—"

As if he'd heard Janice's remark, a disheveled man walked into the restaurant, marched over to them and demanded service.

"I'd like a steak delivered to my room please," he barked at both girls. "A rib-eye, rare. Mashed potatoes and a bottle of merlot as well."

"I'm sorry, sir, but we don't cook our steaks rare," replied Mary before Janice had a chance to say anything. "And we don't serve rib-eye either. We only serve New York strip."

"Are you fuckin' kidding me?" the man exclaimed, garnering Janice's attention.

Mary squeezed Janice's leg and moved in front of her to keep her from lunging at the man.

Janice took the hint, grinding her teeth in frustration, and walked away to release her rage in the kitchen. "Hey, boys," she shouted at the cooks lingering behind the line, "just one more to-go order."

"Ah! Are you joking, mami?" they shouted back in disdain and broken English. "We closed!"

"Not yet. We've got fifteen more minutes of time to serve, and some fucking jerkoff is about to order a steak to go. Mary's taking the order now."

"Fucking *pendejo*!" the cooks cursed in Spanish and stopped wiping down the stainless steel countertop.

Janice walked back out in time to see Mary putting the order in. "So what did the jerk get instead?" she asked.

Mary pursed her lip and gave Janice a look before tilting the computer so she could see. "He actually quieted down when you walked away. I think you scared him," she joked.

"Well, good. I mean, seriously, the nerve of some people to just stroll in here right before we close and start making demands like they own the place, bossing us around like they own us too. We're people, ya know, not slaves."

"He left us a twenty-dollar tip."

"Really?" Janice asked as she looked over his order again. "Well, that was nice of him."

After a few seconds of silence, Janice cracked a smile. Mary broke out laughing.

"Makes him look a lot better, doesn't it?" Mary asked.

"Yes, yes it does."

"Come on, girl. Let's do this checkout and get outta here."

They printed out their receipts and moved to the small office in the back of the kitchen to fill out the paperwork.

"What were your sales?" Mary asked.

"Just under a grand," Janice lied; her actual sales were only a little over $800. "What were yours?"

"Just over a grand," Mary lied, as hers were actually closer to $1,200. "We should make two today."

"We would have made $250 if people had tipped appropriately."

"Yeah, and we woulda made $150 if those guys hadn't hooked you up for being so sexy," Mary said, bumping her hip against Janice's.

Janice blushed as she stapled her checks together. "You comin' or what?" she asked. She already knew the answer, but she wanted to hear it anyway.

"No, Noah's actually on his way here now. He wants to take me out tonight."

"Oh."

"I'd just be in your way anyhow. Go get your knight, girl."

"Right."

Mary and Janice squeezed into the tiny, closet-sized office where Chef Nobles was checking off his inventory lists.

"Hello, girls. How was your night?" he asked without looking up.

"Fine…uneventful," Mary replied quickly.

Janice stayed silent.

"Hmm. All right, Mary. Everything looks good," Chef Nobles said reviewing her sales. "Just, uh, do me a favor if you can.

All the runners are cut. Do you mind taking that last strip up to the guest's room?"

"Sure, no problem."

"Thanks again, Mary. See you tomorrow."

Mary scooted out of the office, lightly squeezing Janice's hand as she did so.

"And how are you today, Janice?" Chef Nobles asked.

"Just peachy, Chef."

Chef Nobles set his clipboard down and looked over Janice's checkout receipts. "My boys told me they had to redo two halibut dishes earlier today," he said, and then paused for her explanation.

Janice stayed silent, holding back the urge to spit in his face.

"Why did they have to redo the dishes?" Chef Nobles asked.

"The gentlemen at the table decided after the halibut came out that they did not like the sauce on the fish."

"And did you explain to them what the sauce was when they ordered? As I recall, you seemed a bit confused about the sauce in our pre-shift meeting."

"Yes," Janice said, "I told them exactly what you told me, that it was a shellfish nage, a very thin cream sauce made from shellfish."

Chef Nobles pinched the bridge of his nose and closed his eyes. "That was not what I said, Janice."

"Yes it was," Janice replied, her tone adamant and defensive.

"No, I said the shellfish nage is a thin sauce made from white wine and shellfish stock, not a *cream* sauce."

"You said it is a cream sauce, Chef."

"Why would I say that when it isn't correct? I am a chef, aren't I?"

"Allegedly, Chef, but those were your words exactly," Janice snapped. Her blood was reaching boiling point, and she could feel her muscles clenching for a fight. "You said it is a thin cream sauce made from shellfish, and that was exactly how I described it to the guests, and they said it was fine. Then, once it came out, they tasted it and changed their minds."

"Janice, when you don't pay attention in pre-shift, it carries over to the service and costs the restaurant money."

"I'm afraid you're wrong about that too."

"Excuse me?"

"Your top chefs back there took the same fish filets and re-cooked them in something else, then re-plated them. They used the same fish the guests sent back. I know because I was paying attention. You described the sauce wrong, and then the line cooks just re-fired the fish."

Chef Nobles paused, unaware that his cooks were employing such methods. "I expect you to write things down from now on during pre-shift meetings," he said.

"Yes, sir, Chef, sir," Janice replied, patronizing the best way she knew how, which was over the top. There was a moment or two of an awkward silence before she added, "If that's all, sir, I have a very busy night ahead of me."

Chef Nobles tapped his fingers on his desk before brushing her off and turning his attention back to his inventory sheets.

"Just lock the front door when you leave," he said as she turned around.

Janice stomped out in a huff, her fists clenched and sweaty. She was sure that if she'd been forced to stay another minute, she likely would have physically assaulted the man.

The checkout interrogation had taken so long that Mary was already gone. Janice exited out the front, not locking the door behind her out of spite, and took the elevator to the fourth floor, and then walked into the small room the hotel provided for service staff on long shifts. She plopped down on the bed and closed her eyes, imagining a place far away, somewhere much better than the Reverie.

TWELVE

11:21 p.m. – Suite 2

"If anyone is fucking in here, I call next!" Dan's voice echoed as he shouted throughout the empty suite.

Alex and Martin followed him into the room.

"Guess that's a no," Alex joked as he walked over to the mini-bar.

Martin took a seat on the couch in the middle of the room. He hadn't said a word since his earlier blow-up in the casino, and for the time being, he postponed his steak dinner.

"Yo, Joey, you here?" Dan asked the empty room.

"Which room is his?" asked Alex.

"Fuck if I know, but watch this. Joey, we're about to smoke a joint! You wanna hit, you best get your ass out here!"

The words only echoed throughout the lavish suite, followed by an empty stillness.

"He's definitely not here," Dan said, pulling the joint out and burning the tip with a lighter.

"Hey, Martin, you want a drink, man?" Alex asked, holding three mini-bottles of Bombay Sapphire.

"Sure," Martin replied as casual as he could. Secretly, he was ecstatic that Alex had offered.

"What, no vodka?" Dan asked.

"Nah. Looks like Joey got to it first."

"Damn. So what's left? Rum and gin?"

"Or cold whiskey," Alex said, holding up a miniature bottle of Maker's Mark bourbon.

"Why the hell would they put whiskey in a mini-fridge?" Dan asked, shaking his head. "Who the hell drinks cold whiskey?"

"Apparently the guy who stocked this mini-fridge."

"What about tequila?"

"Nope."

"Whatever. Fuck it." Dan unscrewed the gin and raised the little plastic bottle in the air with the joint dangling from his lips. "To old friends, new friends, and Mary Jane!"

Alex and Martin rose their bottles, tapped the plastic bases together, and all three men slung them back. Dan and Alex each took a short sip, but Martin killed his bottle in a couple of swallows.

Dan took several puffs from the newly sparked joint before passing it to Martin. "Here ya go, buddy. This'll cure what ails ya."

Martin inhaled the joint like a cigarette, taking a big drag and pulling the smoke down his throat. What came back up was much rougher than any cigarette he'd ever smoked before, throwing Martin into a coughing fit; clearly, it was his first time smoking pot. The opportunity had presented itself many times before in his younger years, but Martin had always turned it down—partly because he'd always been too busy gambling to bother with any other vices. This night, though, was the perfect time to broaden his horizons. He took another puff and passed it to Alex. Then he unscrewed the cap of his gin bottle before realizing, embarrassingly, that the bottle was already empty. When Alex passed him another without saying a word, Martin thanked him with a silent nod.

"So what happened, man?" Dan asked Martin. "I'm sorry, but I gotta know."

"What happened with what?"

"With your woman, the one who left you?"

"Oh." Martin took a much smaller swig of gin this time as Jenny's image appeared in his mind. "Well, really what happened was…she saved me. Jenny, that is. She came out of nowhere when I was at my lowest point, and she saved my sorry, worthless ass. I've always been a gambling addict, but a gambling addiction is a lot harder to spot than other kinds of addictions. At times, I was everybody's friend at the craps table, hitting every number on the roulette wheel. People thought I was lucky, but I wasn't. They never saw how much I lost before that, and they rarely stuck around long enough to watch me lose it all again." He paused to take another swig. "I was down in Atlantic City a year ago and had just lost everything for the thousandth time. Jenny worked there and had seen it all, witnessed the carnage."

The joint came around again, and Martin took a couple more puffs. He didn't understand why people liked the stuff so much. He wasn't feeling anything. "So," he continued, "she was there when I was at yet another low point, maybe my lowest—well, my lowest until now. She bought me a drink and we started talking, and we didn't stop for hours. I know it sounds corny and cliché, but it was as if we were kindred spirits who'd been missing each other for several lifetimes, as if we'd known each other forever. It was just…beautiful. I mean we really hit it off on every note, having the kind of conversation that never lacked or struggled or sputtered. I went to her place that night, which was good, because I didn't really have a home. Don't get me wrong…her home wasn't much. She was just a cocktail waitress. Still, it was special. I stayed and fixed it up while she worked. I washed the dishes, swept the floors, and even painted her bedroom a God-awful, high-gloss purple. It looked terrible to me, but she loved it."

When the joint came around again, Martin took a couple more, bigger puffs, but he was sure he still wasn't feeling anything. "Over the course of the year we were together, things started getting much better for both of us. She got a better job as a floor manager in one of the city's nicer restaurants, and I landed a job as an assistant manager for a marketing company. It sucked, but it was honest work, and it made Jenny happy. I didn't gamble in casinos at first, because I knew Jenny would leave me if I picked up the habit again, but the bug never left. Any extra money I got was spent on scratch-off lottery tickets or anything I could bet on without her knowing. Then we came here, to the Hotel Reverie, for a vacation to celebrate Jenny's promotion. Our budget was tight, so our plan was just to go out West and see the ocean. This was supposed to be just one of the stops along the way."

Martin began to laugh out loud. He smiled so wide that some spit dribbled down the side of his mouth. He wiped it off with his sleeve and took another sip from his plastic Bombay Sapphire bottle. "Shit, if either one of us had known there was a casino here, I'm sure we would have just gone to a Motel 6. I was so happy when I first found out though, even though I couldn't let on to Jenny. Not only was I back in a casino, but I had about a thousand bucks' worth of vacation money and a five thousand dollar deposit check from my boss." Martin laughed again as he talked, shaking his head and gripping his knee tightly. "Holy fucking shit, man! Of everything that's happened, losing that five grand on the Lakers was one of the craziest. My fucking boss is a prick. I'm glad he's never gonna get his hands on that money."

"Shit, Marty, you put five grand on the Lakers?" Dan asked, remembering back to the roulette wheel.

"Yep, and I woulda bet ten if I'd had it. I still can't believe how that game went. A twenty-two-point spread, and they almost beat it. They should have. They were going to, supposed to. Unbelievable! Imagine how different things would have turned out for me if that one fucking Pistons point guard had missed that last shot." Martin replayed the game in his mind, the moment that had cost him everything.

"So she left you after you lost the five thousand?" Dan asked, snapping Martin out of his painful memory.

"What? Oh, Jenny? No, I don't think that was the only reason. I spent every last dime of our vacation money and all the money that was in her checking account too. I'm sure all of that had something to do with it. Honestly, though, I think she would have left me even if she had found out I was buying scratch-offs. She'd made me promise that I'd never gamble again. It was a condition, a rule for us to be together, and I actually kept that promise for a while, hard as it was. I genuinely really wanted it to work between us, but the longer we stayed together, the more I sneaked around and gambled our money away. I think she just needed to see it for herself. You know something, man? I don't deserve her. That's why this happened, because it was supposed to. I was never supposed to have her in the first place. I don't deserve her."

Martin took a couple more drags from the joint that was still being passed around. He had to pinch the end to keep it from falling apart, but he figured out how by watching Dan. "Damn, man, I think this shit's finally kicking in," Martin said as he carefully handled what remained between his fingertips. "I feel great."

"First time?" Dan asked, already aware of the answer.

"Yes, sir."

"So, knowing what you know now," Alex began, "after all this, would you say coming to the Hotel Reverie was a good thing or a bad thing?"

"What the hell kind of question is that?" Dan asked. "Of course it was a bad thing. He lost his money, his woman, and his job. How could that possibly be a good thing?"

"Yeah, but the man hated his job," Alex said, using both hands to gesture at Martin. "And he said himself that Jenny just needed to see that he was still gambling."

"But she left him, dude."

"Well, if he wasn't supposed to have her in the first place, in a way, this isn't the ending of *them* but the beginning of *him*, right?"

"I don't know, dude," Dan said, shaking his head in protest. "That's a bit of a stretch. I think you're just stoned."

"I am," Alex said with laugh. "That's for damn sure, but I don't think it's a stretch."

"Yes it is!" Dan said putting emphasis on each word. "There are much less tragic ways to end a relationship than to gamble everything away so she leaves in the middle of the night."

"Is there?" Alex asked. "If me and Melissa split up, no matter how it happened, it wouldn't be more or less tragic. It'd be horrible either way, right?"

"Melissa and I," Martin corrected, and then took his final swig of gin.

Alex and Dan looked at each other, confused.

"What was that buddy?" Dan asked.

"Before I was a compulsive gambler, back when I was much younger, I taught middle school English."

Dan and Alex hesitated before simultaneously breaking out in uncontrollable laughter.

"Are you fucking serious, Marty? *You* were a fucking English teacher?" Dan chuckled, coughed a bit, and then shook his head in disbelief. "Holy shit! That's hilarious, man." He stretched out on the couch and placed his arms behind his head.

"Oh, man, that makes so much sense," said Alex.

"Why's that?" Martin asked, unaware of the joke.

"Because only an English teacher would think he knows enough about math to be a gambler," Alex said, still laughing.

Martin couldn't control himself. It was one of the funniest things he'd ever heard. He fell off the couch and clutched his side as he hit the floor. The laughter echoed throughout the suite as the men literally rolled on the floor laughing, each struggling to catch his breath as tears streamed from Martin's eyes.

Only when the laughter subsided did the men hear the door to one of the rooms open. They all turned to see Janice walking toward them, emerging from one of the bedrooms. She looked back at the men, and everyone silently addressed the awkwardness of the situation. "Hey, guys," she finally said, breaking the silence.

All three men gave her a nervous, "Hi," in unison, as if it were planned.

Janice smiled and moved toward the doorway, then turned around to face them "So, Alex, it's your bachelor party, right? Have you seen any boobs yet?"

"Um, no, not yet. None so far."

With a coy smile on her face, Janice pulled the top of her dress down, allowing her perky C-cups to fall out. "Congratulations again, Alex. Whoever she is, she's a lucky lady."

Before Alex had a chance to thank her or say anything sensible, she pulled the top of her dress back up and walked out the door.

Dan and Martin shot glances and smiles over at Alex, who was wearing a sheepish grin he couldn't get rid of.

"Hot damn, man! What the hell was that?" Dan asked, punching Alex in the shoulder. "Wasn't that Sean's chick?"

"Who was she?" Martin asked. "I know I've seen her before."

"She's a waitress at Deluxe. Our friend Sean picked her up earlier and apparently brought her here," Alex said.

Martin remembered her as the brunette waitress who'd walked away from his rib-eye rant. He was embarrassed by his previous behavior and hoped she hadn't recognized him.

"Hey, if she was here this entire time, where's Sean?" Alex asked.

"Right!" Dan jumped off the couch and hurried to the rooms to check, only to find them all empty. "Maybe he and Joey went out drinking or something."

"Hmm. I don't know," Alex replied, shrugging his shoulders.

"Let's go find 'em. Marty, you comin' with us, man?" Dan asked, finishing off his bottle of gin and throwing it on the floor.

Martin searched his brain for a reason not to. He knew he had something to do, something planned, something important. He just couldn't remember what it was. All he could see was the right then and there, the moment right before him. He felt good, he was ready for another drink, and there was nobody waiting for him anyway. For the first time in a long time, he felt free. "Yeah, sure. Fuck it."

"That's the attitude, buddy! Fuck it!" Dan slapped Martin on the back, and then lifted himself off the couch. "Honestly, where the hell could they be anyway? This place ain't all that big."

"Ain't ain't a word," Martin corrected.

"Thanks, Professor," Dan said, half-grinning.

"Let's check the bars first," Alex said, heading for the door.

THIRTEEN

10:34 p.m. – McKilligen's Pub

McKilligen's Pub was adjacent to the lobby, forcing Janice to pass by it every shift. She had only gone in there a few times, usually in her Deluxe uniform, to take a bottle of whiskey that she claimed they needed upstairs for the restaurant. Then she would drink it on the rooftop and stash whatever was left where no one would find it. She didn't pull her prank too often, because she didn't want to get caught. It wasn't that she was afraid of losing her job; rather, she was worried she wouldn't be able to get free booze on a semi-regular basis.

The main reason she didn't like McKilligen's was because her guests often drank there after they finished dinner at Deluxe. She was only nice to strangers when she was being paid and tipped to be. In any other case, she could be a real bitch, and she didn't want to hurt her chances of making money later in the week by having a confrontation with a future customer at McKilligen's. For that reason, she hoped she could walk in, grab the cute one, and walk right out.

As she entered the bar, she saw three of the men from the bachelor party sitting in the back corner: the creep, the cute one, and the plain one. She surveyed the room for the fat one and the guy who showed up late, but they were nowhere to be seen. For a second, her mind wandered to Mary and what she was doing with Noah. She wished she were with her friend instead of at McKilligen's. She always seemed to be doing these kinds of things alone. Nevertheless, she gathered up her courage and brushed the thought out of her mind before it had a chance to fester, and then walked toward the table where the three men were seated. "I hope you boys aren't having too much fun without me." She watched their eyes look up, then down, then back up.

"Damn, girl! Look at you," the creep said, standing up to give her his seat.

"Thank you, Sean. Such a gentleman."

"That's my middle name."

"I bet. Anyway, we haven't been formally introduced." She extended her hand to the cute one and flashed her best smile.

He grabbed her hand giving it a gentle squeeze. "Alex, and this is Tim."

"Nice to meet you both." She nodded at Tim, but kept her focus on Alex. He had sharp facial features and great hair and looked like a friendly person. His smile was etched into his face, and just looking at him made Janice feel safe and warm.

"Nice to see you again, Janice," Alex said, locking his eyes on hers.

She was smitten; flattered that he had even remembered her name.

"What are you drinkin', milady?" asked Sean.

"I'll have what I gave you earlier."

"Comin' right up!" Sean walked toward the bar, texting away on his phone.

A second or two later, Alex glanced at his phone and started texting as well.

"So, Janice, busy night tonight?" asked Tim, the plain one.

"Nah, just the normal weirdoes. Hey, Alex…"

"Yes, Janice?" he asked, looking up and catching her eyes again. He had a habit of paying direct attention to her. It flustered her.

"Can you make sure Sean knows it's a raspberry cosmopolitan?"

Alex laughed and slightly lifted his phone. "Way ahead of you."

"Thanks. So, tell me, which one of you guys is the bachelor?" she asked, praying to God it was anybody but Alex.

"That'd be me," Alex replied, crushing her heart with every syllable.

Janice's mood plummeted even lower, and she punished herself for expecting anything other than the obvious. *Of course he's getting married. He's too perfect not to belong to some lucky woman.* "Oh," she said. "The listener. What a lucky lady." She actually thought of his fiancée as a cold-hearted, fat, ugly witch, but she was fairly sure it wasn't a good idea to mention it.

As if to add insult to injury, Sean, in true creeper fashion, returned with her drink. "Raspberry cosmo, just the way you like it," he said as he placed the pink concoction down in front of her.

"Phenomenal. Thanks for remembering."

"I always pay attention to detail."

"Clearly," she said, bringing the rim of the glass to her lips and taking a sip. It tasted terrible, full of sugar and fake lime juice. She almost regretted giving one to him before, but then remembered that Alex was the bachelor and decided any drink thrown her way wouldn't go to waste.

"Look! The highlights of the Lakers game," Alex said, nodding toward the television. "I heard they killed it. C'mon, Tim. Let's go check it out."

Tim and Alex stood and walked over to the bar, leaving Sean alone with Janice at the table.

It wouldn't have taken a genius to figure out what was going on, and in a strange return to the dismal feel of rejection, she didn't even care. She was lonely, and even though Sean was a total creep compared to Alex, he still displayed an air of masculinity that she looked for in a man. *Maybe he'll surprise me,* she hoped.

"So…how was work?" he asked, moving his chair closer as if he gave a damn.

Well, at least he's trying, she thought. "Do you really care?"

"Not really," he said, clearly caught off guard, "but aren't we supposed to make small talk here?"

"Small talk is for men who don't know what they want or don't know how to get it. Don't you know what you want, Sean?"

"I think I do."

"Yeah? And do you know how to get it?"

"I'd like to think so."

"Prove it."

With that, she slammed down the rest of her overly sweet mixture as if it were a shot and stood up; forcing the alcohol down her throat and breathing the fumes back up through her nose. Janice strutted toward the exit, with Sean following behind her. She didn't utter a word and hoped he wouldn't either. It was hard enough for her to lie to herself, to convince herself she wasn't disappointed about Alex. The last thing she wanted was fake, empty conversation just to avoid silence.

Sean led her to the top floor and opened the door to the suite on the right. Once inside he became aggressive. That was good. What was bad was his sloppy performance; it was like the difference between a wrinkled tuxedo and a freshly pressed one. Janice just closed her eyes and imagined Alex had taken her out on a beautiful candlelit dinner. He would have serenaded her with a guitar in the flower garden, and then taken her upstairs so they could make passionate love together. She pictured anything and everything to help her forget that she was actually about to get fucked by some creep she picked up at work.

They moved to the bedroom, and Janice disrobed, all the while fending Sean off; he was relentlessly attacking her from all sides. She reached down and plucked a condom out of the side pocket of her dress. "Put this on…and then fuck me silly."

Once he was all suited up for the job, she turned around, lowered her head, and raised her ass in the air, the universal sign that she was ready for some doggy-style action. When Sean obliged, Janice's mind immediately jumped back to thoughts of Alex. In her mind, that other man was pulling her hair, slapping her ass. As far as she was concerned, it was Alex's cock moving in and out of her.

Sean tried flipping her over, but she stopped him; if she saw his face, it would ruin her fantasy. As her imagination took hold, she could sense the fragments of an orgasm beginning to form. She let out a soft moan and almost immediately felt the condom fill up with Sean's own release. Any possibility of her having an orgasm vanished in that moment, and she laid there silently, hoping he'd just walk away.

Much to her delight, for the first time that night, Sean finally said something that pleased her: "Damn, girl. I think I need a cigarette. You want anything?"

"No, I'm okay."

"All right, baby. Just wait here. I'll be right back."

She didn't even look up to watch him leave. Instead, as soon as the door closed behind him, she jumped out of bed and started putting her clothes back on, hoping to make a quick getaway before he got back from his cigarette run. Most of all, she didn't want Sean to see her cry, and it took everything in her to fight back the bitter tears. As she sat on the bed scribbling a note for him, she heard the door open, but was relieved to hear voices that didn't belong to Sean.

A second later, one of the voices shouted, "Joey, we're about to smoke a joint! You wanna hit, you best get your ass out here!"

As Janice listened through the door, she noticed Alex's voice in the mix. Initially, she didn't want him to see her like that, drowning in tears of regret, and she was terrified to be stuck where she was, but after several minutes of thought, she decided it didn't matter. *He's engaged anyway, right?* Worse, he'd walked off and left her at the bar with Sean; essentially, he was just playing wingman, trying to get his buddy laid. *Mission accomplished,* she thought.

She waited for a while, listening to them without really hearing their conversation, and then made the decision to leave when she thought about Sean coming back. The last thing she wanted was to see him again. She had to leave, even if it meant going through what was about to be a terribly awkward situation. She checked herself out in the mirror and made sure she had everything with her before taking a deep breath and opening the door. It didn't take long for everyone in the room to notice her entrance, and in an instant, all eyes were on her.

"Hey, guys," she finally said, breaking the silence.

All three men greeted her in a nervous unison, as if they'd planned it. Janice smiled and veered toward the doorway. She almost enjoyed the fact that they seemed more nervous than she was; that gave her some semblance of control. They only looked at her as a whore, and she knew that, but as pathetic as it was, it felt good to be noticed at all. When she reached the door, she turned back around and faced the men. "So, Alex, it's your bachelor party, right? Have you seen any boobs yet?"

"Um, no, not yet. None so far."

Then, just like that, Janice pulled the top of her dress down. "Congratulations again, Alex. Whoever she is, she's a lucky lady," Janice said, truly meaning every word. She then covered herself up quickly and made her exit.

A brief, superficial feeling of power engulfed her, and a weak smile formed on her face as she pressed the button for the elevator. But then, standing there alone, hearing the sounds of the elevator approaching her floor, her lips began to quiver, and her smile disappeared. Right before the elevator doors opened, she ran away toward the fire escape. She pushed through the doors and ran down the stairwell as fast as she could. She didn't know where she was going; she just didn't want to be where she was. She kept up her fast-paced descent, going down faster and faster with each passing level.

She was running so fast that one of her heels snapped off, and she tumbled down the stairwell until she hit a platform, where she landed hard on her elbow and slammed her head against the wall. Lying there in a bloody, broken heap, Janice began to lose consciousness, and a moment later, her world went dark.

FOURTEEN

11:59 p.m. – McKilligen's Pub

Tim scratched at the corner of his beer label, attempting to pry it off with his fingernail. He watched as the amber liquid sloshed around inside, bubbling up and foaming in the bottle. He gently tugged at the label, peeling the layer of paper off the glass and exposing the glue. He almost got all of it in one tug, but some remained, creating a frayed, sticky mess around the bottle. He crumbled up the decimated label and knocked back another gulp of the lager.

He'd been sitting by himself for quite a while. It wasn't strange for him to be by himself, as he was often somewhat of a loner, but in this instance, he felt very alone. Perhaps it was the mixture of alcohol and his friends' party-hard attitude, one he did not share, but whatever it was, something about the night depressed him.

The television played nothing but sports highlights. Tim wasn't one for sports, but since there was nothing else to look at and no one to talk to, he tried to follow along with the closed captioning at the bottom of the screen. He could hear the laughter of the strangers drinking behind him, and felt paranoid they were laughing at him. To keep from losing whatever cool he had left, he had to continually remind himself that they weren't.

He watched the players on the screen pass the ball back and forth, occasionally taking a shot. As a kid, he'd never played sports. Instead, he'd spent his free time constructing models and tinkering with computers. For the most part, nothing had really changed. All grown up, he worked with computers for a living, and all things athletic were still a mystery to him. He simply couldn't grasp all the rules, especially basketball. He always thought somebody was traveling when they weren't and could never understand why some fouls were called while others went unpunished. To Tim, watching sports was like talking to women, in that both were confusing, even though every other guy seemed to have no problem with it.

He finished the rest of his beer and scanned the bar for a friendly face. He was embarrassed when he realized he was the only lone drinker in the place, so he chose to pay his tab and leave. It wasn't too late, so he decided to take a walk around the hotel for some fresh air before reconvening with the guys. Outside, he instantly began to feel refreshed. There was so much going on inside, with all that chattering, slot machines ringing, drunken patrons yelling, and glasses clanging around. Outside, it was as if the whole world had been put on mute. Tim could hear the wind whistling around the street signs and the crickets chirping in the distance. The lights from the hotel were not bright enough to outshine the moon and stars, and he gazed upward as he began his walk.

He thought about what Alex had said about Sean, that Sean used to be just like him, more of a romantic than a player. He wondered if he might turn out to be like Sean in the future, but ultimately laughed off the idea almost as quickly as it had entered his mind. *I doubt Sean ever played with models,* he thought, *at least not the same kind I played with.*

When he turned the corner of the building, Tim felt as if he'd entered some kind of dream world. There was a flower garden, which was somehow illuminated, even at that late hour. Red roses, purple lilies, and other, more exotic foliage lined the side of the building, and a cobblestone path lit by small lamps led the way through this serene garden. Tim strolled down the path, inhaling deeply to take in the sweet smell of the floral landscape. On his way, he passed by several small ponds inhabited by playful and happy-looking ceramic frogs and turtles.

He noticed a gazebo off to the left, and he spotted a woman sitting in it by herself. He'd thought he was alone, and when he realized he wasn't he quickly looked away in embarrassment.

The woman didn't respond at all. Instead, she just sat motionless, staring at the garden.

Fueled by the beauty around him and maybe a little more courageous because of the alcohol still filtering through his veins, Tim took a deep breath and approached the gazebo. "Hi. I didn't see you there. My name's Tim."

She glanced at him for an instant before looking away.

Silence filled the air, and Tim's heart started to pound. He felt like a fool. *Why won't she say anything?* he thought. *What did I do wrong?* He stood there, still, before shaking his head and turning his body away.

"Well? Aren't you gonna sit down?" she asked, finally breaking the silence after what felt like an eternity.

"I didn't think you wanted me to. You look rather upset."

"At least you're observant. Come on and sit down."

She patted her hand on the wooden bench by her side, and it was then when Tim remembered where he had seen the woman before. She'd come into McKilligen's earlier, looking like a mess. Sean had tried to hit on her, but she'd shot him down. It made Tim more nervous knowing that even Sean couldn't get her. For a second, he was worried that she—or he himself—was just wasting his time.

Tim eventually sat down on the other side of the bench, leaving enough room for a small group between them. They sat together in silence for a couple of moments, watching the fireflies bounce around the garden and listening to crickets sing in the distance.

Finally, Tim said the only thing he could think of to start a conversation: "So, um…do you, uh…how about those Lakers?"

She slowly swiveled her head around and cocked her right eyebrow, looking at Tim as if he'd just spoken in Swahili. "Are you kidding me right now?" she asked.

"I'm sorry. I just…I don't know why I asked that. I don't even care about the Lakers or sports in general. I'm just…well, I just don't know what I'm supposed to say to a beautiful woman sitting in a gazebo."

She stared straight through him as she tried to determine whether he was spitting a line or being sincere. When she concluded that he was actually being genuine, she couldn't help but break into laughter. "So you decided on 'How about those Lakers'?"

Tim smiled and shook his head. "I know. Dumb, huh? But I was just watching a bunch of highlights in there, and it was the only thing I could think of."

"Why were you watching highlights if you don't like sports?"

"Because I'm *supposed* to like sports."

"What do you mean by that?"

"I mean…I'm a twenty-seven-year-old guy," Tim mumbled, as if he was talking to himself. "I'm supposed to like sports. All of my friends do, and they all have girlfriends. I, on the other hand, have never been into sports, and I've never had…" Tim stopped himself, realizing what he was about to say.

"What? You've never had what?" she asked.

"What they have."

"Oh. So you think watching sports will help you?"

Tim paused and thought about it before answering, "Well, I used to, but not anymore."

The woman started to laugh again and scooted a little closer to him, causing his heart rate to increase. "So…what do you *really* like?" she asked him.

"I like this," he said, gesturing to the flower garden in front of them.

"Stop."

"No, seriously. It's beautiful. I can't believe they didn't mention it in the brochure. They talk about the restaurant and stuff, but this is the real deal. I went to a flower show in Philadelphia once. It took my breath away. I mean, some of the things these people can do is astounding."

"Are you a botanist or something?" she asked.

"No," he said with a chuckle. "I wish. Actually, I'm a computer programmer. I write code that keeps hackers from acquiring people's credit card numbers."

"Oh. How…noble," she said, snickering.

"Yeah, thanks," he replied.

She scooted over a little bit more, and his palms began to sweat. "So…what brings you here?" she asked.

"I just wanted some fresh air."

"No, I mean to the Hotel Reverie?"

"Oh, a bachelor party. My buddy Alex is gettin' married."

"So you picked a place in the middle of nowhere? Why? So you could invite strippers?"

"No! Nothing like that," Tim replied, defensive and embarrassed. A second or two of silence followed before he said, "Well, truthfully, I don't even know what they're doing. I can't really keep up with them. That's why I'm out here."

She scooted over even closer and grabbed his hand, then rested her head on his shoulder and let out a sigh. "That's a good thing, Tim. It really is."

"Sorry. My hands are a little, uh…sweaty."

"It's perfectly all right," she said, smiling and squeezing his hand. "You're allowed to have sweaty hands."

Tim smiled and tried hard to slow his heart rate down. His nervousness was loud and obvious, but she didn't seem to mind. It was as if she was the perfect girl, sent specifically for him. She wasn't intimidating or demanding but kind and warmhearted, the type of person who would stop to take care of a wounded animal. She was an angel, as far as Tim was concerned, and he barely knew anything about her.

He turned his head to look at her. Her beautiful blonde hair hung from her head in knotty clumps. She looked used, beaten, and gorgeous all at the same time.

"What's your name?" he asked, embarrassed for waiting so long to find out.

"Jenny," she said. "My name's Jenny."

FIFTEEN

11:59 p.m. – Main Stairwell, East Side

Janice awoke, still sprawled out in the stairwell from her blackout. Pain surged through her body as blood dripped down her cheek. She could move but didn't want to; instead, she collapsed, curled into a small ball, and began to cry. It was a subtle weeping, one barely acknowledged or detectable. There was no sniffling, no noise—just tears trickling down the sides of her face, mixing with the blood and forming a small pink puddle on the steel floor.

Several levels above, a door creaked open, and Janice scampered to her feet. She didn't want anyone to see her in that condition. She heard no footsteps or voices, but she still hurried in the opposite direction, trotting barefoot down the stairwell, with her heels in hand, including the broken one. The east side stairwell of the Hotel Reverie connected every floor from the basement to the casino to the restaurants to the suites. After jogging down the stairs, she found herself in a spot she knew very well, a gray and blue section of stairs located outside of the Deluxe kitchen. Over the past several years, she'd spent many shifts there, smoking cigarette after cigarette as the hatred of her job built inside of her. As if to pay some sort of sick tribute, she sat back down on the cold stairwell and lit one up. She still didn't want to be bothered, and she knew no one would bother her there. The last six years of loneliness could attest to that.

Janice leaned back and rested her head against the wall. The fall had made her leg numb and sore. Her fingers traced over a ping-pong ball-sized bump on her head, and her elbow was bleeding. Continuing to drag from her cigarette, which at no point left her lips, she cupped her hand around the cut and applied pressure.

As enticing as the temptation was to run away, there was no place to run away to. She was trapped. She was trapped screwing random guys and wishing they were someone else, serving douche bag tourists who tipped her five percent and never remembered her name. Her only real friend was Mary, and Mary had Noah. When those two tied the knot, it would be like tying a noose around their friendship, and Janice would be completely alone. She'd just be a crazy, miserable old lady, still working at Deluxe. *Crazy old lady Janice.* She could almost hear the taunts of imaginary school children from her nightmares. *Crazy old lady Janice, still slinging it away as the rest of the world passes her by.*

Janice inhaled deeply, forcing the smoke down into her lungs and violently holding it there. The smoke came out slow and with it another tear, which she quickly rubbed away.

Her job was a nightmare, one she couldn't wake from. It dragged her down more and more as each day passed, enslaved by the generosity (or lack thereof) of complete strangers who didn't think about her any longer than the time it took them to order their food—even less in certain instances.

Janice breathed in the last of the cigarette, and then snubbed it out on the wall, creating a dark little circle on the stone. In the mood for a drink, she picked herself up and walked into the kitchen of Deluxe, still barefoot and carrying her heels. She splashed some water on her face in front of a mirror and scrubbed away the blood and dirt. Her face still looked awful, and the bump on her head was more than noticeable, but she was glad to see that at least she wasn't bleeding anymore. She walked into the dimly lit dining room and went behind the bar to look for the bottle of Crown Royal she'd grabbed from McKilligen's earlier. When her liquid relief wasn't where she'd left it, the rage began to boil up inside her once again. Somebody had taken her whiskey, and if she ever caught the culprit, they'd be in for a rude awakening. It was her only bottle of booze, and the bars would be closed soon.

She stormed out of the restaurant and headed up to her room, where she threw the broken useless heels on the floor and stepped into some flats. Sore, used, beaten, broken, tired, cranky, on edge, and quickly losing her buzz, she stormed out and walked in the direction of the casino, looking for a thief with a half-empty bottle of Crown Royal.

SIXTEEN

12:16 a.m. – Casino floor

Not knowing what to expect after smoking pot for the first time, Martin was beginning to feel all of its glorious effects. He strolled around the casino floor without a care in the world. The games, the vice that had tormented him for years, seemed to have no effect on him now; he was simply too out of his mind to care about them. It didn't even dawn on him that he had no money to bet on them, even if he had wanted to. Instead, he wandered around, following Dan and Alex, who were deep in their own conversation.

Wait…what am I doing here? Why am I following these two? He had already forgotten. He knew he was supposed to find something, but he forgot what he was supposed to be looking for. Whatever it was, he didn't remember it being all too important anyway.

He gripped the sides of a load-bearing pole and stretched his joints, cracking his shoulders as he twisted his body around. He felt like he was in heaven. Dan and Alex kept walking, but Martin didn't want to follow. He was having too much fun exploring where he was. "Hey, guys! Dan!" he yelled.

Dan and Alex turned around.

"I think I'm gonna break away for a bit," Martin said.

"Huh?" Dan asked, raising his eyebrow and cocking his head slightly to the side.

"I think, uh…" Martin began, and then wondered why it was so hard to put a sentence together. "I think I'm gonna hang out here."

"Oh," Dan said. "Well, hey, man, good luck to you and, uh…Jenny. I hope everything works out, man."

"Oh yeah. Thanks. And thanks for the joint. It really opened my eyes."

"Here." Dan reached into the breast pocket of his blazer and pulled out two joints, twisted in thin white paper. "Enjoy, brother!"

"Oh, man! Thanks!" Martin plucked the two joints from Dan's hand and slid them carefully into his pocket. "Seriously, Dan, it was great meeting you. You too, Alex. Congratulations on the wedding."

"Yeah, man! Nice meeting you," Alex said.

The three men shook hands before Dan and Alex turned and walked away. Martin continued to stroll the casino floor without purpose. He was nervous the joints in his pocket would break, so he decided to buy a pack of cigarettes to have a safer place to store them. Then a sobering thought occurred to him: *I don't have any money. Shit!*

Not sure what to do about it, he walked into the bathroom to take a leak. While he was washing his hands, he noticed a little setup in the corner with mints, aftershave lotion, gum, and—by some miracle of God—cigarettes. *What a break,* Martin thought as he looked around to see if an attendant was watching. After confirming that the coast was clear, he snatched the pack that looked the fullest. It was missing five or so smokes, leaving the perfect amount of empty space for Martin to slide his joints right in. He pulled out one of the cigarettes and lit it with a Hotel Reverie match he'd found lying next to the other packs. With the cigarette in his mouth and feeling like a new man, he strolled out of the bathroom and back onto the casino floor.

There, he caught a glimpse of the brunette waitress they'd met earlier, the one he'd yelled at and who had flashed him in Dan's suite. He walked over to her and immediately noticed the egg-like, swollen bump on her head. "Hi."

"Hello."

"How'd you get that bump?" he asked, wearing a goofy smile.

"Fuck off!" With that, she turned around and started heading toward the elevator. Martin followed like a stupid lost puppy. "Don't you remember me?" he asked.

"How could I forget the douche who freaked out on us because we didn't have any fucking rib-eye?"

"Yeah, that was me," he admitted.

She turned around, confronting him, coming within six inches of his face. "Why were you such a dick?"

Martin hesitated. He felt too alive and free and happy to lie, so he made the incredibly bold decision to be honest. "Because I was gonna kill myself."

"What did you say?" she asked, positive she had misheard him.

"Because I was going to kill myself. I was at the lowest point I've ever been in my life, and I was going to slice my wrists with the knife when I was done eating my last meal, that rib-eye. I love rib-eye, but no one ever has anything but fucking strips." Martin laughed an uneasy laugh, and then smiled. To his surprise, it felt good to talk about it; it felt good to do anything. He brought the cigarette to his lips and took another drag before sticking out his empty hand toward her. "My name's Martin, and I'm very sorry for my rudeness earlier."

Janice stared at him and his outstretched hand, taken aback by his nonchalant, suicidal confession. She hadn't expected him to be so brazen or so honest.

"Janice," she said cautiously shaking his hand. "Mind if I have one of those cigarettes, Martin?"

Martin reached in his pocket and pulled out two more. He gave her one and held up his current smoke so she could light hers with it. Then he lit his new one in the same fashion and flicked his first one toward a nearby ashtray.

"So…if we had given you the rib-eye, would you have done it?"

"I don't think it would have mattered," he said. "I don't want to do it now, so that's all that's important, right?"

"Chickened out, huh?" she asked with a dark, unnerving smile.

"No, definitely not. I just…I found a new reason to live."

"And what's that?"

"Well, shit, I'm not sure exactly. I'm fucking broke, Janice. I lost everything in this casino. My girl left me, and I'm about to lose my job. But you know something? I don't care anymore. None of that is important. Nothing is."

"I'm not so sure about that."

"Look, what's the biggest problem you have? Whatever it is, I have the answer for it."

"Do you now?"

"Yes."

"All right, Mr. Born Again," she said, tapping her ash on the floor in spite of the ashtray six inches away from her. "My problem is that I'm stuck here working this terrible, shitty job, serving dicks like you, most of the time for insulting tips that won't buy me a cup of coffee."

"So quit."

"I can't. I don't have anywhere to go." Janice's eyes drooped toward the ground as the words came out of her. "Like I said, I'm stuck."

"You just said you can't stay here anymore, so you'll have to find somewhere else to go or suffer with dicks like me," Martin said, putting emphasis on the last few words. "You're not stuck, Janice. You just need to make a change, and only you can do that for yourself."

Janice looked back at Martin, still questioning his sincerity. She felt like she should be angry with him for involving himself in her life when he didn't even know her, but she wasn't. Instead, his feistiness was intriguing, if not amusing.

Martin sensed her confusion and admitted, "You'll have to excuse me. It's been a crazy day, and I'm a little high. Would you like to come up to my room with me? I tried pot for the first time earlier tonight, and I think I'd like to do it again."

Janice laughed in the middle of inhaling her cigarette, causing her to choke a little and cough into her hands. She regained her composure, though, and after several seconds, she pulled her hands away from her mouth, revealing an ear-to-ear smile. Her grin held its shape for an instant before fizzling away into the dry smirk that seemed to be a favorite expression of hers, but that one flash of happiness was undeniable; secretly, even she could admit it. "Got anything to drink up there, Martin?" she asked.

SEVENTEEN

12:16 a.m. – Casino floor

Dan and Alex strolled throughout the casino floor, stopping every few feet to stare at a blinking light or a spinning wheel.

"Goddamn, is this the same shit we smoked in high school?" Alex asked.

"Nah. It's a whole lot better."

"You're not kidding. I am stoned as shit. Why are we here again?"

"Uh…" Dan stopped to think for a minute. "We were gonna hit the bars."

"Right."

"But wait…why?"

The two men froze, gazing into the depths of their own brains, trying to remember what they had talked about just ten minutes prior. It was proving to be a difficult task, too difficult for either man to accomplish.

"Seriously, why the fuck are we here?" Alex asked after a minute or so of silence.

Dan laughed and shook his head. "Dude, I honestly don't remember. You wanna get a drink?" Dan asked, eyeing McKilligen's from across the room.

"No, I think I wanna play the slots." Alex walked over to a multicolored *Wheel of Fortune* machine and examined the controls like he was looking at a UFO. "Looks complicated," Alex joked, taking a seat.

Dan sat down beside him, still trying to remember why they were going to hit the bars. Alex reached for his wallet, but Dan had already pulled out a twenty-dollar bill and put it in the machine. "There ya go, man," he said. "Win us some money."

"Sounds like a plan." Alex sat in front of the machine, staring at the pictures as they rolled by.

Dan gripped the back of his chair and turned to look for a cocktail waitress. The casino was as busy as it had ever been, despite the late hour. There were still multiple tables open for dice and roulette and about a half a dozen or so for all the different Asian poker games. Dan felt the itch to get up and try his luck on whatever table his eyes landed on first. He was down for the night by a couple hundred or so, which wasn't too bad, considering he'd been playing for so long. Still, he was bummed he had lost all of his winnings from earlier, and he wanted to end the night in the black.

"Oh shit! The wheel's spinning," Alex said with a laugh.

Dan looked over to see the wheel spinning at the top of the machine. The little needle passed by the $1,000 credit marker and eventually landed on the $200 one.

"Sweet! How much did you win?" Dan asked.

"Meh, ten bucks, but it cost me five to get it." Alex laughed and smacked the machine lightly with the side of his hand.

"Excuse me, gentlemen?"

The two men turned around to see a young guy in his early twenties. He was wearing a maroon bowtie with a matching vest and a pressed, white shirt underneath. "My name's Noah. I work for the hotel. You guys are in Suite 2, right? I just wanted to make sure your friend's okay."

Alex and Dan glanced at one another, each wondering if the other knew what the kid was talking about. For their answer, there lingered an awkward silence.

Noah continued, "I don't mean to pry or anything. It's just that I had to help Mr. Roznick back to the room. He was a little inebriated, and I thought I'd check on him."

"Mr. Roznick?" Alex asked, confident that he'd heard the name somewhere before.

"Yes, er…um…Joey."

"Joey!" Dan and Alex both shouted.

"Fucking Joey," Alex said again, slapping Dan on the back. "That's what we were doing here. We supposed to be looking for fucking Joey!"

"Son of a bitch! You said you took him to the room?" Dan asked Noah.

"Um, yes, sir—well, sort of. I led him to the elevator and I sent it up to your floor."

"Good enough. Thanks again, man," Dan said as he pulled another twenty out of his pocket and handed it over.

"Thanks, but that's not really necessary. Like I said, I just wanted to make sure he's all right."

"No, thank you! Without you, we woulda been sitting here for an hour, losing our asses on this damn game," Dan said, laughing. "You saved us at least $100, so you oughtta have that small cut."

Noah chuckled. "Thanks again, sir. I very much appreciate it."

"No worries, kid!" Alex said, jumping up out of his chair. "Come on, Watson. We have a drunk to find."

"Watson? Actually, I think I'm more of a Holmes," Dan said to Alex. "You should be Watson."

"Bullshit! I called you Watson first. That's all there is to it."

"I think we might need to consult the official rules on Watson and Holmes. I'm pretty sure firsties don't really apply here."

"I'm pretty sure they do, Watson," Alex said, gesturing across the room. "Come, to the elevator!"

The men bounced their way through the casino crowd and arrived at the elevators just as two men speaking Russian were exiting. They sneaked in right behind them as the doors swooshed closed. Dan slid his keycard to allow them access to the suites. Both men practically blasted the door down when they got to their room, bursting in lively and shouting at the top of their lungs.

"Where is that drunk son of a bitch!?" Alex screamed.

"Hey yo, Joey! Your boyfriend Noah told us you're up here. Come on out, would ya?" Dan yelled behind him.

"Wrong. No one's here. The whole fucking place is empty."

Dan and Alex walked into the center of the room to find Sean holding a half-empty bottle of Crown Royal, with six cigarette butts snubbed out on the coffee table in front of him.

"Sean, you smokin', man?" Alex asked, surprised.

"Meh, I stole a pack from the casino bathroom earlier. It pairs well with the whiskey." He shrugged his shoulders and took another swig from the bottle before offering it to the other men.

Both declined.

"So…what's all this about Joey?" Sean asked, bringing the bottle close to his mouth again. "I thought he was with you."

"Nope. He left me while we were playing craps," said Dan. "He got ridiculously wasted and started calling everybody a faggot."

"Hmm. That sounds about right actually," Sean said, stretching his face into a smug and arrogant smile.

"Where'd that Janice chick go?" Alex asked, remembering that she'd left earlier.

"Fuck that bitch. I don't care where she went. What are you dicks up to?"

"Trying to find Joey," Alex said.

"Where's Tim?" Sean asked, not sure if he really even cared.

"I left him at McKilligen's earlier. I'm sure he's fine. The guy's worst offense in life was blowing through a stop sign four years ago. I'm more concerned with Joey. If he's not here, where is he?"

"Wait a minute. Hold up just a second, Watson," Dan said, bent over and holding himself up with the floor.

"I'm Holmes. You're Watson," Alex corrected him.

"Not anymore, because I just found a clue." Dan picked up a small piece of paper from the floor and passed it to Alex.

Alex read it, furrowed his brow, and looked back at him.

"What's it say?" Sean asked.

"Uh…'Room 401. Knock three times.'"

"What?" Sean asked again.

"That's all it says, man. 'Room 401. Knock three times.'"

"Who the fuck wrote that?"

"I don't know, but we can find out," Dan said as he was lighting another joint from his pocket. "Let's just go to Room 401 and knock three times."

"Are you serious?" Alex asked, both about Dan's plan and the burning joint.

"Hell yeah, I'm serious," Dan snapped. "None of us wrote that note. Maybe it was that chick you banged."

"No," Sean said confidently, having already thought of it.

"Well that means it was either Tim or Joey, and since Joey's already been to the room multiple times to drink and whatnot, all evidence points to Joey."

"Or maybe some cleaning lady dropped it and forgot to pick it up," said Sean, lighting up another cigarette.

"We need to go find our missing comrades, littering cleaning lady or not. What's the worst that could happen? We knock on the door, someone answers, and he's not there?"

Dan continued to smoke the joint, never once passing it or even offering.

Sean shook his head and plopped back down on the couch to take another swig of whiskey. He flicked some ash from his cigarette on the table, and then looked over at Alex. "What do you think?" he asked.

Alex thought about it for a minute before nodding at Dan. "Let's fucking do it. Dan's right. What's the worst that could happen?"

"Fine, but I'm not letting you sissies have all the fun. Let's load up before we go," Sean said, and then passed around the bottle of Crown Royal.

This time, everybody took a swig.

Dan offered what was left of his joint, but no one wanted to partake, so he took one more drag before tossing it away. Then the three men gathered themselves and walked out of the room toward the elevator.

"What time is it?" asked Alex.

"Does it matter?" Dan asked

"Yeah. It'd be a pretty dick move to wake somebody up in the middle of the night."

"It's not the middle of the night. It'll be fine," Dan said, even though he wasn't sure either of those was true.

They pressed the button for the fourth floor, and then followed the hallway until they found Room 401. Sounds of music were coming from the other side.

"At least we know we aren't waking them up," Alex said.

"Shit, are you kidding me? Did fucking Joey find a party and keep it to himself? I'm gonna kick the guy in the balls if he did," Dan said as the three men approached the door. He knocked his fist on the wood three times, as instructed.

The door slowly crept open and was held by a Middle Eastern man, thin as a rail and dressed in a hot pink mesh tank-top and ridiculously short denim cutoffs. "Yes? Can I help you, gentlemen?" he asked.

"Uh, we're looking for our friend Joey, and—"

"Joey? Oh! Yes, Miguel is with him. Come on in."

The three men crept into the room slowly, unsure of what to expect. It was very dark, with only mood lighting. There was a large pile of cocaine on a glass table in the center of the room, and a combination of house and techno music was being played in the background.

"Oh shit," Dan said when he saw the snow-white pile. "Do you mind if I party?" he asked the man who had let them in.

"That's what you're here for, isn't it?" the man asked.

"Now it is." Dan walked over to the couch and started cutting up lines. Meanwhile, Alex and Sean walked around the room, glancing at everyone's staring faces.

"Not a lot of girls at this party," Sean whispered to Alex as he walked over to Dan.

"No, not many," Alex agreed. Dan had cut out three lines on the glass table and motioned to Alex to go first.

Alex quickly declined. "No, none for me buddy. I don't touch that stuff."

"Yeah? Me neither," Dan said as he lowered his nose to the tiny metal straw and sniffed the powder until it was gone.

Sean took the next line, and then leaned his head back, pinching his nostrils closed to make sure not to waste a single speck.

All three of the men sat on the couch; completely aware that everyone's eyes were peering down on them. It was hard to see around the room, as the mood lighting didn't illuminate much, but the party certainly appeared to be a younger crowd, all men.

"Total fucking sausage fest, eh, fellas?" Dan said as he straightened up another line.

"That's what I said," Sean added. "Where the fuck is Joey?"

"That dude at the door said he's with Miguel. Who the hell is Miguel?" Alex asked, looking around.

"Excuse me! Where is Miguel?" asked Sean as a twenty-something kid in short shorts and a wife-beater walked by.

The boy pointed to a door on the other side of the room. "He's in there," he said with a meek voice.

Dan sniffed up the last of his line and jumped off the couch. "In that case, let's go fucking get him!"

"Wait, Dan. I have a weird feeling about this party," Alex said, holding him back.

"Yeah, me too," Sean said to Alex, "which is why we need to get Joey and get the hell outta Dodge. Lead the way, buddy."

Dan was already by the door but waited until the other guys arrived before opening it. Initially, the light from the fluorescent bulb on the other side of the door was blinding, and it took a second or two for the three men's eyes to adjust. When they could finally focus again, they saw a tall man with a thin mustache, golden skin, and a lanky build, dressed only in a Hotel Reverie uniform vest and a bowtie. In his hand was a leash, which was strapped around the neck of a very naked Joey. Besides being in the nude, Joey was on his hands and knees, with his mouth wrapped around the strange man's hard cock.

Alex, Sean, and Dan froze, unable to say anything yet unable to look away.

The moment lasted longer than it should have and was finally interrupted by the Middle Eastern man in the mesh tank-top who broke the silence from behind. "You better hurry up, Miguel. It doesn't look like these boys want to wait any longer."

Joey turned his head and saw his best friends staring at him with amazement. Immediately, his eyebrows raised, and he slowly brought his head back, allowing Miguel's cock to drop out of his mouth. A look of horror and shock came over his face; fear engulfing him like a child caught wetting his pants on the playground.

Miguel, unaware of the connection between Joey and the three men standing at the doorway, ejaculated all over Joey's chest. "Whew! Well, fellas, you'll have to wait in the other room for a minute while I clean my little puppy off. What a good little puppy," Miguel said, stroking his hand over Joey's head. "Don't be shy, little puppy. You did an excellent job."

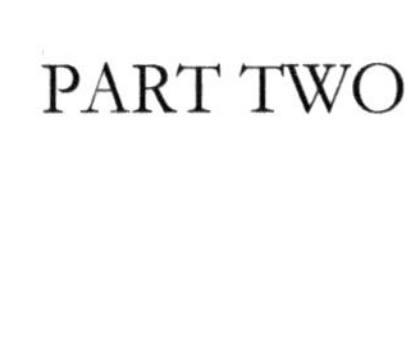

PART TWO

EIGHTEEN

5:35 p.m. – Front Desk

Miguel stood behind the front desk at the Hotel Reverie with the same amount of pride as a guard for the royal family. Never once had he shown up late or called in sick because he was a firm believer in the Hotel Reverie front-of-house slogan, "Everyone is onstage at all times," and that carried all the way down to how he dressed. His pants were always ironed with a perfect crease, and his shoes were always shined until they reflected light when he walked. His shirts and vests never left the house if they weren't starched and fitted, and his bowties were wrinkle free and knotted perfectly. His slicked-back black hair and pencil mustache were always well groomed and appropriate in accordance to the Hotel Reverie Employee Rules and Regulations Manuel. But the boundaries of his attention were not limited to just his looks and attire, for Miguel also cleaned behind the desk in meticulous fashion with an arsenal of various cleaners and disinfectants that he kept hidden away in the coat closet. Attacking smudges and left-behind fingerprints when there was any downtime, he utilized every moment of the day to make the guests' experience at the Hotel Reverie a great one. He was a fantastic concierge with Jedi awareness for guests' needs, but as thorough as he was in every other facet of his life, there was one missing piece: that special someone to share it with. "Welcome to Hotel Reverie. Do you have a reservation?" he asked with full attentiveness and composure.

"Yes."

"And your name?"

"Joey Roznick."

"Very good, Mr. Roznick. Please give me one moment while I pull up your reservation. How was your trip?" Miguel asked, pretending to scan the computer screen while secretly checking out Mr. Roznick. In the homosexual community, Joey would have been considered a bear—a larger, hairier gay. Miguel had never had the chance to cuddle with a bear, and he'd always wanted to.

"Long," Joey answered.

"Excuse me?" Miguel asked, a bit flustered.

"My trip. It was long."

"Oh! Where did you come from?"

"Out east. It's my boy's bachelor party. Needed to get away, somewhere where we can let loose, ya know?"

"Sure," Miguel said. "You need a place where boys can be boys."

"Exactly! You know what I'm talking about, uh…"

"Miguel."

"Right! You know what I'm talking about, Miguel."

Miguel loved the man's cute, pudgy face. With his wide-eyed, innocent smile, he almost looked like a giant teddy bear. "Mr. Roznick, I have your reservation right here. You've requested a suite, correct?"

"That's right."

"And how many are in your party?"

"Five."

"Very well, as long as you're aware that our suites only house four beds," Miguel said, trying to get a read.

"Yeah, I know. But we aren't fags or anything, if that's what you're thinking."

A slight smile formed on Miguel's face. In his experience, the most homophobic people were either religious fanatics or closet homosexuals themselves, if not both. Since Joey wasn't wearing a cross around his neck, Miguel decided on the latter and wanted to pry further. "Oh goodness, no," he said, rather effeminately. "If you fellas were a bunch of faggots, you would have requested a room with only one bed."

"Heh, I suppose that's true. You get a lot of queers here?" asked Joey.

"Now and then. Those boys are a bunch of partiers, so the hotel suits their interests."

"Jesus Christ! Well, I hope they aren't here tonight. Nothing pisses me off more than a fruity little cocksucker."

"Oh? What type of cocksucker do you prefer?" Miguel asked. He smiled and lowered his eyelids halfway in an attempt to lure Joey into the realms of his dirty mind. Joey's blushing red cheeks were a clear sign that Miguel had succeeded, and it only made him want to keep going.

"Uh…well…"

"It's just a joke, Mr. Roznick," Miguel said, lightly tapping Joey's hand.

Joey laughed, although it came out more of a nervous chuckle. "Ha! 'What kind of cocksucker do you prefer?' Very clever."

"Personally, I don't enjoy fruity little cocksuckers either. I prefer bigger, manlier cocksuckers. Why even be a fag at all if you only like girly men, right?"

Joey let out another nervous laugh, this time veering his eyes down and away, as if he was guilty of some kind of naughty thought. "Right! That's funny," he said, nodding quickly like a bird.

"From what I hear, though, those boys have the right idea," Miguel said, leaning across the desk so Joey was the only one that caught it.

"What was that?" Joey asked, leaning in to hear.

"Well, think about it. I mean, honestly, Joey...can I call you Joey?"

"Sure."

"Right. Well, think about it, Joey. Have you ever had your dick sucked by a woman and really enjoyed it?"

"Um..."

"They're terrible! They don't work the shaft right, they ignore the balls, and then they get all pissy when you cum on them."

Joey nodded as his anxiety began to build. He coughed up another nervous chuckle and said, "Damn, Miguel! You make some good points, but what's the alternative?"

"You've got to find yourself a good, old-fashioned fag. They know what you like, and, what's more, they *enjoy* giving it to you," Miguel said.

Joey suddenly felt tense. "Well, I mean, uh...I guess that's probably true..."

"Truthfully, I don't understand why men even go after women," Miguel continued. "All they do is mess things up. Biologically, we're not even compatible. Men have quick orgasms, and then just want to go to sleep. Women are the complete opposite. It makes for some very frustrating fucking, doesn't it, Joey?"

"I guess so," Joey said, the words coming out slow. "I'm not gonna lie. I hate fucking women."

"As you should! You're a man!"

"But I don't think I could ever let another man—"

"No, me neither. I mean, what are we? A bunch of faggots or something?" Miguel laughed off his own question, convincing Joey to laugh as well.

"Right," Joey said, averting his eyes once more toward the floor.

"It's just such a shame, you know? I mean, here we are, two sexually repressed men in our prime, constantly fighting against our desires of having great orgasms, all because we're too distracted with how we're supposed to act around women and pissed off with how they're acting around us."

"Yeah."

"It's such a shame that we could never have such a real conversation with a woman."

"Yeah. So, have you ever, uh…"

"What was that?" Miguel asked, interrupting Joey's question on purpose to keep him in a place of mild anxiety.

"I mean, have you ever, uh…with a man instead of a woman?"

"Well, I'm certainly no fag, if that's what you're thinking!" Miguel roared out in laughter.

"Right," Joey said, nodding his head and laughing along with Miguel. "Me neither!"

"Right," Miguel said, "but I have experimented before with pleasing another man."

"Oh?"

"Sure. There's really no contest. We guys just know what we like."

"Hmm."

"Well, you're all set Joey. Here are five keycards, one for each of you. You'll need them to open the doors and to take you to the top floor in the elevator." Miguel slid the room keys across the table to Joey. When Joey plucked them from the table, Miguel brushed his hand against Joey's lower wrist and let it linger for several seconds, rubbing his thumb over Joeys palm before pulling away.

"Okay."

"And let me give you this," Miguel said as he slid a folded piece of paper over to Joey. "Go out with your friends, drink, and be merry. Later, if you're interested in having a fun time, I'm having some friends over for a party."

"A party?"

"Just a bunch of fags letting loose."

"Oh." Again, Joey darted his eyes toward the floor.

"Another joke," Miguel said, but he didn't laugh this time.

"Oh!" Joey's eyes picked up again, and he returned a smile back to Miguel. "Right. Just a bunch of fags letting loose." Joey glanced at the note, and then slipped it into his back pocket before sliding the room keys into his front one.

"I'll have one of the bellhops take your bags up. Noah!"

"No, that won't be necess—"

"Yes, Miguel?"

"Noah, please take Mr. Roznick's bags to the second suite."

"Yes, sir."

"Actually, we don't have any bags," Joey said.

"My apologies," Miguel said, angry at himself for not paying attention to the guest's needs and wondering if it was because the bear had him so distracted.

"Not a big deal at all," Joey assured them. "Here you go, Noah. Thanks anyway." Joey palmed a twenty-dollar bill over to the bellhop, almost fumbling the handoff when he noticed how sweaty his own palms were.

"Thank you, sir! That's very nice of you," Noah said back.

"Don't mention it, kid. And, uh…thanks again, Miguel."

"Anytime, Joey. Enjoy your stay."

As soon as Joey swiftly walked away and was out of sight and earshot, Noah approached Miguel with a knowing smile on his face. "Joey? That's a little informal, isn't it?" he asked as he tucked the twenty dollars into his vest pocket.

"Oh hush. I think I found me a boy toy for the evening."

"Really? He's gay?"

"Sure," Miguel said. "He just doesn't know it yet."

"That's some pretty powerful gaydar you got there."

"With great power comes great responsibility," Miguel mused, shrugging.

Noah laughed and pulled a stool out of the coat closet. "How many we got tonight?"

"Eh, we're at about 50 percent."

"You think we'll be outta here by eleven?" Noah asked.

"Me? No. You? Maybe. You got plans with Mary?"

"Yeah," Noah replied. He fidgeted around in his chair for a moment or so before adding, "I think I'm gonna propose to her tonight."

Miguel's head shot around in disbelief.

There was a serious look on Noah's face, and he was looking at the ground, kicking his legs under his stool restlessly. He was almost as uncomfortable as Joey had been in Miguel's presence.

"You think?" Miguel asked, prodding his way into Noah's mind.

"You know what I mean."

"Noah, that's fantastic! Let me see the ring!"

Noah reached into his pocket and pulled out a velvet black box, then held it out to Miguel without even lifting up his head. Miguel snatched the box from his hand and opened it. Inside was a quaint diamond, surrounded by several smaller ones, all strung together around a gold band.

"It's beautiful. She won't refuse you, Noah. Oh, I'm so happy for both of you!"

"You don't think it's too soon?"

"No! And don't you dare chicken out! How are you going to do it?"

"I was thinking of taking her to the flower garden. It seems like the perfect place."

"So beautiful." Miguel handed the box back to Noah. "Is she expecting it?" he asked.

"I don't know, but I don't think so."

"I'm so, so happy!" Miguel said, clapping his hands and hopping up and down.

"Calm down, man. She hasn't said yes yet," Noah said.

"She will," Miguel said back. He loved living vicariously through his much younger and straighter co-worker. Thoughts of his own someday wedding played out in his mind daily. With his eyes closed, he imagined himself walking down the aisle, with flower petals strewn about and everyone smiling at him. A soft piano would play in the distance as he walked up to the altar.

When Miguel opened his eyes, interrupted from his fantasies by a gruff clearing of someone's throat, he saw a very large, unattractive man standing at his counter, his face contorted into a discontent and menacing frown.

"Yes, hello. I have a room," he grumbled in a very heavy Russian accent, which was almost as thick as the stench of cigarettes coming off of him.

Miguel mustered his best professional smile, trying hard to conceal how nauseous the man made him. "Welcome to the Hotel Reverie. Your name please?"

"Andrei."

"Very good, sir. And your last name?"

"Tolstokozhev."

"I'm sorry. What was that?" Miguel asked.

"Tolstokozhev. Andrei Tolstokozhev. I requested a smoking room."

Miguel searched for different spellings of Andrei before finding it a minute or so later. "I see it right here, mister." He paused, debating on whether or not he should attempt the man's last name. Opting not to embarrass himself further, he said, "It will be Room 707. Here are your two room keys, and Noah will be happy to take your bag upstairs for you."

Noah dutifully hopped off the stool, but Andrei waved him away.

"That won't be necessary," Andrei replied. "I can carry it myself. Thank you very much."

"And thank you, sir. Enjoy your stay at the Hotel Reverie."

Andrei awkwardly nodded before retreating to McKilligen's Pub opposite the lobby.

"I'm so…unnecessary," Noah said, grinning. "I'll take this all night," he joked as he jumped back on the stool.

"Did that man seem strange at all to you?" Miguel asked with a suspicious edge in his voice.

"Why? Do you think he's gay too?" Noah asked, smiling.

"No, just…bizarre."

"Well, he's Russian. In general, foreigners are pretty strange people. Of course, they probably think the same about Americans in their country." Noah took out his phone and started pecking at it. "I wonder what he's doing all the way out here though?"

"So do I. Maybe he's a terrorist," Miguel said with excitement. "Wouldn't that be something?"

"If a terrorist got a room here?"

"Sure!" Miguel's eyes widened.

"Dude, this is the Hotel Reverie," Noah said. "We're miles away from anything worth blowing up. Why would he get a room here instead of in the city?"

"Because, *dude*," Miguel mocked, trying to sound as straight as he could, which wasn't very straight at all, "This is the Hotel Reverie, and we're miles away from anything worth blowing up."

"I don't follow you."

Miguel didn't explain it. Noah was right anyway; they *were* miles away from anything. It would have been too much excitement for a terrorist to check in to his hole-in-the-wall hotel, far too much for a middle-aged, gay concierge. He fantasized about what it would be like if such a thrilling, unique thing occurred, but this time, his dream was cut short when the phone behind the counter began to ring. He sighed and picked it up. "Thank you for calling the Hotel Reverie. This is your concierge, Miguel. How may I help you?"

"Miguel, it's Fernando. I just have some last-minute details to go over for our party tonight."

"Fernando, what could you possibly be calling about?" Miguel rolled his eyes. He knew there were plenty of reasons for Fernando to call, but none of them were good, and he was somewhat nervous about what Fernando had in store for him.

"I was thinking…wouldn't it be nice if it was snowing?"

"Snowing?"

"Yes, honey, snowing. I'd love to have a big ol' pile of snow to play in, and I think the other boys would too."

"All right, Fernando. I know better than to try to talk you out of it, but why are you calling me?"

"Well…you're the concierge, right? Do you know where we can find some?"

"No."

"Come on, baby! You know all the guests who are staying in that oversized shoebox of yours. Spill the beans already. Somebody must be packing."

"Fernando, I don't—"

"Fine! There's no need to be a wet blanket. I guess I'll just tell the rest of the boys that there will be no snow to ski on."

"I guess so."

"Miguel!"

"No, Fernando! I'm not going to give you any information about our guests. It's bad enough I let you convince me to have this party, but—"

"It didn't take much convincing."

"I could lose my job!" Miguel said. He was determined to win this argument.

Right in the middle of their phone conversation, a young, distraught-looking woman approached the counter.

"I'm sorry, sir, but, uh…there's nothing I can do," he added.

"Sir? Miguel, don't you dare hang up this phone, or—"

"Thanks again for calling. We'll see you tonight, sir."

"Miguel, don't you hang up on me!"

"All right. Bye-bye now." Miguel hung up and looked over at the woman. "Hello. Welcome to the Hotel Reverie. How may I help you?"

"Yes, hi. Um, uh…I need to know how to get back to town," she said, sounding nervous and erratic.

"Well, I'm pretty sure the last bus back has already left. Is there a problem?"

The woman burst into tears, sobbing over her hands and smearing her makeup as she tried to talk between gasps. "My boyfriend…the jackass lost all of our money." She stopped to sniff. "In the casino. I have nothing and…" She sniffed again. "I need to go back home!"

"Get this poor woman some tissues!" Miguel shouted at Noah.

Noah jumped off the stool and ran into the coat closet.

Miguel turned back to face his frantic guest. "All right, honey. Tell me what happened."

"He lost everything we had. It's my fault. I-I never should have trusted him. I never should have come here."

Noah arrived with a tissue box and set it down on the desk.

Miguel plucked four sheets out and handed it to her. "Where is he now, honey?" he asked.

"I don't know. I'm scared to go back to the room."

"What's your name?"

"Jenny."

"Jenny, I'm gonna move you to another room for the night. What room are you in now?"

"Um…302," she said. "It's under my boyfriend's name, Martin."

"Here is a key for Room 812. Don't worry, Jenny. Everything will be fine. Noah, here, will go to your old room and get all your things." Miguel glanced over at Noah, who nodded back and started walking toward the elevator. "Just stay there for the night. He'll never find you. We'll get you back home in the morning."

Jenny just stood there, holding the keycard in her trembling hand.

"What's wrong, honey?" Miguel asked.

"I don't have any money to pay for this."

"Don't worry about that. I think losing everything you have deserves a comped room for the evening. In fact, it deserves a comped meal too. There's a menu upstairs for our restaurant, Deluxe. Call down here and order anything you want, and I'll have it sent up, no charge."

Jenny blew into the tissues and shoved the wrinkled remnants into her pocket. "I don't know how to thank you," she said.

"Thank me by leaving that deadbeat boyfriend of yours. You're a catch, woman! Every straight man in this hotel will be trying to hit it. Hell, you're even getting *me* hot."

Jenny giggled through the tears and smiled with endearment at Miguel. "Stop."

"Just enjoy yourself tonight, honey. Go back home tomorrow and start a new life."

"I appreciate it, but I think I'd like to leave now. Is there any way I can get back to town tonight?" she asked.

Miguel shook his head.

"Most of the staff basically lives here. You could try asking Harold, the bartender at McKilligen's right over there. He drives in sometimes."

"Thank you, um…"

"Miguel."

"Miguel, thank you. A thousand times, thank you."

"Don't even think about it. Harold works till twelve, so even if he can help, you'll have to wait till then. Why don't you go to the room and eat something first?"

Jenny leaned in and gave Miguel a hug over the counter. She then slid her new room key into her pocket with the tissues and walked toward the elevator.

Miguel sighed and watched her slink away. It seemed someone lost something every day, and their better halves always came crying to Miguel. He had always hoped it would be a dreamy, muscular man, begging to cry on his shoulder. Even just the thought brought a smile to his face as he continued to daydream about his fictional wedding and his make-believe husband.

NINETEEN

6:31 p.m. – Casino Floor

"Holy shit, Liam! They have a casino here! Did you know that?"

"No."

"Well, we should—"

"No way, Hector. We're not doing any gambling. I want to get in and out."

"Sure, sure. We get a call to drive out into the middle of nowhere to do a deal, and—"

"Not so loud."

"I gave up a night at Tracy Loretta's house, man! I'm missin' out on all that alcohol, drugs, and—"

"Hector…"

"I gave all that up just so we could do this fucking deal, but at least there's a casino, right? Maybe we stand a chance to actually have some fun tonight after all, but—"

"Enough."

"But noooo. Why? Because big, bad Liam' is putting his foot down, demanding that it's all business all the damn time. Well, fuck you, asshole. After this shit's done, I'm playing baccarat."

"No, you're not."

"Liam, you dragged me away from Tracy Loretta's place. You remember how voluptuous her titties are, don't you?"

Liam's eyes shifted back and forth as he kept a lookout for anyone who seemed to be paying extra special attention to them. Nobody knew they were there, and it needed to stay that way. He just wished Hector would keep his big mouth shut. He pulled a cigarette up to his lips and lit it with a match from a matchbook with "Hotel Reverie" written in script on the back. Liam stared at the matchbook before he threw it away. "Very voluptuous," he said after an elongated pause.

"Very fucking voluptuous, Liam. Very fucking voluptuous." Hector's whole body was electric as he described Tracy Loretta's curvaceous figure, emphasizing her shape in the air, something Liam felt was obnoxious and unnecessary. "Some might even call them gargantuan," Hector continued. "Not me, of course. I've seen actual gargantuan titties before, the kind that give bitches a bad back. Still, Tracy Loretta's girls are very fucking voluptuous indeed. I've been chasing that bitch for weeks now, and—"

"I think you mean days," Liam corrected.

"Whatever. But there we were, Liam, smoking a blunt on her couch while I gave her a back rub. A fucking back rub, Liam! And I was getting all into it; really working her shoulders and shit. Then I moved my hands down her backside and around front. I squeezed those fucking titties so hard, man. I flopped them bitches around like bags of Jell-O, like I was on the damn set for a commercial with Bill Cosby, trying to make them sons of bitches look alive. God, Liam, I grabbed those fucking tits and flung that bitch backward and stuck my dick right in her asshole."

"No, you didn't."

"You're right. I didn't!" Hector shouted. "Do you know why? Because during that back rub that was gonna turn into so much more, I got a fucking phone call from you, demanding that I come outside and take off with you for a job."

"Hector, I—"

"I begged, 'Please, Liam! Please let this bitch touch my dick first. Please let me shove it in her mouth just one time. You could watch, man. Hell, you could join in. You could just sit on the couch and do line after line until you spin out of control and OD right there. Please!' I said, but no dice. You insisted that we leave right then to make this sale."

"Hector—"

"Don't you 'Hector' me! You said we had to leave right fucking then. So, I had no choice but to toss Tracy Loretta's very fucking voluptuous titties aside and get in the car with you. Liam, I'm tellin' you once more. After this shit is done, I am playing fucking baccarat. Now, excuse me while I take a shit."

As Hector walked toward the men's room, Liam stood with his back facing the far wall of the casino, shaking his head in disgust. He weighed whether or not it would be a wise decision to leave Hector at the hotel and drive back to town without him. After a brief moment of calculating the pros and cons, he decided it would be impossible. He hated working with Hector, but he had no choice; neither Vinnie nor David was available.

Liam tossed his smoke and pulled out a piece of paper with a phone number scribbled on it. He walked out of the casino, through the lobby, and to the payphone on the corner. He dialed the number from the paper.

On the fourth ring, someone answered. "*Hola*!"

"Fernando?" Liam asked, masking his voice to make it sound slightly deeper.

"That depends on who's calling, sweetie."

"It's Frosty."

"Frosty?"

"Yeah. As in, Frosty the snowman."

"Oh, I get it! Very clever, Frosty. I'm on my way, so just amuse yourself for the time being."

"I'm on a tight schedule here. When can I expect you?"

"Gimme an hour, baby. I'll be there as quick as I can. Should I call back at this number?"

"No, I'll call you." With that, Liam hung up and walked back inside. He grabbed a second matchbook from the front desk, and then stood outside the men's room to wait for Hector. He lit another cigarette and threw the nearly full matchbook away. He almost had the whole cigarette finished by the time Hector finally came out.

"Damn, that was a stinker," Hector said, waving his hand in front of his nose. "You were smart to stay out here in the fresh air," he joked.

"We've got an hour to kill," Liam said. He snubbed his cigarette out on the side of an ashtray and dropped the butt in the center.

"Baccarat?"

"No. Let's get something to eat. There's a sign over there for a restaurant."

"Fine," Hector conceded, "but since you won't let me gamble, and you made me miss out on Tracy Loretta, you're buying. I figure it's the least you can do."

The two men followed the signs that led them to Deluxe. Hector liked the place because it looked expensive; Liam liked it because it looked empty. Rather than waiting for anyone to seat them, they walked to a booth off to the side and toward the back. The only other patrons were a couple of older men, who were sitting at the opposite end of the restaurant. Liam relaxed as the waitress walked over.

"Hello, gentlemen. My name is Mary. Can I start you fellas off with distilled or sparkling water this evening?"

"No need," Hector said. "Just bring us two dirty Hendricks martinis, shaken, not stirred."

"Just one," Liam said.

"Nah, make it two, Mary. My friend here desperately needs to relax," Hector said, giving Liam a punch to his arm.

"Fine, but listen…ignore the idiot trying to be James Bond. Forget about the shaking and stir them. Add only a half-ounce of olive juice and don't put any more than a thimbleful of dry vermouth in them."

"Um…yes, sir," Mary said, feverishly attempting to write down all of Liam's detailed instructions. "Comin' right up."

"What the fuck is wrong with you?" Hector asked when she walked away. "Everybody knows it's shaken, not stirred."

"Sure, double-oh-asshole, and everybody is an idiot. If you shake gin through ice, it turns cloudy, bruises, and has inconsistencies in flavor depending on the strength of the shake. James Bond may have known how to save the world from imminent disaster, but he couldn't order a drink for shit."

"Oh yeah? Well, you may be able to order a proper drink, but James Bond has hit more bitches than Chris Brown."

"Who?"

"If Mr. Bond asks for fucking turpentine in a sneaker, I'll ask for it too."

"You're an idiot, Hector."

Mary returned with the two martinis and took their order, chicken Florentine for Liam and a veal chop topped with *foie gras* and a grilled shrimp skewer on the side for Hector.

Almost as soon as they finished giving their order, four men entered the restaurant. They sat in the center of the dining room and started ordering drinks.

Liam watched them with full attention, trying to spot any peculiarities in their behavior. He watched their faces, looking for red flags like wandering eyes. Rarely would eyes wander if they were honestly engaged in whatever they were doing. Wandering eyes usually meant something else was on the mind. For example, four undercover cops looking to bust a couple of coke dealers would be looking at exits, civilians, and everything else. The four men seemed to be engaged with only each other, but it wasn't until the fifth man showed up that Liam breathed a sigh of relief. In the history of all stings, no cop had ever shown up late for the bust.

Liam glanced at his watch and started tapping his fingers on the table, apprehensive about the pending exchange.

"What did he say?" Hector asked, sensing Liam's anxiety.

"He said he's on his way."

"Goddamn it."

"What?"

"If we knew he was gonna be late, we could have just come later."

Liam agreed, but he stayed silent anyway. He rarely felt the same way as Hector about anything, and on the few rare occasions when he did, he didn't want Hector to know it.

"I mean, shit, man, I coulda given it to Tracy Loretta twice. How much is it for anyway?" Hector asked.

"A quarter."

"Quarter of a key?"

"Yup."

"Damn. Those fags can't get enough."

"Nope."

"Do they always get a quarter?"

"Only about once a month. Most of the time, it's little balls here and there."

"No shit?"

"Yup, but every now and then, I'll get a call for a small blizzard."

"So…who is this guy?"

"His name's Fernando," Liam said. "He's a prissy little faggot, from what I hear. I don't trust him with my real name, so make sure not to mention it."

"Got it. Where'd you meet him?"

Liam shrugged. "Lorenzo's the operator."

"So where'd Lorenzo meet him?"

"No idea. Not sure I wanna know, so I never thought to ask."

The two men continued to drink their martinis. With each sip, Liam loosened up a little; Hector, on the other hand, seemed to become more professional.

"Good customers?" Hector asked.

"I don't know that either. This'll be the first time for me, but they've been talking to Lorenzo for at least half a year or so."

The food arrived, and the two men continued to talk as they ate.

"So what's the play?" Hector asked, digging into his shrimp skewer.

"Standard protocol. Point guard off to the side. That's you. I'll be the arbitrator. Get in, get out—no mess."

"Is everything all right, gentlemen?" Mary asked, stepping back to their table.

"Just fine. Can we have the check please?" When Mary gave it to him, he paid in cash and left a twenty percent tip.

"I don't understand why you leave that much," Hector said as he fidgeted a toothpick around his teeth.

"Twenty percent is a standard tip. Any less, and the waitress will hate you for it. Any more, and she'll love you. Either way, if you don't leave 20 percent, she'll remember you. The last thing I want is to be remembered."

"Fair enough. C'mon though. Let's get this over with."

"What about baccarat?" Liam asked. He ate his words as soon as they came out, realizing he'd just reminded Hector of it.

"I'm full, horny, and missing Tracy Loretta's sweet, sweet girls," Hector said. "I'll come back another time for baccarat."

Liam was happy to hear it, and the two men climbed out of the booth, walked back toward the lobby, and made their way outside to the payphone. Liam dialed the number as Hector lit up a cigarette.

"Hola."

"It's Frosty."

"Ah! Just the man I need to talk to."

"Are you here?"

"Room 401, baby."

"On my way."

Liam hung up the phone and reached for a cigarette. Hector lit it with the Hotel Reverie matchbook he had grabbed before, then took a cue from Liam and threw it away. They walked side by side around the building and down toward the parking garage.

"So…I've been thinking—" Hector started to say.

"Uh-oh."

"I think I'd make a good arbitrator."

"No."

"Come on, Liam. I'm always the point guard."

"That's because you make a great point guard. Play to your strengths, buddy. Everybody's got a role."

"Thank you…and you make a great arbitrator."

"Thanks."

"Still, I think I'd make a great one too, and I'm sure you'd make a damn fine point guard."

Liam unlocked a black Lincoln Town Car and popped the trunk. The two spun their heads around, surveying the scene for any watching eyes. Once they were sure the coast was clear, they reached in and pulled out an assortment of handguns. They each strapped one to their lower back, masking the shape with their bulky coats, which were far too big to be considered in season. Liam also attached a small six-shooter to his lower leg.

"How about we flip for it?" Hector asked.

"No."

"Liam!"

"The point guard stands in the corner and looks tough," Liam said, facing Hector square in hopes of squashing his dreams of playing the arbitrator. "That's got you written all over it. As for me, I'm great with handling problems. That's why we do this for a living. If this was football, and you were a great wide receiver and I was a great quarterback, why the hell would we switch positions? Why fuck up something that works?"

"I'm always the fucking point guard." Hector grabbed another handgun from the arsenal and tucked it into his front pants pocket before buttoning up his coat.

"Tell you what. Tonight we'll stick to the plan. The next time we work together, you can be the arbitrator, and I'll be the point guard," Liam said, hoping he wouldn't have to work with Hector again for a long while. He then added, just to be safe, "As long as it's less than a quarter."

"I wanna argue with you, Liam, but I know how much it hurts you to say that."

"It hurts a lot."

"Finally!" Hector said with giddy enthusiasm. "I can't wait to be the fucking arbitrator."

"Next time!"

"Right, right. Next time."

Liam pulled a small suitcase out of the trunk. He unzipped it and moved the contents around until he spotted the package: a quarter-kilo of cocaine neatly wrapped in clear plastic, laced with a ribbon of duct tape to keep it nice and packed. He closed the suitcase again and slung it over his shoulder. "Let's move," he said.

"Where are we headed?"

"Room 401. And remember, no real names."

"What's your name again?" Hector asked.

"Frosty."

"Right. Just call me Rico," Hector said, buttoning up the remainder of his coat to hide the weapons underneath.

"Rico?"

"Yeah."

The men walked through the garage and to the elevator attached to hotel.

"Why Rico?"

"I don't know. I just like the sound of it," Hector said. "Plus, it sounds Puerto Rican, and I kinda look Puerto Rican."

"Wait…you're *not* Puerto Rican?"

"No. I'm *sorta* Rican. My mom was Puerto Rican, but Pops was Mexican."

"Oh," Liam said, letting out a mild laugh and following with, "I'm sorry to hear that."

"Fuck you, Frosty."

The elevator arrived, and the two men stood awkwardly silent as they waited for a family to exit before entering behind them. The doors swooshed closed, and Liam pressed the button for the fourth floor.

"I don't think Frosty suits you," Hector said.

"You don't?"

"Frosty was a happy, magical snowman. You, on the other hand, are a sad, lonely drug dealer."

"Hence why it's an alias, a fake identity."

"You don't go around calling yourself Frosty on every job, do you?"

"Only when the shoe—or the snow boot—fits."

The doors opened, and they walked down the hallway to the last room on the right, Room 401. Liam pounded his fist on the door.

A moment later, a frail-looking Middle Eastern man opened the door wide. He was wearing a hot pink, mesh tank-top and cutoff denim shorts. "Frosty?" he said, arching a perfectly plucked eyebrow.

"Fernando."

"Perfect timing, boys! The guests are just beginning to arrive. Come on in and have a seat."

Liam took a couple steps in and stood slightly to the right of the door. Hector walked toward the back of the room and placed himself opposite Liam, inspecting his surroundings to ensure there would be no surprises.

Fernando bounced around the room changing light bulbs and hanging multicolored cloth everywhere, unaware of the men's purposeful, strategic placement.

"Ugh, what a nightmarish day I've been having," Fernando said, flailing his arms to accentuate his points. "I'm trying to plan this party, but I'm getting absolutely no help. The boys will be arriving soon, and look at me, still decorating! Thank the Lord that at least the party favors arrived."

"Where's the money?" Liam asked.

Fernando reached into a box on the desk and pulled out a wad of $100 bills wrapped in a rubber band. He walked over to Liam, swaying his hips as he moved, and dropped the green bundle in Liam's outstretched hand. Liam pocketed the money, unzipped the duffle bag, and pulled out the plastic-wrapped coke.

"Oh goody!" Fernando grabbed a pocket knife from a drawer and cut into the plastic as Liam unfurled the money and counted the stack. Some cocaine fell out onto the desk, and Fernando dropped his face down and sniffed a bump. He came up squeezing the back of his nose, and he sniffed several more times to inhale any excess. "Well done, Frosty! Geez! That's gonna work just fine," he said, shaking his head. He was still pinching his nose, so his voice sounded reverberated and nasally.

"You're short," Liam said.

"What's that?"

"There's supposed to be four and a half large. This is only four." Liam held up the stack of bills in the air, waiting for Fernando's explanation.

"Lorenzo told me it was only four."

"I don't give a damn what Lorenzo told you," Liam said. "I'm telling you what it is. A quarter-key has always been four and a half. This is only four. You're short."

"No, *you're* short, sweetie," Fernando said, smiling. "I was told four, so that's all I'm paying."

Liam shook his head, giving Hector the warning signal, and they simultaneously drew their guns.

"Whoa! Slow down, fellas," Fernando said. He finally stopped pinching his nose and put his hands out in front of him.

"Fernando, I've been doing this for a very long time, and I've always worked with Lorenzo. Never in the history of my very long career have I ever sold a quarter-key for less than four and a half. My partner Rico knows that, Lorenzo knows that, and now, Mr. Fernando, you know that."

"Okay, okay! Calm down, baby. Everything's negotiable if—"

"Negotiable my ass! Where's the fucking money, Fernando?"

"All right! I got your other five, sweetheart. Geez! No need to get all hot and bothered."

The two men stood with their guns drawn until Fernando counted out another $500 from his box: one hundred, fifteen twenties, six tens, three fives, and twenty-five ones. Even though Fernando was down to only ones, it appeared he had about a $100 in singles. He held out the pile of cash for Liam, who tucked his piece away so he could count it; meanwhile, Hector kept his gun leveled at Fernando's head. Liam confirmed the extra $500 and nodded, calling Hector off before putting all $4,500 in his inner coat pocket.

"Will you gentlemen be staying for the party?" Fernando asked, the sarcasm not lost in his voice.

Hector slinked his way over to the door, keeping his back to the wall, while Liam stared at Fernando, answering his question with silence. The second Hector exited the room, Liam followed. He closed the door behind him, and the two of them walked in silence to the elevator. They stayed quiet during the elevator ride. It wasn't until they reached the parking garage that Hector finally spoke up.

"What was all that about back there?" he said as they were walking toward the car, "I thought a quarter-key was four."

Liam paused, and then turned to look at Hector. "It's not four and a half?" he asked.

"I don't think so."

"Are you sure?" Liam asked again.

"Pretty sure."

"Oh, well. Oops."

They walked over to the Lincoln Town Car and stowed away all their firearms in the trunk. Liam climbed into the driver's seat, and Hector got in the passenger side. Both men sat in silence. When Hector lit up a cigarette, Liam followed suit. The smoke bounced off the windshield in front of them and danced around in the air.

"How sure are you that a quarter's only four?" Liam asked, still staring at the swirling smoke in front of him.

"Pretty sure."

"On a scale of 1 to 100?"

"Ninety-eight."

"That's rather confident."

"Like I told ya, I'm pretty sure."

"Well shit. Now I kind of feel like an asshole."

"Don't let it get you down," Hector said. "I woulda charged that fruitcake an extra $500 just for being a fag. Come on. It's not that late. Let's suck on some titties."

Liam didn't start the car.

"What?" Hector asked, afraid he already knew the answer.

"Maybe I should call Lorenzo."

"Fuck that shit! Are you kiddin' me, man? So you charged the faggot and extra $500 by mistake. Big shit! Are you really gonna drag this out for that? What's Lorenzo gonna do anyway, huh?"

Liam churned away at his cigarette as he weighed his options.

"Listen, Liam, I may be wrong, man. Fuck it, I *am* wrong, now that I think about it. A quarter-key has always been four and half. Now let's just go."

"Nah, I need to call Lorenzo."

"Son of a bitch! Fine. Here, call him," Hector said, passing Liam his cell phone.

Liam snickered, pushed it away, and got out of the car, without Hector bothering to follow. He headed up the stairwell and down the path to the payphone on the corner. He dropped a couple quarters in the slot and dialed Lorenzo's number.

"Lorenzo's Italian Eatery. Pickup or delivery?"

"It's Liam. Lemme talk to Zo." He heard some shuffling on the other end of the phone before an old man's muffled voice sounded through the receiver.

"Hello?"

"Zo, it's Liam."

"What's wrong?"

"A quarter-pie…is it four and a half or four?"

"What?"

"Is a quarter-pie four and a half or four?"

"A quarter-pie is four and a quarter, you fucking retard."

"Four and a quarter?"

"Yes! Four and a quarter!"

"Are you sure?" he asked Lorenzo.

"Yes, I'm fucking sure!"

"So…on a scale of 1 to 100…"

"Listen to me, you fucking asshole. A quarter-pie is four and a quarter! It's what I told those fags, and it's what you're gonna charge them. They buy a lot of fucking pizzas, so don't screw this up!" Without another word, Lorenzo hung up the phone.

Liam stood for a little while longer with the phone to his ear as he thought about what he was going to do. He hung up the phone and walked back over to the stairwell, back down the stairs, back to the Lincoln Town Car, and climbed back inside.

Hector watched him, anxious as he waited to hear what he was going to say.

Liam lit another cigarette and breathed the smoke out through his nose. "Lorenzo said it's four and a quarter."

"Four and a quarter?" Hector asked. "Are you shittin' me?"

"No."

"God fucking damn it! God-fucking-son-of-a-bitch-mother-fucking-damn it!"

"Yup."

"I bet he wants us to fucking give it back, doesn't he?"

"Yup."

"Shit! Fucking son of a bitch! Fuck!"

"Yup."

Hector punched the dashboard with his fist and kicked his legs out from under the glovebox. His body flailed and spasmed into a grown man's temper tantrum, but a minute and a half later, he'd already worn himself out. He panted, brushing the sweat from his brow, then lit up another cigarette. "So…how the hell do we go about doing this?" he asked Liam.

"No idea."

"Great. Just fucking great."

TWENTY

12:25 a.m. – Room 302

When Martin entered through the doorway he felt as if he were time traveling. The emptiness enveloped him and refreshed his memory. He could still smell the depression from several hours earlier, and the mirror on the wall was a painful reminder of those dark feelings that had nearly consumed him only a short time ago.

Janice followed behind him and noticed the bottle of merlot. "Well, well. What do we have here?" she said more than asked, grabbing the bottle for closer inspection. "Look at this! My luck's turning around already." She rotated the twist-off cap and poured herself a tall glass from the two provided by the hotel. After a rather large sip, she passed the bottle over to Martin, who wasn't paying any attention.

Martin was far too busy staring at the steak knife with a seven-inch, serrated blade, and a "Hotel Reverie" inscription printed on the side. His knuckles brushed over the handle, but he didn't seem to have the strength to lift it.

Janice looked at him with a morbid curiosity, as if she were watching a nature show in which an unsuspecting gazelle was about to be pounced upon by a hungry lioness. "So…were you really gonna do it?" she asked.

Martin took a deep breath and nodded.

Janice could tell by the amount of energy that response seemed to take that he had been quite serious. Before, when he'd talked about killing himself, he had attempted to make it sound like a lark. He'd been so upfront and bold about it that Janice couldn't discern for certain whether or not he was sincere. Now, by the way he was staring at the knife, the way the back of his fingers grazed the handle, and the deep thought he seemed to have sunken into the moment he saw it on the room service cart, she knew he'd aimed to end his own life. In a strange way, it was somewhat pleasing for her. Of course it wasn't because he was in such a terrible emotional state, but it was comforting to know she was not alone. "Why?" she asked.

"A woman. Why else?"

Janice couldn't help but laugh a little. She then rolled her eyes as if to say, "Of course."

Martin smiled and sat down next to her on the bed. He pulled a joint out of his coat pocket and held it up in the air. "Do you mind?" he asked.

"Not at all."

He stuck the joint in his mouth and patted his pockets for a lighter, but Janice had already pulled one out and lit the tip for him; he was fairly taken aback by the gesture. He'd never been much of a smoker, and he concluded that Janice was the first person in his life to light a smoke for him. It was a strange feeling, and he felt as if he was suddenly someone else, living a different life.

"What was her name?" she asked him.

"Jenny."

"And what did this Jenny do that would make you want to kill yourself. She couldn't have been that bad."

"She wasn't. I was," he said.

"Oh?"

"I'm not sure I want to get into it."

"Well…tough shit," Janice said, raising her voice. "You told me you were thinking of killing yourself, and then you brought me up here. We're not gonna fuck, if that's what you're thinking, so we might as well talk."

Martin inhaled the joint and felt the bite in the back of his throat. Not yet used to its full effects, he held the smoke in his lungs a bit too long, and it all came up in a coughing fit. He jumped off the bed, embarrassed, and covered his mouth as spit and smoke hacked their way out.

"That's right," Janice said, smiling as she climbed off the bed. "You told me you never got high before either." She followed Martin across the room, pressing her right hand on the small of his back and grabbing the joint with her left.

Martin watched her put the paper to her lips, inhale what seemed about a third of the joint, and then slowly exhale a cloud of smoke without so much as blinking, let alone erupting into a coughing convulsion like he had. He felt a strange, unwarranted sense of familiarity with her, where he wasn't sure if she still hated him. Regardless, he was happy she was there. Her brashness excited him. It made her seem dangerous, which coupled very well with how he felt about himself. When she walked back over to the bed, he followed suit and poured himself a small glass of wine in the process.

"So, Martin, spill the beans. What happened?"

"There's not much to tell," he said. "I'm a horrible addict when it comes to gambling. Neither of us knew this place had a casino. She trusted me to stay away, but I couldn't, and I let her down. I lost everything—all my money, all of hers, and all of my boss's. I really only feel bad about losing hers though." Martin took another drag, being careful this time not to inhale too much.

"What'd she do?" she asked.

"This. An empty room," Martin said, using his arms to indicate the space that surrounded them. "She left me. She took everything and left me."

"And that made you want to kill yourself?"

"Sure. She stuck with me through my gambling addiction, and I let her down. I did the one thing she was always afraid I'd do, and now I have nothing."

"It doesn't really sound like you care at all about having nothing," Janice said, unaffected by his suicidal confession. Her tone was plain as if she were talking about something as menial as going to lunch.

"I don't. I've had nothing before."

Janice reached over and stretched her arms around Martin.

He was confused at first and thought she was trying to make some sort of move on him. Only when she plucked the joint from his hands and receded back to her side of the bed did he realize what she was after.

"So, basically, you're saying you wanted to kill yourself, because you love this one fucking girl so much that her leaving you is too much for you to bear?"

"Yeah, I guess," he said, following along and dissecting every word she said.

"And you killing yourself would have made her feel…?"

"Probably terrible," he answered.

"Right. So if you care about this woman half as much as you say you do, why on Earth would you wanna kill yourself and make her feel a thousand times worse?"

Martin paused to think about the question. He had never imagined the aftermath of what would have happened had he actually gone through with it. He wasn't sure if Janice was making a good point or if he was just high. After some hesitation, he answered, "I already told you that I don't want to do it anymore."

"Right. You chickened out."

"No, I said I didn't chicken out."

"You might have said so, but that's exactly what you did."

"No, I-I just…found a new reason to live."

"You're just high, that's all," Janice said. She rolled over and looked at him before continuing, "When you're all out of weed, you'll come back down and remember how shitty life really is. It's all gonna come back to you in some awful way…the fact that you're alone, with no money and a terrible addiction to deal with. And when it does, when the pot wears off, you'll be just a tiny bit closer to not chickening out."

"Hmm. Sounds like you're speaking from experience," Martin said.

An awkward silence followed while Janice slowly inhaled on the joint.

"Okay," she admitted after some time. "So you're not the only person who's ever thought of just ending it. Can anybody really say they've never thought of it? I mean, thinking about death is natural. Hell, maybe it's the most natural thing we do. We wonder what life's all about and what lies beyond it. Once we discover that it's really all about nothing, that it's just the general day-in/day-out bullshit, we begin to yearn for true nothingness."

"There are so many reasons why I don't agree with that."

"Really? Well, don't let me stop you from setting me straight."

"First off," Martin said, "thinking about death is not the most natural thing we do as human beings."

"No? Then what is?" Janice asked, her voice raspy as she held a cloud of smoke in her lungs.

"It's a toss-up between eating and fucking, but definitely not pondering about life after death. To think about oneself and what it would be like after your conscience is gone is a trait, a curse that only human beings must deal with. The rest of the natural world fears death and doesn't want anything to do with it. Only we willingly take our own lives, not to protect those we love or for any noble cause, but solely because we make the conscientious decision to no longer exist. Maybe it's a sign of intelligence that the more we think, the more we're a danger to ourselves. But if that were true, every brilliant man or woman who has ever lived would share the same final chapter, and that hasn't been the case. The likelier answer to why we do it is that people like you, Janice, and me…well, we're really fucked up people." Martin stopped for a moment and watched Janice. He wasn't sure if he had crossed the line or if he should stop talking altogether, despite the fact that he had more to say.

"Go on," she said, sensing his need for approval.

"You said that once we discover that our lives hold no purpose or meaning, we yearn for death, because we're sure that only death can take us to nothingness. But to be fair, none of us really knows what death brings."

"C'mon, Martin!" Janice said, rolling her eyes. "Don't tell me you believe in God!"

"The jury's still out on that," he said, looking away, "but even if there is no God, that doesn't mean we understand death. To fear death, my friend, is only to think ourselves wise without being wise, for it is to think that we know what we do not know. For all we know, death may be the greatest good that can happen to us, but we fear it as if we know quite well that it is the greatest of evils. And what is this but that shameful ignorance of thinking that we know what we do not know?"

Janice held his words in her mind for a moment, breaking them down into segments, grasping each one separately and piecing them back together. "Wow. That's really deep," she said.

"That's Socrates, paraphrased a little," Martin said. "He was a really deep man."

"Right, but that only proves my point," Janice said, lifting her finger and visually alluding to her point as if it was floating in the air on the hazy cloud of weed smoke she'd just exhaled.

"How so?" he asked.

"Well, as Mr. Socrates said, it's foolish for us to believe death is evil when it could be good."

"He was trying to illustrate the point that we blindly put our faith in something we know nothing about," Martin explained, "sort of how you put your faith in nothingness after death. You really have no idea if that's true. For all you know, you'll wake up the second you die and spend the rest of eternity with all the people you used to know."

"God, talk about hell! That'd be terrible."

"Worse than the life you're living now? Because if so, it's not worth risking."

"You make some valid arguments, Martin, but let me ask you something."

"Go ahead."

"Were you thinking of all this when you ordered that steak?"

"No," Martin confessed. "I guess it all really started when I began smoking this joint."

"Ah, just as I thought. But what were you thinking about when you ordered the steak?"

Martin let his thoughts carry him back to earlier in the night. He remembered talking to himself in the mirror. He shuddered as he looked at the mirror, remembering how dark his world had been such a short while ago. "I guess I was thinking about how pathetic I was for doing what I did," he said. "Nobody could depend on me or rely on me, not even the person who loved me the most. I wasn't a man. I was ashamed, embarrassed by my own behavior. I was so…alone. I think that really did it. If there was anybody within reach, I probably wouldn't have even thought of it, but I was just too isolated from the world, like everyone else had forgotten about me. Do you ever feel like that? Do you ever feel that people are laughing at you? That everyone else is having a good time, but you're the butt of their jokes?"

Janice didn't answer. Instead, she snuffed out the joint in the ashtray on the side table to her left. "Do you have any more of these, Martin?" she asked, changing the subject.

Martin passed her the second joint from his coat pocket without saying a word. She lit the joint, inhaled, took a sip of her wine, and then released the smoke from her lungs.

"So…what are you gonna do when you run out of pot?" she asked.

He shrugged. "I don't even know how I'm gonna pay for this room," he said. "Will they give you the tip I left from the dinner I ordered, even if I don't pay the bill?"

Janice's eyes grew wide, and a high-pitched laugh escaped her mouth. "They damn well better!" she said, smiling at Martin. "It's their problem if they rent a room out to a deadbeat, broke-ass gambler, not mine."

Martin laughed with her and grabbed the joint from her fingers. "So, uh…what were you thinking?" he asked.

"Huh?"

"Right before you chickened out."

Janice pursed her lips. "The same thing I always think of."

"Which is?"

"How easy it would be."

"Hmm. Well, clearly something stopped you," he said.

"That's true. Isn't this beautiful, Martin? Just two people, enjoying a real conversation? Not worrying about what the other one thinks because we're practically strangers anyway? Just letting go and falling into the moment? Unfortunately, it never lasts long enough. You always end up coming down, back to reality. You always have to get back to the daily grind. Let me ask you something, Martin. If I gave you $100 right now, would you save it, spend it, or gamble it?"

"I don't know."

"Yes you do."

"No I don't."

"You want yourself to save it," she answered for him. "You'd want to use it to help you restart your life, the life you think you're going to be living from here on out, but you'd still be content if you spent it, as long as it was on a necessity, like a bus ticket or a cheap meal. Really, the most important thing would be that you don't gamble it, right? That you don't go down to those tables like a moth to a bug lamp and get zapped?"

Martin smoked the joint in silence, patiently waiting for Janice to get to her point.

She continued, "It's fun to daydream about what life would be like without the struggles that weigh us down. I like to think of myself as a nicer, happier person. I put on a positive attitude and, lo and behold, run into the man of my dreams." She closed her eyes and wrapped her arms around her torso, hugging herself as she smiled. "He's single, and he loves me because I'm happy and sweet. I'm happy and sweet because he loves me. And he takes me away, somewhere far away from here." Janice opened her eyes and released her grip on herself. She finished her wine and gently placed the empty glass on the nightstand as her smile faded away. "But then I always wake up in reality, this terrible world," she said, "where people try to drag me down and make me miserable. Mr. Right comes by ever so often, but there's always a Mrs. Right. Or worse, he's just traveling through. When that happens, we love each other till the sun comes up, and then I never see him again. With each passing day, my vision of my savior gets just a tiny bit blurrier, and I become a tiny bit more miserable. Eventually I won't be able to see him anymore, and when that happens, when I no longer see my dream, I…" She paused to shake her head. "I just don't know. I don't know whether or not I'll be able to allow myself to chicken out, just like I don't know whether or not you'd be able to keep yourself from gambling that $100. Because you, Martin, and me, well…we're really fucked up people."

Martin's silence was his only response. The weight of Janice's words fell upon him all at once, and he was too taken aback to say anything. She had said it all, had blurted out the real, harsh, nasty truth. He was so captivated by her poetic admission that he hadn't realized the joint was finished. The tarpaper burned his fingertips, and he tossed it away. He wanted to say something, but he couldn't find the words. He wanted to love her but not for any reason other than for her to be loved. He wanted her to know. He just didn't know how.

She curled up into a ball and buried herself in his chest. "I'm sleepy," she whispered.

Martin held her tight. He knew that while they were together, they were at least safe from themselves, and he hoped she knew that too. His eyelids closed, his head dropped toward hers, and at that very moment, every light in the room shut off.

TWENTY-ONE

12:25 a.m. – Courtyard

"Come on!"

"I'm not…I don't know if—"

"C'mon! You have to hurry. That's the whole point."

"But I don't wanna kill anybody."

"You have to. It's part of the rules."

"I can't…I mean, I still don't know—"

"If you give me your answer in the next five seconds, I'll kiss you."

"What?"

"Four seconds."

"Ugh!"

"Three…two…"

"Fine! I'd bang Snow White, marry Cinderella, and kill the little mermaid."

"You'd kill Ariel?" Jenny asked with a shriek.

Tim threw his hands in the air in frustration.

"I thought I *had* to kill somebody?" he asked.

"You do, but you chose the prettiest of the three."

"Well, she's got a fin down there, so I'm not sure how things would be in the bedroom, and it isn't like we could start a family or anything. She's eliminated by default."

"Okay," Jenny admitted. "But why would you bang Snow White over Cinderella?"

"It's not that I would. I'd really just prefer to marry Cinderella over Snow White."

"Interesting. Go on."

"Well," Tim explained, "Cinderella had a hard childhood, so she probably grew up to be a good person of strong character. She'd appreciate the little things and would also most likely raise our kids to be kindhearted, thoughtful individuals. She certainly wouldn't have them scrubbing floors or doing what she was forced to do as a kid."

"Wow. So your main line of reasoning is based on Cinderella's back-story? That's why you'd marry her?" Jenny asked.

"Yeah, I guess," Tim said, scratching the back of his head. "I've never really played this game before."

"No, you did fine. I think it says a lot about you. Most guys first choose the one they'd bang. You took the long way around, like a real gentleman."

"Yeah, I guess."

Jenny leaned in and gave Tim a kiss on his cheek, as promised.

He blushed and turned away.

"Now do me," she said.

"Um…should I pick Disney characters or—"

"Pick any three guys you want."

"Uh…okay. How about…Batman, Superman, and Spiderman."

"Oh, that's a good one!" Jenny thought for a minute, closing her eyes and tapping her fingers on her chin.

Tim didn't want to stare at her while she thought, but he found her too beautiful to look away. He quickly averted his eyes when she reopened hers.

"Hmm," she said. "I'd bang Superman, marry Batman, and kill Spiderman."

"Any reason?" he asked her.

"Sure. Superman is Superman, but he's also Clark Kent, so he'd be powerful yet gentle in bed. Batman is Bruce Wayne, who's loaded. And I hate spiders, which makes it a no-brainer that I'd want the webby one killed."

"I guess that makes sense," Tim said, nodding his head in agreement but feeling a strange, new contempt for the Man of Steel that he'd never felt before.

"Of course, I hate killing spiders," she said. "I may need your help with that."

"Anytime. I don't mean to brag," Tim said, pointing at his feet, "but this shoe has stepped on its fair share of creepy-crawlies."

Jenny laughed and tugged on Tim's arm gently.

Just like that, he was in love.

"This is fun," she said. "Thanks for making me feel better."

"It's my pleasure. So…what are you doing here?"

"Huh? Oh, I just needed someplace to think."

"No, I mean what are you doing at the Hotel Reverie?"

"Oh." She rolled her eyes and slightly shook her head. "Well, that's sort of a crazy question. I'm not sure what I'm doing here. I brought my boyfriend, Martin."

Tim's soaring heart sank. All the air got knocked out of him, like an old boxer up against a prize fighter, and he felt just as foolish.

"I knew there's a casino here, but I didn't tell him. He has a gambling problem, but he hadn't walked into a casino in at least a year. I wanted to see if he could handle it, I guess."

"And he couldn't?"

"Nope. He lost all of our money almost immediately. I don't know why I expected anything different. I guess I just secretly hoped he'd changed. All I wanted was for him to stop making gambling his number-one priority, ya know? Like, I don't think I would have hurt so much if he'd broken up with me and fallen in love with some other girl, just as long as that other girl wasn't a roulette table or something. I don't know. I tried to change him, but I guess I couldn't."

"He lost *all* your money?"

"Not exactly," Jenny said. "He lost all of our *vacation* money. I'm no dummy, and I've been putting money in a secret savings account over the past year, just in case. But he lost all of his money, my checking account money, and his boss's deposit money. More importantly, he failed the test. He chose gambling over us, and now gambling is all he has left. The sad part is that I still want to save him. I just know I can't."

"Some people don't wanna be saved, I guess," Tim said, already finding fault in a man he had never even met.

"I don't believe that. I believe everyone wants to be saved," Jenny said. "But sometimes other people can't save them. Sometimes people have to save themselves."

"What do you do for a living?" Tim asked, wanting to change the subject as quickly as possible.

"I actually just got a new job."

"Yeah?"

"Yes, sir. Not too long ago, I became floor manager of a rather nice restaurant in the city."

"That's fantastic!"

"Not really."

"What are you talking about? You don't like it?"

"No, I love it. It's the best job I've ever had. It's just...well, the money isn't that great—not that being a cocktail waitress was much better, which was what I did before."

"So? If you like it, who cares if the money isn't good?"

"My parents, for one," Jenny said, rolling her eyes again. "I'm almost thirty. I can support myself off this job, but I'd never be able to support a family."

"You're not supposed to support a family by yourself."

"I know that, but look at me. Newly single again, right back to square one and creeping up on being over the hill."

The inflection in Jenny's voice told Tim how distraught she really felt about the whole idea. There were so many things he wanted to say to her. He wanted to tell her that if she were with him, she would never have to worry about money or family or anything, because he would always support her and do whatever was in his power to make her dreams come true. He wanted to say all of that and more, but he couldn't find the right words or put them in the right order. He couldn't find the nerve either.

As if to save Tim from the awkward quietude that followed, a young couple strolled into the courtyard, hand in hand.

Tim and Jenny remained silent as they gazed upon them from the gazebo, watching as the young man led the girl to a bed of roses located in the center of the flower garden. Tiny accent lights revealed the roses with pure splendor creating a picturesque still image of the couple embracing in front of the blooming symbols of love. It was a poetic masterpiece, a picture of true love demonstrated right before the very eyes of two people who felt so estranged from the concept.

Tim and Jenny both let out a small gasp when the man knelt down on one knee and pulled a ring box from his pocket. For a stretch in time that lasted only several seconds, the world froze for both Tim and Jenny. They watched the moment transpire from the comfort of their gazebo as the man whispered his confessions, his dreams, his secrets, and his promises to the love of his life about fifty feet away in the near dark. The young girl released an inevitable shriek and cried, "Yes!" with a triumphant enthusiasm before she fell into the arms of the young man, releasing a simultaneous tingling feeling in the bodies of both Tim and Jenny.

"They're beautiful together," Jenny whispered as the couple walked even farther into the darkness and out of sight.

"How does that even happen?" Tim asked.

"What?"

"How do two people meet, build a relationship, fall in love, and then feel so passionately about being in love that they decide they simply cannot live without each other?" Tim asked, staring at the empty space where the newly engaged couple had previous stood. "How does that even happen? It's like something out of the movies."

Jenny thought of Tim's question as somewhat rhetorical, but that was only because she didn't have an answer. She wasn't sure if she was seeing him for what he was or was just seeing what she wanted to see. Martin had never spoken of marriage, not once. She wondered what he might have said had he seen that young man propose.

Her silence made Tim feel uncomfortable and embarrassed for revealing so much about himself to a stranger. "Um…I should go," he said, standing from the bench.

"What? Why?"

"I-I don't know. I just—"

"Stay with me for a while," she pleaded, tugging at his arm.

He nodded and wiped his sweaty palms on his pant leg before sitting back down.

She scooted closer to him and let her head fall down into his lap, holding his arm and curling her legs up onto the bench. They stayed like that, together, sharing stories about themselves as they watched the fireflies sway and move in the moonlight. When the Hotel Reverie lost power, they were too lost in each other to notice or care.

TWENTY-TWO

10:59 p.m. – Front Desk

Miguel tapped his fingers in rhythmic patterns on the front desk. He hadn't had a guest for over an hour, but he couldn't leave his post until the night concierge arrived. She was running late, as usual, so he was at her mercy. He fooled around on the computer for a while, pretending he wasn't thinking about Noah and Mary. After some social networking and world news updates, he logged off and just stared through the empty lobby, watching over his territory as if he were a prison guard looking for possible escapees.

The lobby was the quietest it had been all night, but Miguel liked to dream that somewhere in the hotel, something exciting and fun was happening, maybe even something slightly dangerous. Just the thought brought a smile to his face. He wasn't bored with his life; quite the contrary, he adored it. He loved working in a place where he met hundreds of new people every week. The strangers' stories were fantastic, and the ones he created about them were even better. However, as of late, he'd been feeling as if the hotel was becoming dry, and the stories seemed to be repeats. Excitement was a hard drug to come by, but it was one Miguel craved. He desperately wanted a wrench to be thrown into the dull gears of life, something to disrupt whatever it had originally planned for him and create something spectacular in its place. His fingers tapped away on the desk as he dreamt, drumming to the tune of the boredom that surrounded him and accenting the silence at the same time.

The phone next to his hand lit up, and Miguel took a breath to regain his mental composure before he answered, "Thank you for calling the Hotel Reverie. This is Miguel, your concierge. How may I help you?"

"Miguel! It's Rachel. I'm not sure I'm gonna be able to make it tonight. I know you've been working all day and that this is late notice, but is there any way you could cover for me?"

"Oh my God, Rach! Is everything all right?"

"Yes…or it should be, but I'm definitely not going to make it in."

"I'm sorry, honey, but I can't work. A friend of mine is visiting from out of town. Are you sure you can't come in at all?"

"It doesn't look like it. I'll call Henry. Thanks anyway, Miguel." She hung up the phone before he had a chance to say anything back.

It wasn't the first time Rachel had called last minute, trying to get her shift covered. Miguel remained by the phone, waiting for it to light up with a call from Henry, the General Manager of the hotel. He didn't have to wait long before the little red light next to the receiver illuminated.

"Thank you for calling the Hotel Reverie. This is Miguel, your concierge. How may I help you?"

"Miguel, it's Henry. Any chance you could cover for Rachel tonight?"

"Hi, Henry, and I'm sorry but no. A friend of mine is visiting from out of town for one night only, and I absolutely promised I'd spend time with him."

"Shit. How are we looking over there?"

"A few cancelations, a few walk-ins. It's kind of leveled off since this afternoon. We're at about 50 percent."

"Any issues?"

"No, other than a couple of comps to a woman who spent a lot in the casino."

"All right. Is Noah still with you?"

"Yes," Miguel lied. He had actually sent Noah on his way over an hour ago, and he wondered for a brief moment if the question had been popped yet.

"All right. The two of you can sign off, as long as the guests are taken care of."

"Haven't seen a guest in an hour, Henry."

"Perfect. We'll close down the front desk till the morning, but do me a favor and leave your cell on, just in case something comes up."

"Will do. Have a good one, Henry."

"Yup, you too, Miguel."

Miguel hung up the phone. He was surprised that Henry wasn't going to make him stay another hour, but was pleased well enough by it to not question anything. He tidied up some of the paperwork behind the desk and made a couple of quick notes in the computer before putting up a "CLOSED FOR THE EVENING" sign and clocking out.

He debated about getting a quick drink alone, but decided that Fernando needed his attention now. He took the elevator to the fourth floor and walked down the hall to Room 401, where Fernando had just finished setting up. Inside, the room was decadent and alive, with mood lighting and multicolored cloth draped around the corners and walls. There was some house music playing in the background and what Miguel considered to be a massive mountain of cocaine on the coffee table.

"Miguel, baby! You've finally arrived!"

"Fernando, I hope you're able to have this room back to the way it was by morning."

"Don't worry, sweetie. This is just a little facelift. My boys should be arriving any second, and they may bring a cock or two. Anyone else we're expecting?"

"Hopefully. I could sure use a drink right now."

"How about a bump?"

"No, just a drink." Miguel walked over to the makeshift bar and poured himself a Bacardi and Diet. He sat on the couch and closed his eyes as the rum swished around in his mouth, down his throat, and hit his liver.

Fernando railed a thin line off the desk, and then sat in Miguel's lap. He wrapped his arms around Miguel's neck and started nibbling his earlobe.

"Fernando…" Miguel said, twisting his head away.

"What, baby? Can't we have a little fun why we wait?"

"It's never just a little fun with you."

"C'mon now! Don't be such a prude." He then moved his hand down Miguel's chest and began gyrating his ass.

With his eyes still closed, Miguel intertwined his fingers through Fernando's hair and pulled his mouth toward his. They began to kiss, and Fernando continued to gyrate around in Miguel's lap, causing him to become very hard.

After they warmed up to one another for several minutes, a knock came at the door.

"Coming!" Fernando jumped up, danced around the room, and opened the door to a hefty, unkempt man who reeked of liquor standing in the doorframe. "Is this one of yours, baby?" Fernando asked.

Miguel looked up to the door and opened his eyes for the first time since he'd poured his drink. When his eyes locked on Joey's, a warm smile formed on his face. "Oh my, yes. Be nice Fernando. This is his first time."

"Did you hear that, honey?" Fernando asked Joey, touching his chest. "Don't listen to him. I'm always nice."

Joey staggered into the room, and Miguel embraced him halfway, holding him close and kissing his neck. Joey embraced Miguel back. Several minutes later, Fernando's guests showed up and distracted Fernando long enough for Joey and Miguel to sneak into one of the bedrooms.

"I'm…I, uh…I'm not sure I—"

"Shh," Miguel whispered back. "Let's forget about everything we're sure of. It's only you and me."

Joey whimpered a little as Miguel undid his pants and began stroking his cock.

"Aw, poor little puppy. I promise I'll keep you safe."

TWENTY-THREE

12:25 a.m. – Parking Garage

"Okay, how about this? We just go right back and knock on the door, then explain that we overcharged by $250, hand him the money, and walk away."

"No," Liam said without bothering to even look at Hector.

"Why not? What's wrong with that?"

"He was setting up for a party. It'd be too messy if something were to go wrong."

"What could go wrong?"

"He claimed Lorenzo told him it was four, and we said four and a half. As it turns out, it's four and a quarter. We can't go back and admit that we made a mistake. If we offer to give him a $250 credit, he'll just argue that Lorenzo told him four."

"So?" Hector asked.

"Admitting fault will leave us with very little leverage. He'll also know we work for Lorenzo or, at the very least, that we rely on him for work."

"Liam, we have fucking guns. He'll listen to us."

"If that room is filled with strung-out fags, I guarantee you at least one person won't listen to us. If we have to use guns to make them listen, we might as well have just overcharged them the $250."

"Fine. So let's just leave."

"We can't do that either. We rely on Lorenzo for work. He's the operator in this town, and if we fuck over his best client, we aren't going get any more clients in the future. Lorenzo won't be happy unless we charged them four and a quarter, so we have to make it right somehow."

"Okay, but what about our word against theirs?"

"Too late," Liam said. "I already made the call to Lorenzo asking him the price of a quarter. He knows we fucked up."

"Hmm. Well, why don't we just fucking kill Lorenzo, take over his clients, and get on with the rest of our lives?"

"That's not a feasible solution, Hector."

"Fuck!" Hector reached into his pack of cigarettes and stuck one in his mouth, and Liam did the same. "Man, we've been sitting in this car for fucking forever talking about this shit and we're just going in circles. Let's just go up, hand him the cash, tell him he's got a $250 credit, courtesy of Lorenzo, and bounce. That's it. No mess, no fuss. We don't draw guns. Hell, we don't even walk into the room. We just stand in the hallway, deliver the message and the cash, then turn around and walk away."

Liam sat in an uncomfortable stillness. He hated the idea, but nothing better came to mind. There were a thousand things that could go wrong, but as Hector so eloquently stated, they had been sitting in the car for fucking forever, and it was time to make a move.

"Seriously, what the fuck's wrong with that idea?" Hector asked. When he talked, his cigarette bobbed up and down in his mouth like a buoy in a stormy ocean.

"We walk up—"

"Yes."

"I tell him it's a $250 credit, courtesy of Mr. Lorenzo—"

"Yes."

"And we leave?"

"And we leave."

"We don't say anything else?"

"Not a word."

"Even if he yells and screams about it being four?"

"He might throw a hissy fit."

"But we still won't do anything?"

"Nope. Nothing."

"And we do not, with the exception of an extreme dire circumstance, draw our guns, especially if it's a crowded room?"

"Right. Don't even really need 'em."

"But we're taking them anyway."

"Wouldn't leave the car without 'em."

Liam churned away at his cigarette, reflecting on what he was saying and debating whether or not he believed it himself. He knew Hector would do whatever he said, even if getting out of there faster meant starting a small war. That was why Liam took an extra minute or so to contemplate. By the time his cigarette was finished, Liam had made a decision. "Fuck it. Let's get this over with," he said, snubbing the filter out in the ashtray on the dashboard.

"Yes!"

The two men emerged from the car, grabbed their guns from the trunk, and began walking back toward the elevator.

"No screw-ups. Can't afford any," Liam said. "And remember, no real names."

"You really think I'm that much of an amateur?" Hector asked, buttoning up his coat to once again conceal his weapons.

Liam didn't answer. He just continued talking to himself, bouncing his thoughts off of Hector as an excuse to not feel crazy.

"And different positions this time. I'm still arbitrating, but now you're just muscle. Don't set up as point guard. We're not going be there long enough for that anyway. Just hang by the door. I'll make the delivery to Fernando, and then we bounce."

"Piece of cake."

The elevator doors opened, and Hector pressed the button for the fourth floor. Liam started counting the wad of fives and ones, determined to give back the smaller bills he didn't want to keep. He sectioned off the bundle from the rest and put it in his side coat pocket, then placed the larger wad in his inner coat pocket. When the elevator doors opened, both men moved down the hallway in character. Hector knocked on the door, and a man Liam recognized from the restaurant opened it slowly.

"Where's Fernando?" Liam asked.

The man, with a confused look on his face, opened the door more, and both Hector and Liam saw a group of men gathered around two naked men, one on his knees, with Fernando standing in the center.

"Jesus Christ," Hector murmured, a little too loud for a guy who was strictly supposed to be muscle.

"What are you boys doing back here?" Fernando asked.

"You've got a $250 credit, courtesy of Lorenzo," Liam said, holding the money out.

"What? I don't know what kind of fucking game you boys are playin', but you better tell Mr. Lorenzo that this cocksucker was told four. It's obvious that you meatheads are clueless. Where's my other $250?"

Liam placed the money in Fernando's hand and exited the room, walking back toward the elevator with Hector at his right side.

"Oh no, no, no!" Fernando wailed, waving his finger in the air like a mother scolding her child. "Don't you even think about leaving, Frosty! I have half a mind to call Lorenzo right now, you piece of shit! You dumb, know-nothing piece of shit. You're worthless! You think you can control everybody because you have a gun? You can't control shit!" Fernando chased them down the hall, screaming and gesturing in erratic behavior. He was tweaking from a fair amount of cocaine, a little drunk, and desperate to make a scene. "Where's my $250, Frosty?" he yelled. "You know you're gonna have to make that up. How far are you willing to go, Frosty? How far are you willing to go to please a gay man, huh?"

Hector and Liam stood in front of the elevator, which seemed to be stopping on every floor but theirs.

"I can't believe you bitches," Fernando said. "Who do you think you are anyway? You lying little shits! You give me all my money back, you pathetic excuses for men. That's right! You're nothing! Lorenzo's errand boys, right? Pawns? Fucking pathetic!"

The doors opened, and Hector and Liam moved inside, Fernando still berating them from the hallway.

"Don't even think of pushing anything in this town again! I know every occasional bumper to the scar-faced junkies. You're done, honey! I may even send you to jail, you little bitches."

Liam pressed the button for the parking garage, and the doors began to close.

"What was your name again?" Fernando asked, looking at Hector. "Rico, right? You're a little faggot, Rico."

Hector planted his right foot behind him, swung his left fist out, and hit Fernando with a jab right between his eyes. Fernando catapulted up in the air and came back down on the other side of the hallway, smacking the back of his head against the wall and plopping his meek little body down on the floor, unconscious. Hector waited for Liam to give him a dirty look, but instead Liam shut his eyes. He wanted to pretend, for a minute, that what he'd seen hadn't happened. He kept his eyes closed while the elevator doors sealed shut, still closed as the cabin began moving down. They even stayed closed when the elevator rumbled to a stop with an unnerving thump. When he opened his eyes he did so slow and uneasy, and rather than the doors sliding open, all the lights were off and the "Out of Order" light was flashing in two second intervals on the console.

TWENTY-FOUR

12:50 a.m. – Room 401

"Whew! Well, fellas, you'll have to wait in the other room for a minute while I clean my little puppy off. What a good little puppy," Miguel said, stroking his hand over Joey's head. "Don't be shy, little puppy. You were excellent."

A knock came at the door, and Alex glanced around to see if anybody was going to answer it. Nobody acted as if they'd even heard it, so Alex opened the door himself.

There were two men standing in the hallway, both rigid and serious. "Where's Fernando?" one of the men asked.

When Alex opened the door wider, the two men gazed into the room, taking in the aftermath of Joey's experimentation. One was clearly disgusted by what he saw, and it became all too obvious for Alex that the two men were not part of the party.

"What are you boys doing back here?" Fernando asked.

The first man entered the room, and the bigger one stayed by the doorway, hiding in no way his repulsion for what was happening.

"You've got a $250 credit, courtesy of Lorenzo." He held the money out for Fernando to grab.

"I don't know what kind of fucking game you boys are playin', but you better tell Mr. Lorenzo that this cocksucker was told four. It's obvious that you meatheads are clueless. Where's my other $250?"

The man placed the money in Fernando's hand anyway and began walking back down the hall with the other man in tow.

Fernando ran out of the room, screaming, "Oh no, no, no! Don't you even think about leaving, Frosty! I have half a mind to call Lorenzo right now, you piece of shit! You dumb, know-nothing piece of shit. You're worthless! You think you can control everybody because you have a gun? You can't control shit!"

Miguel began to get dressed. He knew how much trouble Fernando's mouth could get him in, in all kinds of ways. He raced to get his pants on and jammed his arms into his sleeves. Fernando and the other two men were down the hall by the elevator, and Miguel scampered toward them, with Alex, Dan, and Sean leaning their heads out of the doorway to watch. Joey busied himself cleaning up with some nearby towels.

"Don't even think of pushing anything in this town again!" Fernando shouted, waking up all the sleeping staff members on the floor. "I know every occasional bumper to the scar-faced junkies. You're done, honey! I may even send you to jail, you little bitches."

Alex and the guys watched from down the hall, but they couldn't make out what else Fernando said. Whatever it had been couldn't have been good, because a fist came out of the elevator and hit Fernando smack dab in the middle of his face. He flew up into the air and came crashing back down, bumping his head on the back wall and going limp in the hallway.

"Fernando!" Miguel screamed, bending over and clutching his friend's head. "Fernando? Fernando, can you hear me?"

The three other gay men from the party ran out of the room and down the hall, past Miguel and Fernando, where they disappeared into the stairwell.

Alex and the guys turned back toward the room.

Joey was now fully clothed but still looked like a drunken mess. He staggered toward his friends, holding the walls for support.

Before anybody had a chance to say anything, every light on the floor shut off, leaving the six of them blanketed in darkness.

"What the fuck?" Sean said, grabbing another cigarette from his pack.

"You're really smoking a lot tonight," Alex said to Sean. "I thought you didn't smoke."

"Yeah? Well, I didn't really think Joey was a cocksucker either. I guess there's something in the air tonight."

"What's going on with the lights?" Dan asked.

"I don't know. Maybe we should just go back to the suite," Alex said.

"You can't unless the power comes on," Miguel shouted, having overheard their conversation.

"Why not?"

"Because the elevators run on electricity, and we use locks to prevent guests from going through the fire escape to the top floor."

"You work here?" Alex asked Miguel.

"Yes. I'm sorry for not introducing myself. I'm Miguel, the concierge. I've gotta call my boss to explain to him what's going on. Can you help me get Fernando back into the room, please? I just need to get him some help, and then I can get you fellas the key to your suite. Please help."

Dan and Alex walked over and grabbed Fernando's legs. Miguel reached under his arms and pulled him up. Sean used his phone as a guiding light for them, the cherry of his cigarette burning just as bright in the dark hallway. Joey followed them back into the room and stood in silence, too afraid and embarrassed to say or do anything. The men dropped Fernando on the couch, elevated his head with some pillows, and then wiped some of the blood off his face. The wad of bills the two men had given him was still clenched in Fernando's hand.

Miguel dialed his boss's phone number, and used the time it spent ringing to determine what he was going to say.

"This is Henry."

"Henry, it's Miguel. Something's happened at the hotel. It looks like the power's out. All the lights suddenly just turned off."

"What!? What the hell happened?"

"I don't know! I was just, uh…taking a walk down to the vending machine, and everything went dark."

"Do you know if it's affecting the whole hotel?"

Miguel looked at the elevator lights, which weren't moving. "I'm pretty sure. I haven't been off the fourth floor, but the elevator is stuck."

"Shit! Miguel, I'm sorry, but I need you behind the desk right now while I try to find out what's going on. The casino's probably a fucking wreck. Just try to keep everybody calm and tell them it's some sort of rolling blackout or something."

"Has this ever happened before?" Miguel asked, alarmed.

"No, but don't let anyone else know that. Tell them it happens from time to time. If anybody makes a stink about it, let them know we'll take care of them."

"All right, Henry. I'm headed to the desk now."

"Thanks, Miguel. I'll see you soon."

"All right fellas," Miguel said after he hung up. "Follow me downstairs, and I'll find you that key."

"Shouldn't somebody stay with him?" Alex asked, holding a rag over Fernando's nose to keep it from bleeding.

"That's my next call. You guys come with me. I'll take care of it."

TWENTY-FIVE

1:03 a.m. – Room 302

Janice opened her eyes when she heard her cell phone ringing, even though she thought it might be a dream. A second or two later, the phone rang again, and she crawled over Martin to see who was calling. "Mary?" she said when she noticed the name flashing on the screen.

"Oh, Janice! Thank God you're awake."

"What's up? What's going on?"

"I need you…now."

"Where are you?"

"Um, I'm in Miguel's room, and—"

"Miguel's room?"

"Yeah. I'm sort of cleaning up his, uh…I don't know. His, like, boy toy I think."

Janice chirped out a laugh and pulled herself onto Martin's chest. "All right, Mare. Explain to me what's going on."

"Well, Noah and I were in bed, and he got a call from Miguel, freaking out because the power's out."

Janice looked around the room and noticed that all the digital clocks were off. "Wow. You're right. I had no idea. When did it go out?"

"Like just now or something. I don't know. But anyway, Miguel called Noah and asked him to watch over his friend Fernando while he deals with the power."

"Fernando?"

"Fernando."

"So…what's wrong with Fernando?"

"I don't know for sure. I think he got punched in the face. He's bleeding from his nose, and he's unconscious and lying on a couch."

"Go on."

"Well, Noah wants to help Miguel, because he thinks Miguel is gonna get swamped with complaints or whatever, so I offered to watch Fernando for him. But now I'm creeped out, and I want my Janice."

"Why are you creeped out?"

"I'm not sure exactly. I just am. I kinda feel like I'm sitting in a room where a lot of weird stuff happened recently, ya know? There's this weird mood lighting, and, Janice, my God I think there's a pile of cocaine on the coffee table."

"What was that?"

"Please come. I'm seriously gonna freak out if this guy wakes up."

"All right. Sit tight, and I'll be there. Where are you?"

"Room 401. Hurry!"

Janice threw her phone back on the end table and looked over at Martin, who'd woken up during her conversation.

"What was that about?" he asked.

"Uh…I'm not sure exactly." She dropped her head on Martin's chest and listened to his heartbeat.

"Do you need to go?" he asked, stringing his fingers through her knotted hair.

"Mm-hmm." Despite her response, she didn't move; she didn't want to. She laid on his chest, rising up and down with his breathing, feeling calm, comfortable, and safe. After about a minute, she crawled up to meet him at eye level. "You wanna come with?" she asked.

"Kind of."

Janice smiled. She was happy he hadn't pushed, yet she was thrilled that he wanted to go.

They gathered themselves, straightening their wrinkled clothing as best as they could before making their way into the hall.

"So…where are we going?" Martin asked once they were outside.

"Room 401, Miguel's room."

"Who's Miguel?"

"Our incredibly gay concierge."

"Oh! I met him when I checked in. Seems like a nice guy. But why are we going there?"

Janice stopped by the doorway to the stairwell. "Because Miguel's gay lover, Fernando, got punched in the face and is now unconscious and bleeding from his nose. Miguel entrusted Noah, Hotel Reverie's finest bellhop, to watch over him, but Noah instead went to help Miguel handle the array of guest complaints he's getting about the power outage. Noah sent Mary, his girlfriend, to Fernando's aid, but Mary is super creeped out by the whole thing and wants me there for moral support."

"Oh."

"Yes."

"Interesting."

"Quite."

"That brings me to my next question."

"Which is?"

"Why is the power out?"

Janice looked around the hallway, as if the walls could give her answers. She turned back toward Martin and shrugged her shoulders. "Excellent question. All I can say is welcome to the Hotel Reverie."

He smiled. "Heh. Glad to be here."

They climbed the dark stairwell with care, relying on the illumination from their phones, as well as some scant emergency lighting by their feet. Lucky for them, they only had to go up one floor to find Room 401.

The door was already ajar when they arrived, and they found Mary kneeling by the couch, holding a box of tissues over an unconscious Fernando.

"Oh wow," Janice said tiptoeing around the room, guiding herself by phone light. "Miguel, Miguel, Miguel," she said, clicking her tongue.

"I know, right? It's like…" Mary replied, stopping short when she noticed Martin. "Oh. Hi."

"Mare, do you remember Martin?"

"I was the dick who gave you girls a hard time about not having rib-eye," Martin said, smiling.

Mary laughed and nodded.

"Right, right," she said. "How are you?"

"Fine. And you?"

"Fine."

"Great. Now that the small talk is over, what happened here?" Janice asked, still exploring the room. She dragged her fingers through the pile of cocaine and slid the remnants into her mouth and around her gums with the nonchalance of a chef tasting a sauce.

"Geez, Janice! How the heck would I know?" Mary said. "Somebody didn't like Fernando much and gave him a shiner. I don't even wanna think about what was going on before that. Oh my God, Janice!" Mary exclaimed when she noticed the swollen bruise on Janice's forehead from her tumble down the stairwell. "What happened to you?"

"Never mind that. What happened to your hand?"

"What?"

"Mary, what the fuck is this?" Janice walked over and grabbed her left hand, lifting up the engagement ring and holding it up to Martin's phone light.

"Oh! Well…" But no answer was necessary; Mary's elated face, even shielded in the darkness, was enough to tell the story, and both girls began jumping up and down and hugging each other like teenagers who got asked to the prom.

"Oh my God, Mare! You have to tell me everything."

"It was so freaking cute. He took me to the—"

"Wait." Janice turned, snatched the tissues from Mary's hand, and gave them to Martin. "Watch him. It's girl talk time." She then grabbed Mary's arm and dragged her into the hall.

Martin shook his head and smiled, plucking several of the tissues out and dabbing the blood off of Fernando's nose. He walked over to the makeshift bar in the corner, grabbed a handful of ice cubes from the bucket, and wrapped them up in a napkin. He then walked back over to Fernando and lightly placed the ice on his bruise.

Fernando's head jerked around, his eyes winced, and he began muttering and pumping his fists in the air as if he were having a seizure.

"Take this money, Frosty! Take this money and don't come back until you have the rest of it!" he shouted.

"Whoa! Slow down, guy," Martin said, attempting to hold the ice pack on his nose while at the same time dodging Fernando's flailing fists.

"Take this fucking money, Frosty. I don't need it."

"I'm not Frosty, buddy. My name's Martin. You musta been hit in the head pretty hard."

"You think this is a game? Frosty, you're in big trouble. Take your filthy money, you little shit."

"I'm tryin' to tell you, man, I'm not Frosty!"

"Take the money, Frosty!" Fernando said, holding out the wad of money gripped in his fist. He kept punching the air in the direction of Martin's head with it clenched beneath his fingers.

At first, Martin thought he was having a seizure, but then he remembered that people don't talk during seizures. "All right. Fine. See? I'm taking the money," Martin said, unfurling the cash from

Fernando's hand, all the bills sticky with a layer of sweat. "I've got it, man. Relax."

"Get out!" Fernando shouted.

"Calm down, buddy. I just—"

"Get the hell out, Frosty! I didn't invite you into my home, and I never want to see you again!" After that outburst, Fernando curled up into a fetal position on the couch, tucked his head between the pillows, and knocked the makeshift ice pack onto the floor.

Martin hovered over him, attempting to put the ice pack back on Fernando's bruise. He shoved the cash in his pocket to free up his hand and tried to move Fernando around, away from the inside cushion, but his body wouldn't budge. Exhausted, Martin gave up. He walked out into the hallway, feeling defeated.

The two girls were finishing their conversation when Martin walked up.

"How is he?" asked Janice.

"He's a mess, but I think he was a mess when he started, so he might be fine."

Both girls smiled and nodded.

"I'm gonna go check on Noah. Do you guys wanna come with?" Mary asked.

"No. We'll let you handle that. Oh God! I'm just…I'm just so happy for you guys."

"Thanks, Jan. So much. You two have fun."

Mary walked to the end of the hallway and into the stairwell before Janice turned back toward Martin. She stared at him with a blank expression, almost as if he wasn't there or they were just strangers on the street. Her lips contorted into a smile, and she began walking down the hall in the opposite direction.

"Your friend's getting married?" Martin asked, addressing the obvious.

Janice said nothing and kept walking down the hall.

"Do you wanna hang out? Maybe talk about it?" he asked her.

"Ha! Talk about my best friend getting married to a stranger I just met?" Janice picked up her pace.

"I'm sure it was shocking news, so—"

"Really, Martin? You're sure?" she said, still walking. "Well, you're wrong. I'm fucking ecstatic. I'm just…" Janice couldn't finish the sentence before breaking into tears.

Martin walked over to hold her, but she pushed him away.

"Get away from me, you pathetic creep!" she shouted.

"What did I do?"

"Just stay away!" She ran to the end of the hallway and around the corner.

Martin chased her until he saw her disappear into a stairwell on the other side of the building. He didn't want her to be alone with all those terrible, self-loathing thoughts in her mind; she reminded him too much of himself. If she felt anything like him, she was desperate and feeling isolated, like the whole world was against her. *It's a terrible place to be, feeling like everyone else is the winner and you're the only loser.* He knew from firsthand experience. *It's dangerous, especially when no one else is around to console you.*

Martin turned and went back to Room 401. He popped his head inside quickly to check on Fernando, and then locked the door on his way out. He ran down the hall to the other side of the building and followed Janice down the fire escape. He was afraid it was too late, that he'd already lost her, but he was surprised to find her leaning against a corner of the building on the second-floor platform, smoking a cigarette. Martin sat down across from her and lit one up himself.

For a moment, neither said a word. They sat as the tobacco burned away into their lungs and then was exhaled in clouds of smoke that billowed into the air. They were surrounded by darkness, other than a handful of small, fluorescent lights and two red cherries burning in the void. While their eyes acclimated to the dark, they peered at the other with a morbid curiosity, like a car wreck you just can't help but stare at as you drive past. They felt no pressure from the other's stare, as if the loneliness they both felt was being shared between them, in silence and without pretense or any necessary explanation. Janice snuffed her finished smoke out on the wall, creating a dark, little circle surrounded by several others just like it. She lit another one up and rested her head against the concrete. "This is where I come to unwind," she said, cutting through the silence like a knife.

Martin nodded; quiet, not wanting to interrupt her train of thought.

"Ya know, when I first started working here, I had a serious plan," she said. "On top of that, man, I was so stoked for this job. I thought I'd make decent money and meet interesting people, and it all seemed great, you know? Then, before I know it, seven years have gone by, like it was nothing. Everyone else has made their money or met their people, but here I am, just crazy, old Janice, still serving tables and waiting for…something." She felt the bump on her head and applied a slight amount of pressure to the bruise. It was starting to swell and hurt.

Martin wanted to help, but aided with the wisdom of middle-age he kept his distance.

"Then I met Mary. Mare's my only real friend now, because everyone else is gone. And now she'll be gone too—just…gone."

"You're still very young," Martin interjected.

Janice snickered and smiled. "That's very kind of you to say, but I'm on the wrong side of twenty-five. My hot days are over, and before long, I'll be on my way to Cougar Town."

Martin laughed, choking on his cigarette smoke and coughing into his sleeve.

Janice smirked and passed him a tissue from her purse.

"Thanks," he said.

"Don't mention it."

"So…where do you want to go?" he asked her.

"Where?"

"Yeah. Assume that Admiral Prince Charming walks through the door and recites the most beautiful love poem you've ever heard, causing you to instantly and insanely fall in love. He says he wants to whisk you away from all of this. Where would you want him and his white horse to carry you off to?"

Janice pondered for about a moment, and then shook the notion away when the ridiculous fantasies began to consume her thoughts. "I don't know. I guess I don't have a preference. I guess I'll just have to leave that decision to the first poetic prince who comes my way. How's that?"

"It's your dream," Martin said with a shrug.

"Yes," she said, fantasizing again. "My…dream."

Martin snuffed his cigarette out in the same manner Janice had, creating another little black circle on the wall. He leaned back down across from her.

"Need another?" she asked.

"No. I'm actually not much of a smoker."

"Hmm," she said with doubt. "Not much of a smoker *or* pothead, right?"

He shrugged again. "Tonight seems to be the night of firsts."

"Maybe. It has been rather eventful."

Silence grew between them. They found themselves thinking of the other, not so secretly watching one another in the near dark.

"Tell me something," Janice said, tired of the silence.

"Like what?"

"Something beautiful. Tell me something beautiful—a beautiful poem, one Admiral Prince Charming would tell."

While some men may have been caught off-guard by such a request, Martin knew what to say. Janice was the embodiment of a perfect tragedy, a persona stretched out one too many times to the point of snapping, a gorgeous arrangement of beauty and beast, passion and pain; by the book the best starting place for any poem. Martin knew a thousand quotes penned by famous writers, hundreds of poems and sonnets that would have drawn another smile out of her. Instead, he showed her something he hadn't shown anyone for a long time. He spoke from his soul a poem, a verse he had not recited in many years, one he knew by heart: "An enchanting mind will never be seen. A strong spirit will not be shown. An oversized heart I have found to be rare. Yet, through a miracle that will never be explained, I met you. So astounded by the essence of your charm, I am unable to express my adoration through words and am, therefore, left with a pen. Handicapped as I may be, my vision is clearer than ever, thanks to you. You are the strength that lifts up the obstacles before me, the genius who exposes to me the right path to take. Most importantly, you are the reason that keeps me walking on that path through good and bad and worse. Nothing compares to the sunlight that shines through after the hurricane has passed. The hurricane has passed, and you are my sun shining through."

Janice exhaled when he finished, as if she'd been holding her breath the entire time, hanging on his every word. Her eyes filled with tears, and she hid her face from Martin's view. "Was that for her? For…Jenny?" she asked, trying not to let her voice betray her tears.

"No. Jenny's never heard it. It was for me—or from me. Maybe both. I wrote it when I was young and idealistic, in love with every girl I chased. In other words, I wrote it a lifetime ago. I haven't said it out loud since."

"What made you want to say it now?"

Martin slid over to Janice's side of the wall. He put his arms around her and pulled her close to him.

She pressed her head back into his chest, holding on to his shoulders and breathing in his scent, listening to his heartbeat and rising with every breath.

"Relevance," he said, intertwining his fingers between her hair and brushing it away from the bruise on her face.

TWENTY-SIX

1:03 a.m. – Front Desk

By the time Miguel and the rest of the group made it down to the lobby, a crowd of guests had already formed. Many were more riled up about not being able to gamble than they were about the lack of electricity.

Miguel moved behind the desk, which was illuminated solely by the moonlight outside, and attempted to calm the crowd. "Folks, if I could have your attention please. As I'm sure you all are aware, the power is out in the entire hotel, and we—"

"No shit, Sherlock! I lost $100 in one of your damn slot machines when somebody pulled the plug! What the hell's goin' on?"

"Me too, in video blackjack!"

"I understand your grievances," Miguel said, trying himself to remain calm, "however, I am just the concierge of the Hotel Reverie, and I am not in charge of what happens in the casino. I'm sure someone will address these issues, but for the time being, we—"

"Bullshit!"

"Yeah! I want my money back, so I can go somewhere else!"

"The general manager of the hotel is on his way, and he will make sure everyone is compensated for what was lost. In the meantime, I'm here to help with anything else you folks may need."

"When's the power coming back on?"

"I'm not sure. Rolling blackouts do occur here from time to time. I'm sure the electricity will soon kick back on."

"My room's on the tenth floor. Does this mean I'll have to walk up ten flights just to get there? I'm fifty-six years old, for God's sake!"

"I'm terribly sorry about the inconvenience, sir, but—"

"Inconvenience? This is an outrage!"

"I assure you we will do anything and everything in our power to fix the problem as quickly as possible." Miguel continued to argue with the mob, which seemed to be growing angrier by the second.

Alex looked over at Joey, who was quiet and staring at the floor. "Hey, buddy, you all right?" he asked.

Joey avoided eye contact and staggered away toward the casino with his head hanging low.

"Hey, I'm gonna go with him and make sure he's all right," Alex said to Sean.

"I don't know if that's such a great idea, man. Last time we followed Joey, we found him acting like this dude's little puppy or some weird shit like that," Sean said, pointing over to Miguel. "You might walk into some weird orgy in that dark casino."

Alex rolled his eyes. "He's our friend, and I've gotta check on him. I'll meet you guys back in the room."

Dan and Sean shared a look before nodding at Alex.

Alex followed Joey through the lobby and to the casino floor, where a crowd similar to the one in the lobby was forming around the cashier's cage. Joey collapsed in one of the slot machine chairs, and Alex sat beside him.

"This place seems to be falling apart, huh?" Alex asked.

Joey didn't reply. He just stared at the floor, holding his body up with the chair.

"You okay, man? It's not like you to be so quiet."

"My life is over."

"What? No way, man. Why would you think that?"

"You think I'm a faggot!" Joey broke down into tears, cupping his face in his hands and turning away. Snot drizzled from his nose, and he brushed it away several times with his sleeve.

"So? Even if you are gay, that doesn't mean your life's over."

"You're never gonna want to be around me ever again. Sean's never gonna shut up about it. And the worst part is, I'm not gay!"

"Joey, man, I gotta tell ya the truth here. You haven't exactly been fun to be around lately, not since a couple years after high school. I mean it's not that I don't like you. I love you, man! I asked you to be the best man at my wedding, didn't I? You were my best friend growing up. Hell, at one point, you were my only friend. But you've always been the crazy one, doing outrageous things without any shame. Truthfully, this is like seeing a whole other side of you, a better side, in some ways."

Joey sat still, sniffling and still brushing the tears and snot away from his face with his sleeve.

Alex continued. "Do you remember when you first started to feel this way?"

"What are you talking about? I'm not gay!"

"All right, all right. Calm down, man. I just want you to know it's fine if you are, so—"

"I'm not!"

"Okay! So you're not."

"I'm not gay, Alex," Joey insisted, growing angry.

"Hey, man, everybody experiments."

"Have you?"

"Um…well, okay, maybe not everybody, but my point is that it's not a big deal. Even if you were gay, it wouldn't be a big deal. All that matters is that you're happy. Listen, I love you guys. I do. We've all had some really great times together. But when I met Melissa, I knew I had reached a turning point in my life. No matter how much fun we used to have, I knew I'd never be the same man again. Her love showed me what kind of man I really am."

"What are you saying? That I'm in love with that dude or something?"

"No, I'm not saying that at all. I'm just saying you shouldn't lie to yourself, man. For a while, I lied to myself, acting like I was still young enough to party with the guys. The truth is, nowadays, I'm content to just sit at home with my woman and a bottle of wine. I know it's not as fun and glamorous as hunting for chicks in bars late at night or smoking weed all the time, but it's who I am now. Whether I like it or not, it's just who I am."

"I'm not gay, Alex," Joey repeated.

"I don't really give a damn if you are, but it's not me you need to convince." Alex stood up and arched his back. He peered over to the crowd, around the cashiers' cage and shook his head. "I wonder how many of these people are lying to themselves right now," he said, "telling themselves they lost their money because of the power outage. I wonder how many of them will quit gambling when the power comes back on. My guess is not a single one. We'll be in the suite when all that madness happens, though, assuming we can find a way up there." Alex then patted Joey on the back and walked away.

Joey sat and watched the crowd as they pushed and shoved to get to the front. A large man in a suit stood in front of the cage, handing out tickets that were most likely credits and comps. Joey watched the faces of those who received the tickets; as they held the ticket in their hands, they kept glancing back over to the casino floor, watching the tables with the eagerness of a kid at the front of a rollercoaster line, waiting for them to reopen so they could relinquish their money back to the house. Joey shook his head, stood, and walked as best as he could around the floor to the men's room. He walked into the last stall on the left, knelt down, and threw up countless drinks into the porcelain bowl—beer, vodka, and gin—along with the meal he'd eaten at Deluxe. He flushed the smelly, chunky puke away and stood to rinse the bitter, acidic bile from his mouth with a handful of water from the sink, a pointless gesture since he was about to be sick again.

In a small moment of sobriety that lasted till the next sickening bout of heaving, Alex's words jumbled around inside his head. Joey caught a glimpse of his distorted reflection on the silver flusher, and an epiphany began to take shape in his mind. He hunched over the bowl, stronger now, and hurled the remaining contents of his stomach out, determined to purge every piece of himself that he no longer enjoyed.

TWENTY-SEVEN

1:04 a.m. – Front Desk

"So…what do you make of all this? What are you thinking? I mean, about what we saw?" Sean asked.

Dan shrugged and shook his head. "Truthfully, it kind of explains a lot," Dan said. "I mean he's always acted gay, right? He never got any pussy when we were in high school, and he never really tried."

"That doesn't mean anything. Tim doesn't really try right now, and I'm pretty sure he's not a homo."

"True, but Joey didn't seem to care about not getting any. At least Tim talks about it."

"Good point," Sean said after thinking it through.

"I need some air."

"I'm comin' with."

As the two men walked outside, Sean began to head to the right, but Dan stopped him. "Let's go over there, near that payphone," Dan said.

"Why? There's a bench right here."

"I wanna spark a joint."

"Damn, man. How much weed do you smoke?"

"Evidently not enough. Come on."

They walked over to the payphone, and Dan lit his joint on the way. He offered it to Sean, but Sean turned it down for another cigarette.

"Damn, man. You keep talkin' to me about weed, but look at you. When did you become a chain-smoker anyway?" Dan asked.

"It's been a rough night."

"Rougher for some than others. When I was thinking of the debauchery that was going to go on tonight, I suppose I imagined something slightly different."

"Yeah, you ain't kidding," Sean said, not paying much attention but waiting for a moment to speak. "Hey, do you remember Billy Henderson?"

"Billy Henderson?"

"Yeah, you know—that guy with the hot car, the one who got all the girls and shit in high school."

"Yeah, I remember Billy Henderson."

"Do you know what he's been up to?"

"Billy Henderson?" Dan asked again.

"Yeah."

"He's locked up."

"Locked up?"

"Yup. In jail."

"What?! What for?"

"Statutory rape."

"Oh my God! Are you serious? Are you sure?"

"Yup," Dan said again, puffing away at his joint. "When he was twenty-five, he got caught banging a fifteen-year-old."

"Get the fuck outta here. Why would Billy do that? He could get any chick he wants. Why was he fuckin' around with a kid."

"Don't know, but the girl's parents found out when she tried to run away with him. It was real messy there for a while. You remember his dad, right? Mr. Henderson? Big, important CEO and shit?"

"Sure."

"Yeah, well old Mr. Henderson tried to sweep everything under the rug, to keep it out of courts and shit, but he couldn't. It blew up that his son was in prison for rape, and he ended up losing his job."

"Fuck off, man. You're bullshittin'."

"Nope. True story. It's tough to sweep rape under the rug, ya know?"

"Actually I don't."

"Yeah, well, me neither, I suppose," Dan said as he sucked in the last few bits of marijuana smoke before tossing the roach away. "I'm headed back in. You comin'?"

"In a minute," Sean said, flicking the final bits of ash off his cigarette and tossing the filter into the night. "I'm gonna hang out here for a while."

"You're not turning gay on me or anything, are you? I mean, are you gonna be somebody's puppy or what?"

"You'd like to put me on a leash, wouldn't you?"

"Man, don't even play like that. I've already seen more of Joey than I ever care to see again. That shit will be a recurring nightmare for me for years."

"You mean a wet dream."

"Fuck off, asshole. I'll see you inside."

Dan grinned and strolled back into the lobby, refreshed from his latest blaze.

Once he was out of sight, Sean walked over to the bench next to the front doors and sat down. He gazed up at the stars, trying to spot the constellations. As he did, his thoughts quickly turned to Janice. The dots he couldn't connect in the sky were easy to connect in his brain. She had used him for his body, playing his ego and emotions against him. Then she'd left without so much as a goodbye. He hated her for that, but he also loved her for it at the same time. She'd shown him who he really was, and he'd discovered it wasn't who he wanted to be. *Maybe it isn't who she wants to be either,* he thought, and he found himself wishing he could see her again, that he could just have one more chance. "Plus, she's got a sweet ass," he muttered. He lit up another cigarette, noting the seven remaining in the pack, and he promised himself he would smoke those seven and no more.

There was a noise off to his right, and he peered around the corner to see what it was. Tim was walking toward him, holding the hand of the same girl Sean had seen at McKilligen's earlier.

"Sean!" Tim shouted when he spotted his friend on the bench.

"Tim? What's up, man?"

"Not much. Sean, this is Jenny."

"Hi," Jenny said, extending her arm.

Sean grabbed her hand and shook it. "Nice to meet you."

"Where is everybody?" Tim asked.

"In the lobby. Follow me."

TWENTY-EIGHT

1:20 a.m. – Main Stairwell, East Side

"You think I'll ever get married?" Janice asked, with her head still buried into Martin's chest.

"Yes."

"How can you be so sure?"

"Because you want to."

"So? You can't just want somebody to love you and expect it to happen."

"Who said love has anything to do with getting married?"

"Hmm. Good point. Then I guess I should ask, do you think anybody will ever love me?"

"Yes."

"And how can you be so sure about that?"

"Because I know many people already have. But that's not what you're looking for. You're looking for someone you love who will love you back the same way."

"I guess that's true," she said. "You're pretty good at reading people, Martin. So tell me, can you anticipate my next question?"

"Do I think you'll ever find anybody like that?"

Janice stayed silent, waiting for Martin's answer.

Neither had moved from their corner on the second-floor stairwell platform. Whatever the reason, the darkness mingling with the cold concrete and steel was comforting for both. It was as if they were enclosed in a shell, safe from the outside world, where no one could bother them or even see them.

"Well, how the hell do I know who you love?" he said after some time, much to Janice's disappointment.

"You suck."

"Come on! I can't answer that for you," he said with a smile that went unnoticed. "That'd be like me asking you if I'm ever gonna be able to walk through a casino with money in my pocket and not gamble it. How the hell would you know?"

"I just know."

"You do, do you?"

"Yes."

"Hmm. Well please enlighten me then, oh wise one."

"I can force you to not gamble," she said, playing with the fingers of his left hand.

"How?"

"By making you promise me right now that you won't."

"That's it?"

"That's it."

"I'm not gonna lie, Janice. Sitting with you here, in the dark, it'd be very easy for me to make that promise, but with lights and sounds and people shouting and dice rolling…" Martin trailed off, disappointed with himself for what he was saying.

"Why did you run after me?" she asked.

"What?"

"I called you a pathetic creep and ran away. Why did you run after me? Why are you here right now? I know you're not trying to fuck me, because you had that opportunity and didn't take it. Why'd you chase me?"

"Because I almost fell off the edge today," Martin said, gathering his thoughts. "I came very close, closer than I've ever been before. I know if I ever get that close again, I won't survive. For a moment, my mind left my body, and I became disoriented. Crazy would be the best way to describe it. It's easy for me now to see why I want to live. Money doesn't mean anything. When I don't have it, everything else becomes so clear. Laughing and loving is all free, but when I have money, everything becomes very expensive. The only thing I want when I have money is more money. It's all I strive for, the only thing that seems important. But it's not, Janice. It's not important. I see that now. Whether or not I'll see that later is another story entirely. Essentially, I chased you because you, like me, are at a crazy point in your life. I feel like you are very close to that same edge, too close. I chased you because maybe someday, somebody might chase me, even if I shove them away. Together, we're safe. Apart, we're dead."

"I'm not your responsibility. You hardly know me."

"I know, but I am my responsibility, and if temporarily saving you temporarily saves me, well…I guess I'm just selfish enough to do it."

Janice burrowed herself deeper into Martin's chest like a snuggling child. "So promise me you won't gamble ever again. Promise me here and now."

Martin sighed and loosened his grip on her waist.

Janice bounced off and straddled his legs. She pressed her hands into his chest and brought her face within an inch of his. "No! You promise me right now. You don't get the choice to decide who lives and who dies. You forced yourself into my life, so you're here, and you're gonna listen to me." Janice bit her lip, terrified at what she was saying. "I need you right now. I also need to know that you'll be there for me when I need you in the future. I know this is fucking crazy since we only just met, but I need you, and I think you need me too. So promise me, Martin. Promise me that you'll never gamble again. Then, if you do, if you break that promise, you'll know you're risking more than money. If you're serious about saving me, I'm serious about saving you. On your life and on mine, promise me."

Martin had no words, no response for her. She had backed his spirit into a corner and had attacked him with an ultimatum:

change, or we die. He teared up, realizing how pathetic it was that he couldn't answer right away. He thought about all the lives he'd hurt with his gambling, all the late nights and binges and worrying and lying and hiding. He recalled all the times he had to start over and then start over again and again, and in that moment, he hated himself more than ever before. "I-I don't want to disappoint you, but—"

"You'd be disappointing *you.*"

Martin eased his head back up, aligning his eyes with hers. They rested their foreheads together, and she grabbed the sides of his face. Their noses brushed as the space between their mouths grew hot, and the urge to become one was unbearable. They kissed as if their lips had locked a thousand times before. As he slid his tongue in her mouth, she gripped his hair and exhaled down his throat. Martin's cock started to become hard, and Janice could feel it grow. She pushed him away, and Martin couldn't speak fast enough.

"I promise! I promise I won't ever risk our lives again. I-I won't ever gamble."

"I'm gonna make you prove it," she said.

"I'm up for the challenge."

Janice smiled and removed herself from his lap.

Martin straightened himself out, surprised and disappointed that the moment was already over. It amazed him how infatuated he was with Janice, and he tried to hide his erect penis down the seam of his pants. "So…what do we do now?" he asked.

"Lets take a walk. I think we both need to, uh…cool off a bit," she said, glancing down playfully at his crotch.

He wrapped his arm around her lower back and held her close as they walked. She scratched his back with her nails as they strolled through the pitch-black hallways of the hotel, talking about all the places they'd love to visit.

TWENTY-NINE

1:20 a.m. – Elevator A

"We're fucked, aren't we?"

"Yes."

"How fucked?"

"Excuse me?"

"Like…going-to-get-arrested fucked or gonna-get-killed fucked?"

"Hopefully the former."

"But the second one is a possibility?"

"Always, Hector."

"Fuck!" Hector reached in his pocket and plucked out his last cigarette, then crumpled up the pack and threw it a short distance across the elevator floor. "What the hell are we gonna do?" he asked Liam.

"I don't know. I'm still trying to figure that out. I'm sure that as soon as these doors open, a SWAT team will swarm around us, shoving the barrels of their rifles in our faces. Obviously, that wouldn't be an ideal conclusion to our evening, so if you have any brilliant ideas, I'm all ears."

"You think that fag called the cops?" Hector asked.

"I don't know, but he threatened to just before you punched him in the face, and now our elevator's stuck."

"How could he have stopped the elevator?"

"Hell, I don't know, but it sure would be a weird coincidence if he didn't, right?"

"We shoulda taken the fucking stairs." Hector lit up his smoke, then tossed the match and the rest of the Hotel Reverie matchbook toward the empty cigarette pack in the corner.

Liam smiled at the first intelligent sentence that had come out of Hector's mouth all night.

The two men had dropped down to the floor, sprawling their legs out with their backs against the wall.

Hector continued to talk between puffs from his smoke. "If that fag plans to just keep us in this damn cage till the cops come, we've gotta find a way out," he said, churning away at his cigarette and ignoring the smoke that was filling up the confined space.

"I'm listening."

"Huh?"

"What?"

"You said you're listening," Hector said.

"Yes."

"Listening to what?"

"Goddamn it, you idiot. I'm listening to hear how you expect to get us out of this damn elevator."

"I don't know how. I'm just sayin' that's what needs to be done."

"No fucking shit, Captain Obvious! You sorta-Rican asshole! Do you have a plan, or are you just blabbing to waste what little oxygen you're not polluting with that damn smoke?"

"Whoa! Slow down there, *amigo*. Don't go gettin' angry with me just because I'm working toward a solution."

"You couldn't spell solution, dipshit."

Silence fell upon them as Hector puffed away at the last remnants of his cigarette. He snubbed the cherry out into a dark circle on the carpet and flicked the filter toward his trash pile in the corner. "This never woulda happened if you'd have let me be the arbitrator," he mumbled.

"What the fuck did you say?"

"I'm just sayin', ya know? If we'd have switched roles, things mighta turned out differently."

"I'm sorry, but I fail to see that."

"Remember how this whole thing started? You arbitrated with the fag when we were all alone. I was in the corner, playing point guard, which I did perfectly, but you fucked up. *You* charged the fag four and a half when it was only supposed to be four and a quarter."

"You thought it was four even!" Liam said in his own defense.

"Furthermore, you called Lorenzo, solidifying the shit we're now in. If we had merely left after you overcharged, as I suggested in the first place, we woulda been fine, but your stupid ass couldn't leave it well enough alone."

"We would not have been fine, and I guarantee you Lorenzo wouldn't have left it alone."

"Had *I* been arbitrating and undercharged the son of a bitch, we would have simply made up the difference to Lorenzo when we saw him in the city."

"No, because I thought it was four and a half, and I woulda called him after you charged the fag four."

"Why the fuck do you have to tattle to Lorenzo with every fucking detail?" Hector exclaimed, his hands flying in the air in desperation. "That's why we're in this shit."

"Because, you retarded down syndrome reject, Lorenzo leads us to our customers. He's the fucking operator! Without him, we've got nothing. No customers means no money."

"We didn't lose Lorenzo."

"We would have for not charging his clients the quoted prices, you idiot!" Liam shouted. The smoke from Hector's cigarette still lingered in the cabin, causing Liam's eyes to water, which only infuriated him more. "I thought it was four and a half, and you thought it was four even. It was four and a quarter, which means we were both wrong. You have equal blame in this, asshole."

"But you agree that if I'd have been the arbitrator, we wouldn't be sitting here, right?"

"What is your problem, man? Can't you get it through your thick skull that you're just as much to blame as I am? Hell, I'd actually go so far as to say it was your shitty muscle that landed us here."

"What? My shitty muscle?"

"Yes!"

"What the fuck are you talking about? I knocked that fag out cold."

"No. Goddamn it!" Liam took off his coat, weaseling his arms out like a contortionist to avoid having to stand up. He unbuttoned several buttons on his shirt and patted the sweat off his neck with a napkin. "Not your actual muscle, you inbred piece of shit. I'm talking about your role as the muscle. You were supposed to stand still and act tough. That was it. You were only supposed to act if shit flew off the handle, but you overreacted."

"The dude was whiling out!" Hector argued. "I would say he flew off the handle."

"I knew he was going to go ape shit! I said so in the car, and we agreed that even if he did, we wouldn't do shit."

"So I knocked the cocksucker out. Big deal."

"Yes, Hector, it was a big deal. It was a big fucking deal, one that got us stuck in this elevator. If the Feds send us to prison, it's gonna be a big deal when some fat, tattooed motherfucker tries to ram his cock up your ass, right? Then again, maybe you'd like that."

Ignoring the insult, Hector protested, "You honestly think this elevator is stuck because of that little fag?"

"You honestly think this is a total coincidence?"

Hector reached his arms around his back and removed his coat in the same fashion as Liam had. The sweat began to form on his brow, and he wiped it away with his sleeve. The smoky cabin made Hector's eyes tear up too, and the humidity began to rise. "Fuck," Hector exclaimed. "And to think, if I'd only told you to fuck off earlier, I'd be chin deep in Tracy Loretta's titties right now."

Liam shook his head in disgust. "Tracy Loretta's a professional."

"Huh?"

"I said she's a professional. You weren't working her, you idiot. She was working you. Tits cost money, my friend, and you were nothin' but a john to her. If anything, I saved you some cold, hard cash."

"Fuck you."

A sinister smile formed on Liam's face as he folded his discarded jacket behind him for back support. "You seriously think a gorgeous, big-tittied blonde living all by herself in some fancy metro apartment is waiting tables? That bitch is pulling tricks."

"Fuck you twice! You shouldn't talk shit about shit you don't know."

"Vinnie already hit that, man."

"Who?"

"Vinnie Tuscaloosa, Georgie's boy."

"No way."

"Yep, like six months ago. He said she's pimped out by some punk from the north side."

"That's bullshit."

"Why? The bitch even looks like a whore. She saunters around town in that short red cocktail dress, using those monstrous titties to get guys to pay for all of her addictions."

"Addictions?"

"Coke, vodka, shopping—pretty much your standard, typical whore."

"And you say Vinnie Tuscaloosa hit it?" Hector asked after a pondering pause.

"Straight from his mouth."

"Why didn't you say anything before?"

"Fuck, man. I'm not sure why I even bothered saying anything now."

"Yeah? Well, me neither," Hector said. "I coulda lived happily the rest of my life without ever knowing that."

The "Out of Order" light flashed, illuminating the smoke hanging in the stale, humid air. Liam's eyes had adjusted to the darkness, and they were beginning to acclimate to the smoke as well, but he couldn't seem to look away from that awful blinking light. It was tortuous, and it began to drive him crazy. He closed his eyes and looked away for a moment, but he kept seeing the red light flash through the cabin, like a red laser through the smoke. *Blink, blink, blink…*

"You all right?" Hector asked, noticing as Liam began to tilt to the side.

"What?"

"You good, man?" Hector asked again.

"Yeah. It's just so fucking hot in here."

"I know. So you think we're really fucked, huh?"

"Yup."

"Shit. We shoulda took the fucking stairs."

Liam wanted to argue with Hector some more, but he couldn't seem to find the strength. Sweat began to bead all over his body and trickled down in rivers. His legs started to cramp, so he repositioned his body opposite Hector's, turning to face the back wall, partly to stretch out his cramp but mostly to avoid having to stare at the blinking light any longer.

"I'd like to go on record saying that I don't think it was the fag who stuck us in this elevator," Hector said.

"No?"

"No. I knocked him out cold, and the elevator was stuck ten seconds later. There was no way he could have done it."

"Maybe one of the other fags did it."

"But how?"

"Maybe one of them works here." Liam tried to refute Hector, but in secret he started to believe him; things just didn't add up.

"Then why aren't the cops here by now? How long have we been here?"

"I'm not sure," Liam said, thinking about it. "Twenty minutes? Thirty?"

"They woulda been here by now."

"What do you think?"

"I think it's all a coincidence."

"So, just to be clear, you're going on record to say that even though we used this same elevator frequently before with no problems, now, after we pissed off our clients and royally fucked up the deal, the elevator just happens to get stuck?"

"Maybe God had something to do with it."

"Jesus Christ."

"Exactly."

"No," Liam said, propping his back up against the wall to better communicate with Hector. "I'm thinking God has better things to do with His time than stop a fucking elevator."

Hector paused for a minute as Liam watched the wheels turn in his head. "Maybe, but I don't think that fag did either. I gotta say it's just a coincidence."

"Record noted. Maybe you can tell Bubba your side of the story when he's makin' you dance around the cell in your damn boxers."

The smoke flowed around the cabin, twisting and swirling with every movement and breath. It wafted upward, touched the roof, and then floated back down with the grace of a feather falling from the sky. The sight of it discouraged Liam; if there was not even enough space for smoke to escape, there certainly wasn't room for him to get out of there. He patted some of the sweat off his forehead and dropped his head toward his chest to think.

"I still say we wouldn't be in this mess if you'd have let me arbitrate."

"And I still say we wouldn't be in this mess if you weren't such a fucking asshole," Liam snapped, growing weary of Hector's ranting.

"How am I the asshole?"

"You knocked the guy out, idiot."

"I don't think that matters. Besides, he shouldn't have said what he said."

"What? That you're a faggot? You are a fucking faggot, Hector."

Hector's eyes zeroed in on Liam; when Liam didn't seem to notice the nasty look, that only infuriated Hector more. "I'm sick of your shit. Take that back," he said.

"Fuck you…and that's not an offer."

Without another word, Hector leapt up and drilled his elbow into Liam's stomach, then demanded, "Take it back!"

Liam curled around, placed his hand on the back of Hector's neck, and pressed his face into the elevator door. Hector kicked out, shoving his heel into Liam's ribcage, allowing him to be momentarily free. The two men stared at each another for another five seconds, both panting and wheezing before lunging at one another with clenched fists. They each threw their arms around the other's torso, and both tried using the small amount of space to their advantage. Liam hit Hector in the jaw, and Hector in merciless rage punched Liam's eye. They were so distracted with one another that they even continued to fight when the elevator lights turned back on and the cabin began to move.

THIRTY

1:32 a.m. – Front Desk

Dan entered the lobby and walked over to Alex, who was standing off to the side, monitoring the swarm of angry guests. Several times, the crowd came close to jumping the desk and overtaking Miguel. Alex felt it was his moral obligation to at least stand watch.

"Any updates?" Dan asked.

"Not really. That bellhop from before, Noah, is helping out now."

"Doesn't seem to be doing much. Looks like the mob's out for blood," Dan said. "What's the big deal? It's just the power."

"I think most of 'em had money in play at the casino."

"Oh. Well, I guess that makes sense," Dan said. "I'd be pissed too."

"Yeah. It's a good thing that Miguel is gay, 'cause it looks like he's about to get fucked."

"Heh. Good one."

"Where's Sean?" Alex asked, only now noticing that he wasn't with Dan.

"He's outside, being weird. Where's Joey?"

"He's in the casino, doing the same."

"Great bachelor party, Alex. After this, you're never gonna want to spend another minute away from the wife again. The white picket fence will seem like a dream after all this crazy shit."

Alex laughed and nodded. "I miss her already, but hey, at least my party will be unforgettable."

"You got that right," Dan said, looking around. "Hey! Look who it is."

"Who?"

"That other waitress from the restaurant," Dan said, pointing through the dark. "Damn, she looks good."

"You should make a move."

The men watched as she snaked through the horde and sneaked behind the counter. She gave Noah a quick kiss, and then sat on a stool off to the side.

"Or not," Alex said, shrugging his shoulders and laughing. "What's Sean being weird about?"

"I don't know. He was asking me about Billy Henderson."

"Billy Henderson?"

"Yeah. What happened with him tonight? He hooked up with that other waitress, right? That Janice chick, the one who came out of the room and flashed us?"

"Yeah. Tim and I were with him in the bar, and when she showed up, they left together. Then you and me saw her in the room, and then we see him. Shit got kinda crazy after that with Joey and all, but I don't know what coulda happened to make him act so weird. He's gone through a whole damn pack of cigarettes tonight. I've never seen him smoke like that."

"I was just saying the same thing to him," Dan said.

"What did he say?"

"Nothing really, except that it's been a rough night. That Janice girl really musta messed with his mind, but it's not like Sean to be bothered by hitting it and quitting it, ya know?"

"Yeah, I know."

"Hold up. Here he comes."

Dan and Alex watched Sean walk back into the lobby, followed by Tim and a blonde woman Alex vaguely remembered from the bar.

"Look who I found outside," Sean said, walking up to Dan and Alex.

"Hey, Tim. We thought we lost you," Dan joked. "Who's your date?"

The girl smiled and interlocked her arm with Tim's.

"Guys, this is Jenny," Tim said. "Jenny, this is Dan and the bachelor, Alex."

"It's nice to meet you both. Congratulations," Jenny said.

"Thanks," Alex replied. "It's nice to meet you too, Jenny."

"So...what brings you to the Hotel Reverie?" Dan asked Jenny.

Jenny and Tim exchanged a quick look before Jenny replied, "I guess I just needed to get away, but now I think I'm ready to go back. What's going on here?"

"The power's out for some reason," Alex said.

"Oh my God. That sucks."

"I know. We're waiting for the concierge to give us a key so we can go back to our suite. Apparently, we can't get there without it."

"Oh? I've never seen a hotel suite," Jenny said, excited.

"Me neither. I haven't even been up there yet," Tim added.

"Tim, you mean to tell me you've been spending all this time with me, abandoning your friends and a hotel suite at the same time?"

"Trust me, Jenny, Tim was better off with you," Sean interjected with a smile.

Alex and Dan both nodded in a nervous agreement.

"Speaking of which, where is our little puppy?"

"He's in the casino somewhere," Alex said, pointing down the escalator.

"Gotcha. Well, I don't know about you assholes, but I could use a drink, and I do believe I have some whiskey upstairs. I say we get this show on the road." Sean walked over to the desk to join the angry mob.

"What have you guys been up to?" Tim asked Dan and Alex, smiling like an innocent child.

"Oh, nothing really," Alex said. It sounded rushed and unnatural.

"Yeah," Dan added. "Nothing at all. Just…nothing."

"Hmm. Well, that's cool I guess."

The four of them stood there, an awkward pause grew between them, not knowing if any one of them should add anything to the conversation, or at that point the lack thereof.

Jenny gave Tim a look, and he said, "Well, we'll be over there by those benches. Let me know when Sean gets the key."

"Yup."

"Will do."

Tim led Jenny to a bench on the far side of the lobby, and Dan waited until they were sitting down before speaking up. "That's Martin's Jenny."

"I know," Alex said back.

"Holy fucking shit! I wonder where Martin is."

"For all our sakes, I hope he's nowhere nearby."

"Goddamn Tim. The fucking guy never talks to girls, and tonight he talks to the one chick that left the dude we hung out with earlier. What the hell?"

"Seriously. Although I am happy for him," Alex said. "It seems like he's having a great time with her. He looks…happy."

"Oh fuck."

"What?"

"And there it is. The perfect storm of perfect storms."

"What are you talking about?"

Dan stretched his arm out and pointed his finger to the stairwell; emerging out of the doorway were Martin and Janice, hand in hand.

Alex looked over at Tim in the corner with Jenny, then over at Sean, who was attempting to flag down Miguel for the key.

"Listen, Alex, I'm way too high to figure out what we should do, but this doesn't look good from where I'm standing," Dan said.

"Nope, not at all. I think the only thing that may save us is the darkness. If nobody sees each other, we should be all right."

"Please, everyone, if I could have your attention for one second!" Miguel said, now standing on top of the front desk and projecting his voice over the restless crowd. "Please listen to me! This is a temporary blackout. The power will return, hopefully sooner rather than later. The general manager is on his way here and will be happy to take care of you folks as best as he can. If you lost money due to the blackout, please proceed to the cashiers' cage in an orderly fashion, and you will be issued a credit. If there are any other problems or concerns, please form a line, and I will be happy to assist you to the best of my ability. Again, my name is Miguel. I am the concierge on duty, and I am confident that the power will—"

As if he were flicking the switch himself, every light in the room sputtered on, flashing sporadically for the first couple of seconds, before returning to full strength and causing those in the lobby to go temporarily blind.

"See?" Miguel said, as if he'd performed some amazing magic trick. "Again, I apologize for the inconvenience. If you wish to receive a credit for your losses due to the blackout, please proceed down the escalator to the cashiers' cage in an orderly fashion."

Like a herd of wild antelope, the crowd flooded down the escalator and rushed toward the casino, emptying out of the lobby faster than water from a draining tub, leaving only Alex, Dan, Sean, Tim, Jenny, Martin, Janice, Mary, Noah, and Miguel.

"Finally," Miguel said stepping down from the desk, "back to normal."

Before anybody had a chance to recognize what was going on or who they were sharing the lobby with, the elevator doors opened, and out came the two men Alex, Sean, and Dan had seen earlier in Miguel's room. They toppled out of the elevator, throwing punches as they rolled onto the floor of the lobby, wrestling around, ripping their shirts, and splattering blood everywhere.

One man finally pinned the other down while the captive tried to wiggle his way free. "Stop, you stupid fuck!" he shouted. "Stop! We're free!"

The pinned man looked around, realizing that the man on top of him was correct. Both then jumped up and bolted out the door. They made a sharp left toward the garage, and disappeared from sight.

Everyone remaining stared as they left, distracted by the bizarre scene. Noah, however, spotted their discarded coats in the elevator and picked them up, then carried them behind the front desk as the rest of the onlookers began to turn their heads around.

"Dan! Alex!" Martin shouted in their direction, as they were the first faces he recognized when his eyes adjusted to the light.

Neither replied as they gazed in his direction, knowing that what was about to happen next was not going to be good.

Jenny turned her head. "Martin?" she said, seeing him for the first time since his casino confession.

"Martin?" Tim echoed with a soft voice, following her eyes.

Martin's head turned toward hers. "Jenny?" Martin replied.

"Jenny?" Janice asked in the same manner as Tim.

"Janice!" Sean shouted from across the room.

"Shit," Janice said, looking away.

Then, the room fell silent, like high noon at the O.K. Corral, everyone just waiting to see who would draw first. Miguel and Noah looked around in complete confusion. Mary was only a tad less confused. Sean's eyes shifted from Janice to Martin; he was curious who the man was and jealous that Janice was standing with him.

Janice held on to Martin, steering her attention away from Sean and over to Jenny, then back again. Tim passed glances from Martin to Dan and Alex, wondering how they all knew each other and what the strange rendezvous had to do with Jenny. Mary looked over at Janice before directing Noah's attention there as well, sensing something terrible. Dan and Alex surveyed the whole room, unable to move as they both waited for the inevitable, tumultuous clash.

Despite all the eye-shifting, Martin and Jenny never lost sight of each other; they stared into one another's eyes, falling into their memories and both wondering how it had gotten to this point, trapped and frozen by the love they both still felt and consumed by the guilt of what they'd done.

Martin was especially shocked and regretful all at once. Janice tugged on his arm to try to bring him back, but he was too far gone. Jenny stood up and broke away from Tim, and she and Martin, as if on cue in some awkward dance, walked toward the center of the room. They held each other while the whole world watched.

"Can we talk?" he whispered in her ear.

"Of course. We…should."

She led him outside, and they turned toward the courtyard. Janice ran away the second they disappeared, sprinting toward the back stairwell and now wishing more than anything that she and Martin hadn't walked into the lobby. Sean followed her, Mary followed him, and Noah followed her.

Tim walked up to Dan and Alex, who still hadn't moved since seeing Martin walk into the lobby with Janice. "Should I go after her?" Tim asked.

"No!" they both said in unison.

Alex added, "It's better to let them work it out, ya know?"

"But I really like the girl, and—"

"And I'm sure she really likes you," Alex said to Tim, "but you have to give her space right now. They just broke up earlier tonight, and she needs closure. Right, Dan?"

"Yeah, man. What Alex said…closure."

Tim scratched his head and looked around. "What the hell just happened here?"

"My thoughts exactly," Miguel chimed in as he joined the group.

Dan and Alex exchanged a look before shrugging their shoulders.

"I don't know," Alex said

"Me neither," Dan said. "Let's go back to room."

"Good idea. You coming with?" Alex asked Tim.

"No. I think I'll just wait down here for a minute."

"Don't let that girl drive you crazy, buddy. Chicks can do that, even when they don't mean to."

"She's not driving me crazy."

All three men smiled, making it clear that not even Miguel believed Tim.

"Well, if you're staying here, would you mind watching the desk for a minute?" Miguel asked.

"Um, I'm not exactly a concierge. What am I supposed to do if anyone shows up?"

"Just tell them I'll be right back. I have to check on my friend Fernando."

"Okay."

"See ya later, buddy," Alex said, waving back to Tim as the three men walked to the elevator.

"Yeah. See you guys."

The men entered the elevator, and Tim watched as the numbers illuminated, stopping at four before continuing on to the top floor. He sat on the bench with his legs crossed, clicking at his phone on occasion to check the time, and to keep himself from falling asleep. He let out a deep yawn and stretched to get as comfortable as he could on the hard wooden bench. His eyes closed for a second or two before several gunshots woke him up.

PART THREE

THIRTY-ONE

1:32 a.m. – Pokrovskoy, Soviet Union, Fifty Miles West of Moscow, 1969

Sergei Orlov became an orphan the day he was born. His mother died giving birth, and his father was nowhere to be seen or found. He grew up under the care of an elderly woman who his mother had known from the market, and she fostered the boy until he reached the ripe old age of eight and made the conscious decision to become a thief.

As is the case with every thief, the loot started out small, just the necessities. He would slyly grab an apple or a bag of nuts off a cart and disappear into the crowd. As he grew older, he became more confident in his craft and began swiping clothing and cigarettes. What began as a way to survive sparked a desire to take, and nothing became too sacred for his little hands to grab.

When the woman who had raised him for eight years decided she could no longer be responsible for a child who wasn't trustworthy enough to leave alone, she booted him out with the intention of sending him to an orphanage. Before the ink was dry on the paperwork, Sergei escaped. For several years, he lived as a migrant, a runaway, squatting in abandoned buildings and stealing whatever he could to survive.

When he grew skilled enough, he started swiping wallets and purses, and then used the stolen money to pay for things he couldn't steal, like shelter. By thirteen, Sergei was totally self-sufficient. Everything he needed, he stole or bought with the money he took.

One day, he was making his rounds through a nearby town when a patrolman, who was very adept at spotting young crooks, followed him with discretion. Sergei picked his mark and played his usual bait-and-switch maneuver, asking the salesman for something he knew the man would require extra assistance to get, this time a canister on the top shelf. When the man climbed the ladder, Sergei jumped over the counter, grabbed handfuls of cigarettes and bottles of vodka, and ran away before the clerk could climb down. The tactic had worked very well up until that particular day, when the discreet patrolman met him outside and knocked him clear off his feet.

Sergei was taken to a youth disciplinary center and was put to work for several years, doing menial and monotonous tasks like cleaning floors and peeling potatoes. Both degrading and painful, he had never hated his life more. At the age of eighteen, he was given the option to join the Soviet Army, and he accepted with pleasure. He was trained as a soldier and spent the next five years being deployed here and there. He was stationed primarily in Afghanistan, and that was where he met Nikolai.

Nikolai was much like him, an orphan who had taken to a life of crime before learning how to fire a gun for his country. They became good friends, and that bond lasted until the day they both died.

In 1991, the Soviet Union fell, and both Sergei and Nikolai were discharged from the military. Sergei was twenty-two at the time, and he and Nikolai used what little money they had to leave Russia and travel west, toward Europe. Both men were accustomed to not having anything, and they soon fell back into the pattern of stealing to get what they wanted. Now, though, they were much older, much smarter, military trained, and working together. The cunning duo formed scams and cons galore. Their favorite was when one would take a woman out on a date, long enough for the other to ransack her place.

They survived off of these crimes, and others pettier, until they both decided it was time for something bigger, a heist that would allow them to take a large enough amount of money that they wouldn't have to con to stay alive. After much research, they chose a small bank in the outskirts of London. Their plan was simple and militaristic. They waited until late in the day, just moments before the bank was set to close, then stormed in when the only people inside were a handful of guards and bank employees. They killed everyone with a single shot to the head; there was no screaming or pleading, for Sergei and Nikolai didn't allow time for such noises to escape the victims' mouths. They walked through the coldhearted bloodbath and, with an eerie calmness, hauled over a quarter-million British pounds out of the bank.

They spent years running from the law. Their names and faces were plastered everywhere and, after several close calls, they both decided it would be wise to leave Europe altogether. They boarded a shipping boat bound for the United States. Since they were wanted men who couldn't get passports without being arrested, they stowed away in a large container of liquor bottles. When the boat docked, they snuck away and blended in with ease in New York City. They converted all their money into U.S. dollars and lived for several more years in New York before venturing out toward the Midwest. The Big Apple was too populated for them too enjoy, and they needed to find another mark soon, because their stolen bank money was starting to dwindle.

After months of traveling, Sergei stumbled upon a small hotel and casino in the middle of nowhere. They staked the place out for another month, paying attention to the shift changes, as well as the casino's busiest and quietest times. Their research had taught them that by U.S. law, every casino had to carry enough cash in its vaults to cover every bet on the table.

Sergei and Nikolai planned for weeks before making their move. They drew out detailed floor plans of the place and even went so far as to acquire a safe similar to the one the casino used so they could practice. They conducted time trials and drills, and acted out various scenarios. Realizing the danger of robbing a place with more than just a handful of guards, they took extra precaution to diagram their plan without the intention of killing anyone. The goal was to be as discreet and stealthy as possible, without adding the risk of murder to the mix.

On the day of the robbery, they drove their Jeep into the garage and parked it next to a service door that led to the power supply for the entire hotel. They walked into the lobby, and Nikolai veered toward the bar for a drink. Meanwhile, Sergei walked up to the counter and checked them in under a fake name.

"Yes, hello. I have a room."

"Welcome to the Hotel Reverie. Your name please?"

"Andrei."

"Very good, sir. And your last name?"

"Tolstokozhev."

"I'm sorry? What was that?"

"Tolstokozhev. Andrei Tolstokozhev. I requested a smoking room."

"I see it right here, mister…it will be Room 707. Here are your two room keys, and Noah will be happy to take your bag upstairs for you."

Noah hopped off the stool, but Sergei brushed him away.

"That won't be necessary," Sergei replied. "I can carry it myself. Thank you very much."

"And thank you, sir. Enjoy your stay at the Hotel Reverie."

Sergei walked over to meet Nikolai at the bar, room keys in hand. "What are you doing?" he asked.

Nikolai was sitting with a glass of vodka in front of him, watching basketball on the television. "This basketball team, the Los Angeles Lakers…I think they are very good."

"So?" Sergei asked, turning his head to watch. "It is only basketball. Do they play hockey?"

"Perhaps. I think we should move there, to Los Angeles."

"Hmm. It would be more wise for us to leave the country."

"Perhaps, or perhaps no."

"We can decide that later. Come on. We have work to do."

In their room, Sergei placed his black duffel bag on the bed. He unzipped the sides and started unpacking the articles in a meticulous fashion, inspecting them before setting each one in its own reserved spot: two pistols, two extra-sharp switchblades, a box of latex gloves, a blowtorch, a small pack of self-contained explosives, two casino employee uniforms, a small wiring set, a lock-pick, two heavy metal clubs, and two synchronized watches.

"Are we prepared, comrade?"

"Yes, Nikolai."

"Wonderful. And how much time do we have?"

"A while longer," replied Sergei. "We must wait until the middle of the night."

"Of course."

"Let's get something to eat in the meantime."

THIRTY-TWO

12:45 a.m. – Casino Floor

Leonard wobbled when he walked, just one of the side effects of being so obese. He waddled through the alleys of the casino, moving the velvet ropes rather than ducking under them, knowing he could never contort his large body that way. He wasn't just fat; he was also big. At six-five, he towered over most other men and was rather intimidating. His dark suit jacket, tailored to meet his special dimensions, wrapped around his body in an awful attempt to help him appear slimmer than he was. The suit did, however, give the impression that he was a VIP, a man who should not be tangled with, making him the perfect casino pit boss.

Leonard made his rounds near the roulette tables, checking in on some of the wannabe high rollers and keeping an eye on anyone who was on too much of a hot streak. As pit boss, he was only concerned with winners and high rollers. "All that matters is the size of the bankroll," he often said.

At this point, it was late, and most of the tables were empty. He closed some of the outer tables to consolidate everybody toward the center, knowing that when gamblers felt alone, they'd be less inclined to continue. This brought everybody to the same space in the center of the casino floor, allowing for a more friendly, fun, and sociable atmosphere in which they could lose their money.

Leonard then walked over to a nearby computer and entered his information. Details sprouted up about everyone on the casino floor. Those who gambled at the Hotel Reverie casino used rewards cards to rack up points and comps. The casino then used that information to determine how often each individual gambled, as well as how much they won and lost. At this particular point in time, Leonard saw there were about a hundred people playing mixed table games and just over three-dozen on the slot machines. For the middle of the night, the numbers were right around average.

"How's the nightlife, Boss?"

Leonard looked over at Jimmy, a security guard who handled the transactions between the casino floor and the cashier's cage. He was holding a clipboard, with counts of all the chips he was taking back to the safe. Leonard looked over the notes as he answered, "Oh, you know, Jimmy—wild as ever."

"I hear that. Any high rollers tonight?"

"Nah, not really—just a handful of luck buckets."

"Yup. Just a head's up though. I think Mark's looking to go on break soon."

"Oh?" Leonard asked.

"Yeah. I overheard him talking about how he's been on his feet since seven," Jimmy said.

"That's strange, considering he clocked in at eight."

Jimmy laughed. "The fun never stops," he said with a smile.

Leonard initialed the report and winked at Jimmy. After Jimmy pushed the cart away, Leonard walked over to Mark, who was dealing blackjack to a couple of older Asian women. "How's tricks, Mark?" he asked.

"You know, Boss. Same old, same old."

"I hear you're lookin' to go on break."

"If I can, yeah."

"All right. Gimme a couple minutes for Sam to get back, and I'll send him over to relieve you."

"Thanks, Lenny. I appreciate it."

"No problem, buddy."

Leonard walked over to the center of the craps tables, where most of the excitement and confusion happened in the casino. People were shouting at one another to put this bet here and that one there. Dice often flew off the table, and there was always one stupid drunk who would jump over the velvet rope to get his lucky one back. Leonard pulled up a chair, reached in his pocket for a bandana, and then used it to pat the sweat away from his brow and neck. He saw Sam coming out of the bathroom and flagged him over.

"What's up, Boss?" Sam asked.

"I need you to cover Mark over at Table 32."

"Table 32?"

"Blackjack."

"Damn it. I hate blackjack."

"It'll only be for a half-hour or so, just to allow Mark to go on break."

"Damn. The guy acts like he works ten-hour days."

"Yeah, yeah, and you bitch every time I make you deal blackjack. We all got problems."

"All right, Boss. Whatever you say."

"Thanks, Sam."

As soon as Sam walked away, the table grew rowdy. The shooter was on a hot streak.

"Hard eight," said the dealer.

Everybody at the table cheered.

Chips were pushed and shoved around as the shooter scooped up the dice again, said his prayers, and cradled the plastic cubes in his hands. "No whammy, no whammy, no whammy, no whammy, no whammy, no whammy, no whammy!" He threw the dice and watched, holding his breath, as they bounced off the back of the table.

"Easy four," said the dealer.

The table cheered again

"You're watching the shooter at Table 12, right?" said the voice from the eye-in-the-sky, talking through a microphone attached to Leonard's ear.

In true 007 fashion, Leonard pressed a button on his watch and spoke directly into it. "Yup. You think there's something dirty?"

"Nope. Just a lucky son of a bitch."

"Heard that."

"No whammy, no whammy, no whammy, no whammy, no whammy, no whammy, no whammy!" The shooter lobbed the dice across the board, and it bounced off a stack of chips and ricocheted again off the other end of the table.

"Easy six."

The table cheered.

"Right around now is where I'd start betting against the shooter," said the eye-in-the-sky.

"I'd say I'd kick you out for gambling in the casino you work for, but I think the rest of this table would tear you to bits before I had the chance to do it."

"Good point, Lenny," the eye-in-the-sky said, laughing into the microphone.

Leonard leaned back in his chair and took a deep breath.

The shooter scooped up his dice and said his prayer again to the press-his-luck gods: "No whammy, no whammy, no whammy, no whammy, no whammy, no whammy, no whammy!" He threw the dice in the same manner as before, but this time with a much different outcome.

"Seven," said the dealer as his aides scooped up all the chips off the table and dragged them to the casino's side.

The crowd moaned, and some people began to walk away.

"Can I call 'em or what?"

Before Leonard had a chance to reply, everything went dark. The overhead lights shut down, the slot machines stopped beeping, and in one fell swoop the casino was blanketed in blackness. Every gambler looked around for answers, and every dealer looked at Leonard.

"What's going on up there?" Leonard asked through his watch.

"I was just about to ask you the same question. Lost power. We're totally blind up here. All the monitors shut off, but we've still got our ears on ya."

"What the hell's going on?" the dealer asked Leonard.

"Temporary power outage," he replied, hoping that was all it was.

"What should we do?"

"Don't let anybody make a bet or cash out with anything other than what they have in front of them. I'm gonna call Henry." Leonard wobbled through the crowd of gamblers, who were starting to grow restless, and over to the cashier's station.

"What's happening?" the cashiers asked.

"Lost power. I'm about to call Henry. Nobody cashes out till the power's back on."

"Um…people are going to get real angry about that real quick."

"What are you complaining about?" Leonard said. "You're in a cage."

"Good point."

Leonard stepped off to the side and flagged Mark down from his aimless walking around. "Mark, do me a favor."

"I'm on break."

"Forget your break for one minute, would ya? Can't you see there's some shit going on? I need a favor."

"What's up?"

"Go to all the dealers and tell them not to allow any bets till the lights come back on. I'd do it myself, but you move a lot faster than I do. Plus, I need to call Henry and see what he wants me to do."

"Okay, but after that—"

"Yeah, yeah. After that, you'll get your precious break."

After Mark scampered away, Leonard pulled out his phone. He started paging through his contacts when his phone lit up to alert him that Henry was calling. "Henry?"

"Leonard, Miguel called me and told me there's a power outage."

"That's right. I was just about to call you."

"Shit. How's it look?"

"The eye-in-the-sky is down, and the guests are starting to become agitated. I told all the dealers to not accept any more bets and told the cashiers not to cash anybody out till the lights are back. Any idea what's happening?"

"No not yet, but I'm on my way down now. Just hang tight till I get there. Hand out some room and meal comps and throw in some twenty-dollar slot credits too. Any high rollers?"

"No."

"Well, that's a relief."

"How long till you get here?"

"Like I said, I'm on my way. Maybe twenty minutes at the rate I'm goin'. Don't worry. You'll be the first person I see."

"If I'm still alive by then."

"Come on now. You're the biggest lug there. Plus, you're about to hand out a shit ton of comps. How angry can they get?"

Leonard scanned the room as people started to yell and scream at the dealers who were huddling behind their tables like scared dogs. "Um…just hurry." He then hung up the phone and pulled over a chair. With the help of a nearby slot machine, he propped himself up and balanced carefully, so as to not topple over.

"Folks, if I may have your attention for one moment! Folks, if you'll please just quiet down and give me your attention! My name is Leonard, and I am the pit boss for the casino. What we're experiencing is a temporary blackout. Unfortunately, there can be no more gambling at this time, until power is restored."

"I had $100 in that machine!"

"Me too!"

"I had fifty on black, and it hit after the lights went out!"

"Yeah! I had twenty on it!"

"Folks, please calm down," Leonard said, projecting his deep voice over the crowd as best as he could. "I assure you that we will refund all bets placed at the time of the blackout. Unfortunately, we have to wait until the power returns so we can check the validity of your claims with the security monitors and—"

"That's bullshit, mister!"

"I can assure you that all valid bets will be paid in full," he continued. "In the meantime, I am authorized to hand out some room, meal, and slot comps as a token of appreciation for your patience."

"The woman behind the cage said I can't cash out my chips!" a man shouted from across the room.

"We cannot cash out any chips until the power returns. It is an insurance and security issue. I apologize for the inconvenience, and I can assure you that this is only a temporary blackout."

"That's fucked up, man!"

"I'm gonna sue the ass off this place! I've got all my money tied up in your damn chips, and now I'm stuck here!"

"You can't do that! This is my money!"

Leonard tried his best to remain calm. "At this time, I'm going to start issuing the room, meal, and slot comps. Please form a line outside of the cashiers' cage, and I will be over momentarily."

He then again used the help of the nearby slot machine as he climbed down from the chair. He wobbled as fast as he could toward the cashier's station while trying to calm down the irate guests in his path. He knew that not all the gamblers were telling the truth; after all, he'd just checked the numbers prior to the blackout, but he also knew it was best to remain relaxed, poised, and professional so the guests might mimic his demeanor. If he tried to call the liars out, he knew he might spark a small mob, and that would be disastrous for everybody, especially him.

The cashiers were hiding behind the desk in their cage when he approached. He directed them to pass over a stack of room, meal, and slot comps, and he began dating and signing them as fast as his hand would move. The crowd behind him was growing bigger by the second, and he knew it would take the whole stack of comps to quiet everyone down. Before turning around to hand them out, he plucked his bandana out of his breast pocket and patted down his brow and neck. The cloth soaked up the sweat to the point where it was useless, and he tucked it back in his pocket before turning around and passing out the comps to every waving hand he could find. "Folks," he shouted, "please form a line! Everybody will get their comps, but for the time being, I need you to line up in an orderly fashion so I can hear your issues one at a time."

Several people veered toward the center to form a line, but the rest just remained where they were, irate as ever. The people who did move jumped back to their original spot when they realized the rest of the horde wasn't going to obey the pit boss's orders.

Leonard's heart raced as he passed out the comps, and the crowd did begin to shrink, albeit at a snail's pace. After about thirty minutes or so, he had finally gotten the group down to a select handful of people, whom he assumed were most likely the only ones telling the truth about their lost bets. Leonard concluded the liars disappeared as soon as they got their free meals and rooms.

"What I want to know is what this casino's gonna do for me."

"Sir, I can assure you we will do everything in our power to make your stay here as comfortable as ever."

"That's correct, sir," Henry said, barging into the conversation. "My name is Henry, and I'm the general manger for the Hotel Reverie. I can tell you there is nothing we won't do to remedy this situation to the best of our ability."

Leonard sighed with relief as Henry started addressing the small group. It gave him a minute to take a step back and breathe. He walked over to the bathroom to grab some paper towels. He again wiped the sweat from his neck and brow but left when he heard someone throwing up in the stall behind him. Normally, he would have alerted an attendant, but right now he was more than happy to just pretend he hadn't even heard the gagging and upchucking. He walked back over to Henry, who had somehow managed to whittle the crowd down to just one person.

"This is outrageous! I flew in all the way from Maine to be here! When is the power gonna be back on?" the remaining guest complained.

"Sir, we're working on it now. It should be up and running again shortly, and—"

Then, as if Henry's words were God's, commanding the darkness to dissipate, the lights returned. Machines began flashing and beeping, and a cheer rippled through the casino as gamblers rushed back to the tables. Ironically, all those who'd complained about not being able to cash out forgot about that as soon as the power returned.

Henry gave Leonard a nod and thumbs up, who then gave the sign to the rest of the staff to reopen, and in no time at all, the casino was booming, as if nothing had even happened to interrupt them. A crowd from the lobby stormed down the escalator, and Leonard shook his head.

"Relax, Lenny. I got this," Henry said, sensing Leonard's frustration.

"Thanks, Boss."

"Just do a round on the floor and make sure everybody's happy."

Leonard was walking to the tables when the eye-in-the-sky started to talk to him.

"Uh, Lenny, we're still dark up here. I mean we have power, but no eyes. All the cameras are showing static."

"Why? What's going on?"

"We're not sure exactly."

"What do you mean, you're not sure?"

"I mean we're not sure. Everything's back on except the cameras. Do you think they short-circuited or something?"

Leonard did not believe they short-circuited. He grew very anxious and paranoid at the thought of no cameras, but before telling Henry, he decided to investigate himself.

"Send down two guards. I want to check out the safe but I'm not going alone. Try rebooting the computer or something in the meantime."

"Good call. Hang tight, help is on the way."

Leonard waited by the cashier's cage until the men arrived. The three of them then walked down the hallway and into the main corridor. Leonard swiped his card and entered his PIN, allowing the vault doors to open. Documents and folders were scattered everywhere, and that was enough of a sign for the guards to draw their weapons. Leonard told the eye-in-the-sky to be alert.

The men entered the room with military-like strategy, checking behind corners and desks and using their hands to send silent commands to one another. One motioned to Leonard when he saw a pair of feet sticking out from under the safe.

Leonard wobbled over to find Jimmy lying on the floor. He pressed his hands to the guard's neck and was relieved to feel a beating pulse. "He's alive…just unconscious." Leonard then looked up at the safe. All the shelves were empty, chips were thrown everywhere, and every $10,000 stack of hundreds was missing.

"Well? What's going on down there?" the eye-in-the-sky asked. "Everything okay?"

THIRTY-THREE

1:37 a.m. – Main Stairwell, East Side

Sergei and Nikolai moved with cheetah-like swiftness through the stairwell, each toting a large burlap sack over his shoulder. Sergei pushed a door open, and they made their way into the parking garage. They jogged over to their black Jeep and loaded the bags into the back seat.

It was five dollars to park in the garage, which was enforced by an electronic gate by the exit. The gate was made of cheap wood and could easily have been broken by the Jeep, but Sergei wanted to remain as inconspicuous as possible and decided the best course of action would be to turn the electricity back on after the mission was complete and exit the garage paying the five dollars. The entire heist was in jeopardy if they peeled out of the garage, breaking the wooden gate, all in front of the eyes of unaccounted for witnesses who just happened to be standing outside. This was a risk Sergei was not willing to make.

He descended the stairs opposite the Jeep and headed toward the power supply in the sub-basement while Nikolai stood watch. Sergei twisted together the wires he'd clipped an hour or so earlier. After many weeks of studying the circuitry, he knew where all of the connections were, what every wire controlled in the large building. Considering the thick layer of dust everywhere, he assumed he knew more about the circuit board than the electrician who had designed it, and clearly, no one had fiddled with it in quite some time. He twisted together two pieces of a green-encased wire, then a red, and then a yellow—everything except the security cameras—then he flipped the main power switch up. The stairwell illuminated again, and a loud *thump* alerted him that the power was on in the rest of the building. He ran back up the stairwell and greeted Nikolai with a smile. "Success, comrade!"

"Excellent, my friend. Let's go."

The two men piled into the Jeep, Nikolai into the driver's seat and Sergei riding shotgun. "A toast!" Nikolai said as he reached into the glove compartment and pulled out a bottle of Russian vodka. "To another lifetime of loot." Nikolai took a swig, then passed the bottle over to Sergei, who followed suit.

The men smiled and embraced in an awkward fashion over the shifter, patting one another on the back as they leaned in sideways from their seat. "Alright," Sergei said, "let's rejoice elsewhere."

"Agreed." With that, Nikolai pulled the Jeep around the corner and toward the exit, only to see two men arguing with one another in the middle of the garage blocking their escape.

Whoever they were, they were screaming and fighting, shouting obscenities and accusations. Without warning, both pulled out handguns and aimed them at one another. Sergei and Nikolai watched in silence as the two strangers positioned the barrels of their guns at the other's temple, still screaming and shouting.

"What do we do?" Nikolai asked.

Sergei didn't respond. He hoped the problem would correct itself, but he knew that with every passing second that they lingered near the hotel they risked getting caught. The entire robbery had gone off without a hitch up until then, and it hadn't cost one single life, and it somewhat saddened Sergei that blood might be shed; somewhere beneath all that crime and evil, there lurked a bit of a heart, a small spark of the woman who'd mothered him. In spite of their guns and their brawn, the two men seemed like amateurs, possibly two drunks fighting over a woman, so Sergei deduced they weren't a danger of being foes or witnesses. "Scare them away," he said, when he grew tired of watching them argue. "They'll scurry like rats."

Nikolai pulled out his gun and opened the door of the Jeep. "Drop your weapons!" he shouted, his accent making the demand seem all the more menacing.

THIRTY-FOUR

1:38 a.m. – Front Desk

Hector and Liam fell out of the elevator, entangled like wrestlers. They threw punches at one another, tugging on each other's shirts and kicking with their knees.

Liam grabbed Hector by his collar and hurled him down toward the floor, then jumped on top of him and used his forearms to brace Hector's shoulders. Hector struggled, but Liam pinned him down, long enough to look around and recognize where he was. "Stop, you stupid fuck!" he shouted. "Stop! We're free!"

Hector glanced around to confirm that Liam was telling him the truth and not just trying to get in a cheap shot. Without a second thought, they both jumped up off the floor and ran out the door. They sprinted left, toward the parking garage, and headed back to their Lincoln.

"Open the damn door, man!" Hector demanded, tugging on the locked door handle. "Hurry the fuck up before SWAT gets here! Let's go!"

Liam patted his pockets in search of the keys. When he felt nothing, his mind scrambled, trying to recall where he'd last seen them. In a moment of distressing sobriety, he realized where the keys were. "Shit. I don't have the keys," he confessed.

"What!? Where the fuck are they?" Hector screamed.

"In my coat pocket, next to the money."

"What the hell?"

"In my fucking coat pocket, next to the money from the deal, the four and a quarter."

"So where's your fucking coat, man?"

"In that goddamn elevator, same as yours."

"Fuck!" Hector yelled, then pounded on the roof of the car with his fist. He began pacing like a madman, muttering to himself, then turned back to Liam and said in a cold voice, "Go get it."

"What?"

"I'm not playing, Liam. Get the fucking coat."

"Shit, I ain't going back in there alone."

Hector reached behind him for his piece. Liam, realizing what he was doing, did the same. Before either man had any time to think, they were glaring at each other, with their guns leveled at the other's forehead.

"Get the fucking coat, Liam! Get it now!"

"You took your coat off too, fucker!"

"Yeah, but mine doesn't have the keys and the goddamn money in it, shit for brains! I'm sick and tired of your shit. You overcharged that faggot in the first place. Then you called Lorenzo like the damn mama's boy you are, and then you insisted that we go back in there to—"

"Wrong! *You* wanted to go back to deliver the money, dumbass!" Liam shouted.

"Just get the fucking coats!"

"Not unless you go with me. I mean it!"

"Drop your weapons!"

The strange voice came from about fifty feet away. When the men turned to see who it was, the first thing Liam noticed was the handgun the man was holding, aimed at both of them.

"Piece!" Liam shouted.

Hector unloaded three rounds at the man, hitting him twice in the chest and once in the head.

As the large man fell to the concrete, Liam saw another man emerge from a nearby Jeep, pulling out a gun of his own. Liam aimed and fired two shots, hitting him once in the chest and once in the head.

Hector and Liam stood frozen, holding their smoking guns as the sound of gunshots echoed and faded away in the parking garage.

"I didn't tell you to fucking shoot him!" Liam shouted at Hector.

"You screamed that he had a piece, man. I turned around and saw a dude with a gun pointed at my fucking head. What the fuck did you expect me to do?"

"Oh shit. Shit, shit, shit, shit, shit! We are so fucked now."

"This is bad, isn't it?"

"Shit!" Liam repeated. "Bad isn't the word for the shit we're in."

The men jogged over to the Jeep for a quick inspection.

"Are they cops? They look like cops."

"I don't know," Liam said to Hector. "They don't look like cops to me."

"Then what the fuck were they doing here? Oh man, we're in really big trouble. What the fuck were those guys doin', man? Huh? I mean, shit, who the fuck are they, and what were they—"

"Hector…"

"We're completely fucked! We gotta run. That's it. That's what we gotta do. We gotta just bite the bullet, leave the fucking car and cash, and just fucking bolt. This shit is too fucked up."

"Hector…"

"Maybe we can hide the bodies and go get the coats."

"Hector…"

"You're right. It'd be too much work. How far is it to town? Can we make it there on foot?"

"Hector…"

"It's probably too far. Maybe I could hotwire the car while you get the coats. Somebody must have heard the shots, so we don't have long."

"Hector!"

Hector looked over to see Liam holding a stack of hundreds. His eyes traced his arm to the burlap sacks in the back seat, where piles of cash were falling out onto the floor. Hector glanced at the dead bodies, and then darted his eyes around to see if anyone was watching them.

"Fuck the coats and the car," Liam said. "These guys weren't cops. I don't know who the hell they were, but I say we take their Jeep and this cash and get the fuck outta here."

"Right. Sounds like a plan. Let's go."

Liam jumped into the driver's seat as Hector climbed in the other side. They peeled out of the parking garage, snapping the wooden gate in the process, and sped onto the highway. Hector drank from a bottle of vodka he'd found on the floor, and Liam couldn't resist taking a swig as well.

A few miles down the road, the Jeep disappeared into the darkness. Not even the moonlight could catch up to them. Not Lorenzo, nor Tracy Loretta, nor anybody else who had known of Hector or Liam ever saw them again.

THIRTY-FIVE

1:45 a.m. – Courtyard

"So…here we are."

"Right. Here we are."

In the lobby, Jenny's gaze had held Martin captive, but in the courtyard, he was too intimidated to even look at her. He felt as if he was finally paying for his crime, and there was no plea he could think of to excuse himself. "I'm not exactly sure where to begin," he admitted. "I mean, I could apologize again, but what good would that do? The truth—the real truth—is that I'm sorry I met you a year ago. I used you for security or something. I'm not even sure what. I wish I could have been a better person for you. For your sake, I wish you never would have spoken to me."

"Just stop. You're a fine person," Jenny said. Seconds later, she summoned up the courage to say, "Though you do have your flaws."

"I let you down."

"No, you let yourself down. Look, I knew you were damaged goods, but I almost found that endearing. I was naïve and thought I could fix you somehow, but I couldn't. I know it's a little too late, but I see that now."

"There's no fixing me."

"There you go again. Just stop. You're not as wounded as you like to believe you are."

Martin smiled. Jenny had always had a way with words, a way of easing even the most jarring truths into his ears.

"Ninety-nine percent of you is perfectly fine," she said. "It's just the one percent you need to work on controlling, the bad side."

"So what now?" he asked.

She folded her arms and sighed. "I think you already know. When the sun comes up, I'm going home, alone. I love you, Martin. I really, truly do. You're a beautiful man with a beautiful soul, but I can't enable or babysit you anymore. I can't be your excuse." Jenny teared up a little as the sound of those words hit her ears, ringing of a heart-wrenching finality.

"I understand."

"So what are you gonna do?" she asked, with a genuine curiosity and fear for his future.

"I'm not sure. I'll figure something out."

"Who was that girl you were with?"

"It's not what you think. I just met her, so—"

"That's not what I was asking."

"Her name's Janice," Martin said. "She's a waitress here at the hotel, in the restaurant. We've just been, uh…well, keeping each other company."

"Good."

"Good?"

"I'm beyond being jealous, and I'm glad you're not alone."

"Who was the guy?" Martin asked.

"Tim. I just met him too. He's very sweet."

"Yeah?"

"Yes. He's a bit of a geek." Jenny laughed. "But he's still very sweet."

"I'm glad you found somebody," Martin said, unable to hide the wince of pain that crossed his face when he said it.

"Don't be like that. Tim and I have only shared a conversation so far. Like Janice, he's just been keeping me company." She paused and took a breath. "Can I ask you something?"

"Anything."

"Why haven't you ever tried to go back to being an English teacher?"

Martin took a deep breath. He hadn't expected that question, and he wasn't prepared to answer it. "I don't know," he lied.

"Yes you do."

"Fine," he said. "I just…I don't like the answer, and I'm sure you won't like it either."

"If you don't wanna tell me—"

"I do. It might be too late for us, but you deserve to know the truth." Martin paused and allowed the memories to surface in his mind. He'd gone to great pains to shut them out, and it took him a moment to recall the details: the scenery, the kids, and the looks on their faces. "I used to teach in a small town called Hanksville," he began. "I taught creative writing and English to middle-schoolers, sixth through eighth grade. It was a tiny school, with just over 100 students. I taught for five years before the town decided to close the school and bus the kids up to Fairview, a much bigger town several miles north. When that happened, many of us lost our jobs. I tried to find another one, but when the next school year started, I couldn't even land a substitute gig. I tried again the following year, and I made it clear that I was willing to move anywhere for a job, but no one was hiring. When the money ran out, I ended up selling everything I owned, with the exception of a few choice books, just to earn enough to move back to Bucks County, Pennsylvania, back into my parents' house. To keep busy, I worked part time in a retail bookstore, part of a chain I'd rather not mention. I hated it. The customers were just pretentious, hipster pricks who were more interested reading corny modern books about little kid wizards and sparkling vampires playing baseball than real literature. They wouldn't have known a classic if I'd have hit them upside the head with a copy of *Moby Dick*. It depressed the living hell out of me, and I missed my students dearly. Teaching those kids gave me purpose. It meant that no matter what I did, as long as I helped one of those students, I was doing something real. Something I could be proud of. Without them, I felt like I had nothing to say when people asked me what I did. I was unemployed, a grown man living with my parents, working a part-time job for minimum wage in a place I hated, and I was desperate to find a way out of the funk I'd fallen into. At that point, the only joy I ever felt was winning, whether it be at poker or roulette or even a scratch-off now and then. Winning, whether it was five bucks or way more than that, made me feel like I was in control again, the way I'd felt when I was teaching. It felt so exhilarating to win that I soon became addicted to it, and I was unable to save any money because I just kept pouring every dollar right back into the gambling. Eventually, I just stopped trying to be who I once was. It became easier to live day to day than to focus on any long-term plan that I was sure wouldn't work out anyway. Now it seems so long ago, as if I've lived an entire lifetime already. I guess I haven't gone back to teaching because…well, I don't even know who I was back then."

"And then you met me?"

"Yes, I met you."

"Why didn't you ever talk to me about all this?"

"It's not easy to confess to anyone that your life history consists of being a monumental failure. I'm almost a middle-aged man, if I'm not already, and I'm stuck, so far gone from anything I once had, from anything I once wanted."

"Have you ever stopped to think that maybe the reason why you gamble so much is because you're trying to fill the void that was created when you had to leave your teaching job?"

"I'm sure that's true, but what good does it do to think about it? It's just salt in a wound. It's been nearly a decade since I last taught a class. I have no references and little experience, other than the time I spent teaching in a tiny classroom in a small town, in a school that doesn't even exist anymore. I can't get a job anywhere.

Trust me, I tried. My degree is worthless and outdated, but I frankly don't think it would even matter. I'm not a teacher anymore. I'm just too old for my meager accomplishments to mean anything."

"Maybe you aren't a teacher. Maybe you just need to do something with your life, something you feel good about, something that gives you a sense of accomplishment, other than the temporary one you feel at the slots and tables."

"Like what?"

Jenny sighed and shook her head in frustration. "I can't answer that for you," she said. "Like you said, you're almost a middle-aged man now. That's something you need to figure out for yourself."

"I'll try."

"Don't say that," Jenny said, pushing him away. "You'll do. Just do it…for you. You can't do it for me or for anyone else. You'll only be happy if you do it for you."

"I love you, Jenny…and I'm truly sorry for everything."

"I love you, too, Martin, but I'm not sorry for anything."

BANG! BANG! BANG! The gunshots rang out in the distance, and after a short pause, two more shots were fired.

Both Martin and Jenny jerked their heads in the direction of the noise.

"What was that?" Jenny asked, frightened.

Martin didn't reply and instead crept toward the parking garage. He peered around the corner of the building in time to see a black Jeep barrel through the wooden gate by the exit. He watched as the vehicle sped into the distance, leaving skid marks and shards of wood from the gate on the road. When Jenny tugged on his sleeve, he just shushed her and kept moving. "Stay here," he said, but when he walked toward the center of the garage, she followed close behind.

As they got closer, Jenny recognized a man about fifty feet ahead of them, hovering over something she couldn't quite make out. "Tim?" she called out.

"Jenny! Stay where you are!" he shouted back.

"What's going on?"

"Just stay where you are!"

Jenny obeyed, but Martin kept advancing. He walked over to where Tim was standing and saw two dead bodies on the ground, blood seeping from their heads and chests. "What the hell happened?" Martin asked.

"I've got no idea, man. I just heard the shots and ran out to see. I saw a Jeep pulling out in a hurry, but I couldn't get the license plate. Oh my God! I've never seen a dead guy up close like this. I think I'm gonna be sick."

Martin knelt down to examine the men. He'd never seen a corpse up close either, except those that were already embalmed and clean in a casket. The two dead men were resting in ever-growing puddles of bright red blood, forcing Martin and Tim to step back to avoid a crimson stain on their shoes.

"What's going on over there?" Jenny shouted from across the garage.

"Nothing! Just stay back!" Tim replied.

Martin glanced over at Jenny and then back to Tim.

Tim was ghostly white and couldn't look directly at the recently deceased. He looked as if he might actually cry.

"Go to her," Martin said, looking back down at the two dead men.

"What?"

"Go to her. She needs you. Go to her and take her to the lobby. Tell somebody what's going on and call 9-1-1. I'll stay here in case anyone comes."

"Are…um, are you sure?"

"Yes…and Tim…"

"Yes?"

"Take care of her."

"Uh…okay. Okay, man." Without another word and after a stern nod from Martin, Tim ran toward Jenny and led her out of the parking garage.

Martin watched out of the corner of his eye. Once they were gone, he focused his attention back on the two dead men. The blood puddles seemed to have reached their maximum size, and Martin stood just out of reach. The scene didn't disturb him at all. He found it all quite calming—the still, quiet, lifeless silence in that cold, concrete place. *How Zen,* he thought. He envisioned how his own death would have played out in the hotel room had he gone through with his post-rib-eye plans, had he not chickened out. For a brief, horrible moment, he wondered the same for Janice. As he stood there keeping the dead company, with Jenny's words about filling the void manifesting inside his head, he visualized his and Janice's faces on the two dead bodies, and believed very much that they were both better off alive.

THIRTY-SIX

1:45 a.m. – Sixth Floor, Hallway

The black cloud clung to Janice as she ran down the hallway. She could hear the footsteps hammering behind her, a stampede of shame and embarrassment. Her heart pounded, and her blood was hot. The adrenaline pumping through her veins helped to keep her ahead of whoever was pursuing her, if only for the moment.

"Janice! Janice, wait!"

"Janice, stop!"

The voices mixed together in her eardrums. All she could see was what was in front of her. She ran down the hall and shoved the stairwell door open by throwing herself into the waist-level bar. Gripping the guardrails and hurling herself around the flights of stairs, she flew down levels faster than when she fell. She popped open another door in the same manner and sprinted down the new hallway. The sounds of the black cloud were beginning to trail off, a sign she was winning the battle. She hurled herself through another door and swung around using the guardrails, this time upward, climbing two floors in under ten seconds and sprinting down another hallway.

"Janice!"

"Seriously, Janice! Please stop!"

Despite the begging voices, she kept running, sprinting as fast as she could. Away from the pity and the lectures and the constant display of someone else's happiness, from the judgmental stares and the nasty assumptions, she ran. She decided in that moment that she would run for the rest of her life if she had to, if that's what it took. She made it to another stairwell and threw herself down the landings, bumping off the walls and falling down the staircase like a gumball rolling down the spiral ramp of a six-foot-tall gumball machine, bouncing off the concrete and marking up her arms with scratches and bruises in the process. She could still hear the black cloud close behind, but knew she could escape if she could just keep up the pace.

She found the door for the fourth floor and fell through it, throwing all of her weight into the push bar. The door almost closed behind her before the sound of the stampede busting through it echoed back. She made it to her room and slid the key into the slot. Green became her favorite color when the small light illuminated, allowing her entry, and she twisted the handle and floated in with the breeze, then slammed the door shut behind her, holding it there for extra assurance.

The stampede arrived only a second later, pounding on the door with Mary's voice shouting through the wood, "Janice! Janice, let me in!"

Janice then heard Sean say, "I want to talk with her."

"Just back off, okay? I'm her best friend. Come on, Janice. Let me in."

"Janice, I love you! You've changed me!"

"Seriously, dude, back off," Mary said to Sean.

Janice lowered herself to the floor and sat with her back to the door as she listened to the argument taking place outside.

"She doesn't wanna talk to you right now. You scared her, you asshole!"

"Yeah, well, she was runnin' from you too. Obviously she doesn't wanna talk to you either," Sean snapped.

"Wow. Real mature."

"Janice, I'm not kidding. I love you!"

"Hey, buddy, maybe you should do what the lady says and back off," said another voice, the voice of an angry and protective bellhop.

"Fuck you," Sean shouted. "Don't you have some bags to unload or some shit?"

"Fuck me? No, fuck you!" Noah shouted back. "I'll show you what I can unload!"

"Noah, don't!" Mary's voice pleaded. "Janice, please open the door!"

"Janice, listen to me! You're beautiful. My God, you're just…you're great. Whatever you're running from, we can change it, baby. I can help you—"

"Help her? Leave her alone! You're a creep!" Mary screamed at Sean.

"Man, get the hell out of here, before I have to make you," Noah threatened again.

"Don't fucking touch me, kid."

"Get out of here, dude!"

"Janice, honey, you've gotta open this door," Mary said. "Please let me in; just me. I'm worried about you."

"I told you not to fucking touch me, you little monkey-suited punk!" Sean yelled.

"Get your hands off me!"

"Noah, don't!"

"Stop! Quit it, kid! I swear to God I'm gonna—"

"I told you to get the hell out of here!"

"STOP!"

Janice heard punches being thrown, followed by a loud *thump*. Grunts and squeals followed as she listened through the door and imagined the scene on the other side. When the noise stopped, Janice turned and stared at the door, waiting for it to say something else. She was sure it wouldn't be long before the voices started up again, and she was right.

"Janice, please! I'm your best friend, and you know I love you," Mary said. "Whatever's going on, you can talk to me. Everybody's gone. It's just me out here."

Janice didn't flinch.

"I know you're lonely, sweetie. I know you've been trying to find what I have with Noah."

Janice cringed at the thought.

"But you can't keep doing this. You can't keep running away. Please talk to me."

The silence that followed was thicker than the walls or the floors. Little noises and ticks amplified the quietude, echoing throughout the baron hush in a effort to remind Janice of the silence that enveloped her. She sat bathing in its awkwardness, feeling Mary growing weary on the other side.

A short time passed before Mary finally put an end to the hush. "You know something, Janice? I can't keep watching out for you like this. I've tried to be a good friend, but I guess I just don't have it in me."

Janice could hear Mary's footsteps walking away, and the nothingness that followed was colder than the awkward silence had been. In the same way she knew Mary had been there before, Janice knew she was alone now. The subtle echoes of the building were her only companions, and she began to talk to them as if they could respond. "I suppose you're getting tired of me too," she said. "Are you going to leave now?"

An air conditioner in the room above her turned on, answering her with its low, melodic *hum.*

"Fine. I can't really expect any different, can I?"

She looked at her reflection in the mirror. The woman staring back at her was hideous and frightening, a wicked witch or an old hag. Her skin was withered, dark, and bruised. Lines and bags lingered under her eyes, and her features, once pretty, had been ravaged by torment, stress, and depression. She hated the woman in the mirror.

A door closed in the hallway, and footsteps followed before they, too, faded away.

"It would make sense that you're all alone. Who would want you?" Janice said to the woman in the mirror.

Three pops sounded in the distance, outside her window. A couple of seconds later they were followed by two more. She fell on her bed and swayed from side to side, focusing on every sound: *tick…thump…hum.*

"He doesn't want you. He doesn't even know you. You don't even know him."

"What are you doing?" the haggard woman in the mirror asked.

Janice didn't know how to respond; she rocked back in forth on the bed, looking around the room for an answer. The air conditioner upstairs turned off; now she didn't even have that.

"What are you doing?" the woman asked again.

"I-I don't know."

"What are you doing?"

"I-I thought he—"

"What are you doing?"

Janice rolled off the bed and paced from wall to wall. She averted her eyes away from the woman in the mirror, too frightened to look back at her. Her body and heart felt numb, but her mind was clearer than it had ever been before. She didn't feel the need to cry. She couldn't fathom how she would ever cry again. Her knees tingled as if there were a thousand miniature firecrackers exploding beneath her skin. She paced and thought, thought and paced. Her heart hung in her chest like a dead weight of responsibility, one she'd never wanted. Getting rid of it was the only option.

"What are you doing?" the woman in the mirror asked yet again.

"I know! I know."

"What are you doing?"

"I know what I'm doing. It's okay. I promised him, but it doesn't matter, because he doesn't love me anyway. Hell, he doesn't even know me. It was just…bullshit." She said bullshit with defeat in her voice, the way a child would sound discovering that there isn't a Santa Clause.

"I promised him, but he loves somebody else." Janice walked with an eerie calmness to her bathroom and plucked the top off of her disposable razor. She carried the plastic cartridge out to the living room and placed it on the floor near the desk. She then lifted up the desk, straining her back in the process, and kicked the cartridge into the indentation in the floor from where the stubby wooden legs of the desk were. She dropped the desk, heard the cartridge crack underneath the weight of the desk, and then she continued to lift the desk up and drop it down three more times. The plastic pink shards crushed from the abuse left three small, silver blades bent but intact. She scooped them up in her hand and held one between her fingers, then rubbed her thumb along the blade and peeled a bit of her skin back to feel the pain.

"What are you doing?" the woman asked.

"I know what I'm doing! Leave me alone."

"What are you doing?"

"Shut up! I know what I'm doing!"

With the blade in her hand, she skimmed it along her wrist in a delicate, yet very deliberate, precision, like a baker applying a rim of icing to a cake, scratching the top layer of skin and shooting adrenaline through her vulnerable, endangered veins. The blade twitched in her hand. She thought about Mary and Noah, Chef Nobles, and Sean. She thought about how miserable she felt all the time and how bitchy she had to seem to everyone else. Self-loathing thoughts filled her brain as the blade trembled in her hand. She clenched it. "One quick slice," she said aloud. "One quick slice from north to south, and it'll all be over, Janice. That's all you need to do."

"What are you doing?"

Janice jerked her head upward, confused by the very male tone of voice. When she looked into the mirror again, she saw Martin staring back at her instead of the old, haggard woman she thought herself to be. Her bottom lip began to quiver. "I-I thought we had something," she said back.

"What are you doing?"

"Saving us."

Martin didn't respond, although the disappointment on his face said more than words could have.

She looked away, and then looked back. She felt as if his eyes were burning through her, as if his harsh stare might turn her to stone. Furious, she threw the blades across the room and ran toward the mirror. "Why did you leave me like that!? Why!?" she demanded of the reflection. With all the strength she had left, she punched the mirror with both fists, and the glass shattered around her. The shards fell onto her skin, cutting her hand before she dropped to the floor. Janice toppled onto the pile of broken glass and cried from the pit of her stomach. Both of her hands were bleeding from the knuckles, and the glass crunched beneath her weight. A moment earlier, she'd felt she would never cry again. Now she wasn't sure if she would ever stop, and questioned if she even wanted to.

THIRTY-SEVEN

1:45 a.m. – Room 401

Miguel opened the door to his room and was at once taken aback by the odor. It smelled of stale sex, sweat, and liquor. The pungent, miserable aroma hit his nose, and he turned away, cringing in disgust. He knew he had helped create the stench only an hour or so earlier, but it may as well have been caused by strangers. No longer driven by his primal instincts to fuck, he was now back to being a normal, clear-thinking, clean human being, the one who took such great care of the Hotel Reverie and its guests. He stood by the doorway, breathing in the last bit of purified hallway air before entering the aftermath of the smut-storm he'd created.

The mood lighting still made it very difficult to see, despite the power being back on. He saw a lump on the couch and smiled as he tiptoed around the room, cleaning up small pieces of trash and doing his best to tidy up so he wouldn't have to do it later. He opened up his lone window and stuck his nose out, thankful for the fresh desert air.

As he took a couple breaths, a loud commotion sparked up in the hallway. It sounded like Mary and Noah were yelling at Janice. Still, Miguel was more than content to just sit in his room, listening to the sounds of the tranquil night outside his window. He was exhausted. As much as Fernando and his other gay friends loved to party, he felt as if he was growing too old for it. The lifestyle had caught up to him and, more than anything, all he wanted was to meet somebody nice and settle down. "Ah, settle down," he said, quietly so he didn't wake Fernando. Just the words themselves seemed so beautiful. They sounded comfortable and secure. He loved where his life had taken him, but it was about time he shared it with someone else.

When the noise in the hall quieted, Miguel walked over to the door and looked through the peephole. Noah and Mary were walking down the hallway, away from Janice's room. Miguel smiled, glad that the drama was over. He crept over to Fernando. "Hey, sweetie. How's your eye?" He placed his hand on what he thought was Fernando's back, only to discover there was nobody there at all—only a stack of sheets and pillows.

Miguel stood up and explored the rest of the room to confirm that Fernando wasn't on the floor or hunched over the toilet. After discovering that the cocaine was gone as well, he guessed that his lover had left.

A silence engulfed Miguel as he realized that he was alone. It hung in the air and blanketed itself over him as he stood there. He wasn't waiting or thinking. He was just there, just being, tired and alone.

The grim, cold, gray feeling lasted for only about a minute before several pops rang in from outside his window. He wasn't sure what they were, but it was enough of a noise to snap him back to reality. He walked out of the room and into the hallway.

When he passed by Janice's room, he heard her scream, "Shut up! I know what I'm doing!"

He hesitated for a second, debating whether he should knock to check up on her, but decided that he'd done more than his fair share of helping people for the night. He needed to stop thinking of everybody else and start thinking of himself. *I deserve it,* he told himself. *I'm allowed to be selfish sometimes.* Nevertheless, he stood by her door for another minute. It sounded like she was having a conversation, but the only voice he could hear was hers. When Janice started to scream again, Miguel walked away, exhausted at just the thought of dealing with her and her emotional tirade. He headed back down to the lobby. Just as he stepped off the elevator, he saw his boss emerging from the casino entrance. "Hi, Henry."

"Miguel! Where have you been?"

"I was just checking up on—"

"Never mind all that! We've been robbed!"

"Robbed?"

"They cleaned us out. Somebody cut the power to rob the casino."

"Oh my God!"

"Did you see anybody suspicious today? Anybody acting weird?"

"Uh…well, there was this—"

"We need to call the police, the FBI, the CIA. Hell, call the damn President! It's outrageous that somebody could get away with this. Can you believe it, in this day and age? We've got security cameras, pit bosses. My God! Somebody's gonna pay for this. Somebody's gonna reimburse us. You can bet your ass on that!"

"What do you want me to—"

"I need you to stay on duty tonight. I know you're tired, but I need somebody at the front desk. Don't issue any comps or credits for anything; we can't afford it. And the casino is closed until further notice. You got that?"

"Okay, but—"

"No comps or credits! I don't care how shitty their night is. I guarantee ours is worse!"

"Right, so—"

"Thanks, Miguel. You're a good man. Now call the police and message me when they get here." Henry then stormed off in the direction of the casino.

Dumbfounded, Miguel looked around to see if anybody else was within earshot, but the lobby was empty, so he ended up releasing a lonely sigh and trudging back behind the desk. He pulled up a stool and rested his head on his arm. He thought about all the guests he'd seen, trying to discern if any of them seemed suspicious enough to pull off a casino robbery. The only one he could think of was the strange Russian who had checked in earlier, but then he punished himself for fantasizing about a life that interesting, and he dismissed the thought almost as soon as it came. *It was probably an inside job, somebody who works for the casino*, he thought. *It's probably not even as bad as Henry's making it out to be. I might be the queen around here, but that man's full of drama.* Miguel wasn't sure what had happened at The Reverie that night, but he was sure the real story had to be much less exciting than a terrorist or a safe-cracking, casino-robbing Russian.

Just as Miguel picked up the phone and dialed 9-1-1, Jenny ran into the lobby, holding the hand of the man she was with when the lights went on. She spotted Miguel and ran up to the desk with the man beside her. "Help, Miguel!"

"Jenny, what's wrong?"

"There are two dead men in the garage," the man said.

"What!?" Miguel asked, unsure he had heard correctly.

"There are two bodies in the garage!" he said again. "I was outside, and I heard gunshots, so I ran to the garage and—"

"Oh my God! Are you serious?"

"Yes! You have to call the police!"

Miguel held the phone in his hand as all three of them heard a voice coming out of the receiver: "You've reached 9-1-1. What is your emergency?"

THIRTY-EIGHT

2:12 a.m. – Suite 2

Sean's head was throbbing when he entered the suite. He closed the door behind him with a gentle push and walked into the center of the room. He spotted Dan sitting on the edge of the coffee table, breaking up some weed. "Damn, man. Don't you ever stop smoking?" Sean asked.

"Well, well. Look what the cat dragged in," Dan said, glancing up from the coffee table. He squinted his eyes as he focused in on the bruise around Sean's eye. "Damn! What happened to you?"

"Got into a fight."

"Shit. Looks like you lost, Rocky."

"Fuck you. Is there any ibuprofen around here? My head really hurts."

"Only medicine I've seen around here is this here weed and that whiskey you've been drinking."

Sean's head began to pound at just the thought. He sat down on the floor next to Dan and leaned back against the couch. "I'll pass."

"You sure you don't want a couple hits? This is good stuff."

"I guess that'll work. Where is everyone?"

"Alex is in there," Dan said, pointing across the suite. "He's most likely fast asleep. I think we wore him out tonight."

"Yeah, well, I'm pretty tired myself."

"We left Tim in the lobby downstairs. Joey is MIA again, but I'll be damned if I'm going looking for him this time."

"True that."

"Seriously, what happened to you?" Dan asked. "You look like somebody hit you with a Mack Truck."

Sean closed his eyes and pressed his hand against his head, hoping it might subdue the pain, but it didn't. "I don't know."

"You don't know? What the fuck, man? Did he hit you so hard you've got amnesia?"

"You're one to talk about memory lapses," Sean said, motioning toward the pile of pot on the table.

Dan laughed. "Well, at least I don't come out of it with a black eye."

"I was chasing after this girl—"

"Janice? That waitress?"

"Yeah, Janice. Some other people were chasing her, too, including that other waitress from earlier tonight."

"Why were you chasing her?"

"Because she was running away."

"Why? What'd you do to her?"

Sean thought for a minute, recalling the scene from the lobby. He remembered her displaying a look of disgust, then dashing off toward the stairwell. "I'm not sure. I don't even know if she was running from me. She was just…running."

"Okay. So she was running and…?"

"She got to her room, then locked herself inside before we could catch up. That other waitress was pounding on the door, trying to get in."

"And she wouldn't open the door?"

"Nope. While we were knocking on the door, this dude came out of nowhere, a younger guy. He started to get angry with me for some reason, telling me to get out of there. I think that other waitress is his girlfriend, and I was pissing her off because I was trying to get in to see Janice. Anyway, the stupid kid put his hands on me, so I shoved him. He got pissed and tackled me, then threw a punch. The waitress started screaming, and since it was clear Janice wasn't opening the door, I just walked away. The kid's damn lucky I did."

"Wow."

"Yeah. Wow."

"You really like this chick, huh?" Dan asked as he put the finishing touches on his perfectly rolled joint.

"I don't know, man. There's just something about her. I think I may love her."

"Love?" Dan began laughing. "You sure you haven't already been smoking my stash? You're in love. Right. Fuck off."

"I'm serious, man. She's got this fuck-the-world confidence about her. It's sexy beyond belief."

"Wow. You're just hung up on her 'cause she fucked your world, man. At dinner, you didn't give two shits about her. You were just trying to bang her, and that's a mission accomplished, right? It's not like you to be so whipped."

"I know."

"What changed?"

Sean thought back on how he'd felt when he'd come back after his post-sex smoke and found nothing but a note in his room. He reached into his pocket and pulled out his remaining cigarettes. He drew one out and sparked it up. *Love you till the sun comes up,* he thought, recalling the handwritten words that he'd been reading the moment he knew he was in love. "I don't know exactly," he answered, an absolute lie. "She basically left me. She just used me for sex and then left me."

"Hmm. Wasn't that what you were trying to do to her?"

"Yeah, but she did it with such…I don't know. Swagger, I guess."

"Swagger? Are you sure she's not just your unicorn?"

"What the hell are you talking about?"

"Your unicorn," Dan repeated. "You know, a mythical beast that's impossible to capture."

"I know what a fucking unicorn is."

"Then put two and two together, asshole," Dan said. "The reason why a unicorn is so special is because no one can capture it. If you ever caught one, you'd see it for what it really is, and you wouldn't want it anymore."

"And what is a unicorn really?"

"Just some fucking horse with a boner coming out of it's head."

Sean laughed and took a drag from his cigarette. There was an ashtray within reach on the table, but he didn't have the energy to move his arm. Rather, he flicked the butt with his finger and let the ash fall on the floor by his leg, like black snow on the carpet. "Man, you're just stoned."

"I'm serious," Dan continued. "Everyone's unicorn is different. For some people, it's a job or career that seems unattainable, like getting into the NFL or some shit. Maybe it's a lifestyle a person dreams of, or finding some rare piece for a collection, or whatever. If you ever did get that job or found that collectible, you'd realize it's not so special at all."

"A poetic pothead. Nice."

"You hear me, but you're not listening."

"No, I am. Look, I know how crazy this must sound. I guess I've just been in some strange funk all day."

"That's putting it lightly, man. I've never seen you finish a cigarette before, and now you've smoked almost the whole pack."

"Nah, there are still a couple left. My throat feels like fucking sandpaper though."

"Good. Those things are terrible for you."

"And that's not?" Sean asked, gesturing to the marijuana leaves scattered around the table.

"What, weed? Not nearly as bad as cigarettes. Plus, the advantages outweigh cigarettes."

"Is that a fact?"

"Nope, just an opinion," Dan said. "But my opinion. Which is the most important opinion of all opinions."

Sean shook his head, snubbed the cigarette out on the side of the coffee table, and flicked it toward the ashtray, missing by several feet.

"You oughtta at least put some ice on that shiner the kid gave you," Dan said. "You look like shit."

"I don't wanna get up."

"How old was the kid who clocked you?"

"I don't know. Maybe twenty-three or twenty-four."

"Shit! Since when is twenty-four a kid? I remember feeling old at twenty-four."

"It was only four years ago, dude."

"Yeah," Dan said, "but four years from now, we'll all be thirty-two."

Sean smiled and shook his head.

"Fuck," he said. "I didn't think of that."

"Face it, man. We're getting old."

"No," Sean said. "We *are* old. I mean, look at Alex. The fucking guy's getting married. Married! Shit, how long till he starts having kids?"

"Not long," Dan said. "A year, two at the most."

"That fucker's gonna be changing diapers like it's his job, sneaking out of the house just to watch a football game like my old man. I guess he's the first one of us to grow up."

Dan sparked up the joint and inhaled in a soft, almost surgical way, to churn the fire inside, creating a cherry fireball at the end. He passed it over to Sean, and then leaned back, letting the smoke billow out of his mouth and float aimlessly toward the ceiling.

"You know, if we're all growing up, you may need to cut down on this," Sean said, lifting the joint in the air.

"Fuck that. The fact that I'm growing up only makes me want to smoke more."

A short silence followed as Sean pulled the smoke into his lungs and held it there.

Dan, now pondering being an adult, added, "I do think about quitting sometimes though. I gotta admit, in the morning, when I feel energized and awake. At that moment, I'll swear I'm not gonna smoke weed ever again. But then, when bullshit starts happening, like the coffee maker starts acting up or my phone doesn't fully charge overnight, all this little shit builds up and drives me nuts. Then I'm blowing smoke just to make the drive to work a little less shitty. By the time I'm ready to come home at the end of the day, all I have to look forward to is getting high. Sure, maybe there's a game on or something, but everything's better with a joint."

Dan paused again. Sean's mind grew hazy as the weed took over. It didn't stop his headache, but it helped him forget his head hurt.

"When I was a kid, like fourteen or so, I remember getting high the first time," Dan said, bringing Sean mentally back into the room. "Some people don't get high the first time they smoke, but I sure did. I remember saying it would only be a once-in-a-while thing. But the next night, I was smoking again, and before I knew it, it was the thing I most wanted to do. Alcohol was so much harder to get when we were young, and it always makes me feel sick, but weed's great. I remember splitting bags with you dicks and only smoking a little, then wandering around town looking at everything in a new light. Pot's definitely lost a lot of that magnificence since then, but it still takes me to the same place and helps me to enjoy everything and everyone around me. Life's just different now. Instead of sneaking behind corner stores and lighting pinners with you guys, I'm ripping a lot more by myself."

"Do you like it better?"

"Not really," Dan admitted. "Truth is, I'd much rather be sneaking around with you assholes, believe it or not. But like you said, we're all adults now. Alex may be getting married, but as far as I'm concerned, he's already been married for years. Joey's obviously just as much of a wreck as he always has been. And you? Well, you're too worried about bitches, and I don't care nearly enough. We all gotta move on."

"What about Tim?" Sean asked. Dan brushed away Sean's question as if it were floating in the smoke in front of them.

"He's Alex's friend. I've got nothing in common with the guy."

"True. So what do we do?" Sean asked, passing the joint back to Dan.

"About what?"

"About life. What are we gonna do about life?"

"Fuck if I know what you're gonna do. You can keep chasin' that damn horse boner if you want, but I'm just gonna keep doing me. We can't stay young forever, so there's no use even trying. Life will carry us along our own individual paths till it decides were done. Our best years are behind us, ya know?"

"That's pretty depressing."

"Yeah, well, now you see why it's so hard to quit smoking weed."

Sean let out a little laugh. He nodded and stared off toward Alex's room. "He makes it look so easy."

Dan followed Sean's eyes until he realized he was talking about Alex.

"I don't think he makes it look easy. I think for him it is easy," he said.

"Fine, but why? Why's it so easy for him?"

Dan shook his head and tapped the ash into the ashtray. "I don't know. Maybe you should ask him."

The two men sat in silence as they finished the joint, each one diving into his own lost world. Dan contemplated his life and how much of it he'd spent being high, wondering if he had the strength to quit should he ever really decide he wanted to.

Sean couldn't stop thinking about Janice, even though he tried hard to forget. He just couldn't stop seeing her face. His mind carried him back to when his hands were on her hips and he was driving his dick into her. Then, in a sobering moment, he remembered walking back into that same room a short time later. It broke his heart to read the note she left him, and it had been a long time since he'd hurt that way. Sean was convinced Dan was wrong about her, or maybe he was wrong about unicorns in general. Janice was much more than a horse with a boner jutting out of her forehead. She was truly a one-of-a-kind, genuine unicorn.

THIRTY-NINE

4:12 a.m. – Parking Garage

"All right, sir, so let me go over this with you one more time, just so I know I got everything."

"Okay."

"You said you were over by the courtyard, having a conversation with your girlfriend, and—"

"Er, uh…she's actually my ex-girlfriend."

"You're ex-girlfriend?"

"Yes. That was what we were talking about, as a matter of fact."

"All right. So you were over by the courtyard, having a conversation with your ex-girlfriend, when both of you heard gunshots?"

As the police officer read the scene from his notepad, Martin rewound it in his mind. He drew back to his conversation with Jenny, standing next to her in the courtyard. He remembered that she had told him to find something in his life that he could feel good about again, one of the last things she'd said before they heard the shots. He thought about his teaching days and about why it was so hard to talk about it.

The two police officers didn't seem to care too much about Martin's past or his relationship with Jenny. Martin hoped they were much more interested in the two dead bodies by their feet, though overall, both officers seemed to be fairly bored.

"Yes, that's right," Martin responded.

"Do you remember any sort of pattern in which the shots were fired?"

"Pattern?"

"Yes, sir. Were they all fired at once or in succession? Was there any kind of pause or delay?"

"Uh, well, I think I remember three shots, then a pause, then two more."

"Three and then two?"

"Yep, like three bangs, then silence, then two more bangs."

The interviewing officer scribbled something down in his notes, while the beanpole-thin one walked around the scene in pointless circles, gripping the sides of his gun belt as if he were afraid it might fall down around his ankles.

"So you and your ex-girlfriend…uh, what's her name again?"

"Jenny. She's inside with Tim."

"I know that, sir. Officers are questioning them now."

Martin was growing impatient with the cop's arrogant attitude, and he didn't appreciate Jenny being interrogated as if she was a suspect. He also wondered why the cop had asked for her name if he already knew she was being questioned, but he figured it was best for everyone involved if he would just cooperate with the police and get it over with.

"So you and Jenny walked to the parking garage, and you saw a vehicle driving off?"

"Yes, a Jeep. It sped away and left those skid marks over there."

"Can you tell me anything about the Jeep? Did you get any part of the license plate, or do you know what color it was or how many people were inside it?"

"Not really. Maybe a darker color, black or brown. Like I said, it sped away. Everything happened pretty fast."

"Were you able to catch a glimpse of the driver at all?"

Martin was tired of repeating himself. He felt like making a snide remark but instead replied with a solemn, "No."

The officer briefly looked up before continuing, "After the Jeep drove away, you and…Jenny…walked over to the bodies, correct?"

"Actually, Jenny stayed up there," Martin said, pointing to the entrance of the garage. "Tim was already here, and he called up to us and told her to stay."

"But you didn't," the officer said.

"No. I walked over to Tim to see what was going on."

"And what was going on?"

Martin stared at the officer, astounded, wondering if he was serious. "Well, Officer, as you can see, there are two dead bodies lying in the parking garage. That was what was going on."

"You said this Tim was already here. Do you think he had anything to do with it?"

"No."

"And what makes you so certain?"

"Do you mean besides the Jeep that drove out of here like a bat out of hell not more than a minute after the shots were fired," Martin said with a heavy amount of sarcasm. When both officers gave him a menacing stare, he reminded himself that it was in his best interest to calm down rather than throw any more of his impatient attitude in their direction. "I don't think Tim had anything to do with it," Martin said. "I think, like me, he heard the shots fired and came out to see what was going on. When I walked up to him, he looked like he was gonna throw up and cry. He mentioned that he'd never seen a dead body before, and the blood really seemed to be freaking him out. When Jenny hollered at us, asking what was going on, I told Tim to go take her out of here, and I said I'd stay by the bodies till you guys came."

The officers exchanged a brief glance before resuming their roles of nonchalant sidekick and arrogant interrogator.

The questioning one jotted more notes, the sound of the scribbling being the only noise all three of them heard for a full minute. Martin wondered what he could have possibly been writing that would have taken that amount of time.

"Sir, is there anything else you feel you need to tell us?" The officer asked, tucking his pen into his shirt pocket. "Any suspicious individuals you might have encountered in the hotel or just anything out of the ordinary?"

If the sky had turned purple and gravity had ceased to exist, Martin would have given the same response as he did. "Nope. That's pretty much it."

"Thank you for your time," the officer said. "I have all of your information here, and we'll be in contact with you if we require any more details. You're free to go."

Free to go? Martin seethed in his mind. *You're damn right I'm free to go, you fucking moron.* He turned and walked toward the lobby. The questioning had lasted a couple of hours, and Martin was ecstatic to finally be done with it. He was tired from an all-around long night, and on top of everything else, he was no longer high, and the misery of his penniless life had begun to sink back in.

He entered the lobby and saw no one but a very tired-looking concierge behind the desk. Wanting to be alone, Martin walked to the only sanctuary he'd known for years, the casino. It was closed and dark, but he felt a sense of peace there. He sat on a chair and debated about his next move. He wanted to visit Janice, but he wasn't sure how. He didn't know her room number, and he didn't want to ask. It wasn't until that moment that he realized how long it had been since he'd seen her. They'd walked into the dark lobby together, but when the lights came back on, he had left her to walk out with Jenny. *God, what did I do?* He thought, imagining how Janice must have felt. *What if she's all alone somewhere?* He knew she was as fragile as he was, in no condition to be by herself, and he'd left her for Jenny well over an hour ago.

Martin grew anxious as a panic crept through his core. He wasn't sure if he was overreacting or if he wasn't reacting enough. It was late, and the sun would rise soon. In several hours, he would have to check out of the Hotel Reverie, and the thought of doing so without knowing what happened to Janice left him feeling sick. He stood up and began to walk around the empty tables and dead slot machines. The colorful lights and sounds that had occupied the space only hours before were now gone, replaced with soft, fluorescent lighting that blanketed the room in a quiet, somber sleep.

A small assortment of men were scattered around a television in the corner, and Martin walked over to join them. They were watching *The Price is Right,* making prop bets wherever they could.

"I'll bet you forty bucks right now that the KitchenAid mixer isn't worth more than 300 bucks," a stout man in his twenties said to another observer.

"You're on…and it looks like I just made forty bucks," the man replied, a bit older than his challenger but still younger than Martin, at least based on appearances.

"No way! It's just a hunk of metal."

Martin thought about it and concluded that the appliance had to be worth more than $300. He'd gone shopping for one with Jenny once and had been astounded by how much some of the higher-end models cost.

"Actual retail price of the Kitchen Aid Mixer is…$324.95."

"What!? You can't be serious!" the stout man said, pulling out a wad of bills and counting out forty dollars.

"I knew it! Those things are expensive as shit."

"How long have you guys been betting on this?" Martin asked.

"Ever since they closed down the casino. Why? You want in on the action?"

"No, I don't have any money," Martin replied.

As soon as they realized he had nothing to gamble away, the entire group of men turned their backs on Martin and resumed barking out their bets to the old, familiar games.

"I bet you fifty bucks that those golf clubs are over a grand."

"What types of clubs are they?"

"Calloway."

"I won't take that. They look expensive."

"Hmm. Well, I bet they're over $1,100. How about that?"

"Make it $1,200, and you've got a deal."

The two men shook hands, and Martin watched the screen, wiping his palms on his leg with the eagerness of a cat about to pounce. He didn't have any money on it or any stake in the bet whatsoever, but that didn't matter. He was certain the clubs weren't worth more than $1,200, but he had to know for sure. He kept rubbing his leg as the anticipation alone was enough to make his palms sweat.

"Actual retail price of the Calloway golf clubs is...$1,045.75."

"Son of a bitch! They must not be as good as my clubs then."

"Whatever, sucker. Pay up."

Martin again watched the exchange of money and grew excited at the action. He crammed his hands into his pockets this time to wipe off the sweat. As he pulled his hands out, he felt something fall. He looked down at the floor and was surprised to see a wad of cash sprawled out by his feet. He bent over and began picking up the bills, rewinding the night in his head to when he'd taken the money from Fernando's fist to keep the man from screaming.

The other men gazed at him as he picked the money up from the floor. They had hunger in their stare. "Look at this guy," the stout one said. "Says he's broke, and now he's flippin' through bills. You tryin' to hustle us or some shit, buddy?"

"No, it's not like that. This isn't my money. I'm just…I just have it."

"Pssh. Man, this ain't my money either," the other man said with a laugh. "I'm just hanging on to it until the casino opens up so I can give it to them."

Everybody in the group laughed except Martin. He just stared at the $250 for a moment. Then he curled it up into his palm and let the paper soak up the sweat. He crumpled it into a ball, and then fanned it out with his thumb. His vision had shrunken to only the men he was with and the television they were staring at. Trapped in the moment, he forgot about the two dead bodies in the garage, the job he didn't have, and the home and woman he could no longer go back to. In fact, he forgot everything about Jenny and what she had said to him as they held each other in the courtyard about two hours ago. He didn't remember the negative funds in his account or that he had nowhere to go after checking out at eleven a.m. Only briefly did his mind turn to Janice, sitting in the dark stairwell as he conveyed to her his long-unspoken poem. He hated her for not being with him now, without remembering why she wasn't.

"What's the next item?" somebody asked.

"Some kind of leather-bound Charles Dickens set."

Martin looked up and saw the six books on a rotating display table.

"Hey, new guy, you know anything about books?" the stout man asked. "I bet you $50 that set ain't worth more than a $125."

FORTY

9:54 a.m. – Suite 2

Sunlight filtered into the room, painting everything in a warm yellow hue. Dust particles swirled around in the air, some levitating while others danced in patterns. The sunlight brought the temperature of the room up a noticeable few degrees, showering the furniture in warmth and light.

Alex was admiring the sight until he spotted Sean asleep and halfway falling off the couch, his right eye purple and swollen. He tiptoed around, so as to not wake him, and began making coffee.

A door opened, and Dan emerged, his tousled hair pointing in every direction, his eyes droopy and low. Dan spotted Alex, gave him a half-nod, and began to stretch. His bones cracked with each turn and pivot. When all the noise of his stiff joints stopped, he made his way over to Alex in the faux kitchen. "How'd you sleep?" Dan asked, reaching for a cup of coffee.

"Great. You?"

Dan shrugged. "Fine I guess," he said. "It took all my energy last night to pull the sheets out from under the bed."

"Yeah, I know. The cleaning ladies tuck 'em in pretty tight. The coffee's terrible too, by the way."

Dan took a sip and pulled his head away in disgusted agreement. "Damn. The best suite in the hotel, and we can't get a decent cup of coffee? What a gyp."

"What happened to him?" Alex asked, pointing at Sean's black eye.

Dan looked over and saw Sean on the couch, drooping over the side with a string of drool leaking out of his mouth. His eye was puffy and bruised in several shades of purple, yellow, and black. "Well, he's in love with Janice, that waitress," Dan said.

"Really?"

"That's what he said."

"Did she give him the shiner?"

"Heh, sort of. Remember when he chased her from the lobby?" Dan asked. "When the lights went out?"

"Yeah."

"Apparently, a couple other people were chasing her, too, including that bellhop who didn't like the fact that Sean was there."

"He got in a fight?"

"Basically."

"Figures."

"That's our Sean. But anyway, what about you? Did your bachelor party live up to all your wildest dreams, man?"

Alex took a sip of noxious coffee and smiled. "Yeah. I think I'm ready to get married now."

As if on cue, the weight of Sean's body shifted, causing him to fall over the side of the couch and land with a harsh abruptness on the floor. Out of instinct, he grabbed the sides of his head and let out a long, painful moan.

Alex and Dan watched from the kitchen area, both laughing at him out of earshot.

Dan poured another cup of coffee and took it over to Sean. "Morning, buddy! How'd you sleep?" he asked, a little too cheery for Sean's liking.

Sean breathed in heavy, rhythmic breaths for a moment as he struggled to come back to reality, reacquainting himself with where he was and why he was hurting so bad. He stood up with a cautious uncertainty and took the coffee from Dan's hand.

"Damn, Sean. How'd you get that black eye?" Alex asked, as if Dan had not already filled him in.

Sean took a sip of coffee and pulled his head away from the awful taste. He set the coffee down on the table and sat back on the couch. "I don't wanna talk about it," he said, leaning his head down into his hands.

"Our good, dear friend got in a fight over a girl," Dan said, stifling a laugh.

"Get outta here, man! Over a girl? You?"

Sean shook his head and pressed his hands against his forehead, trying to contain the pain.

"It's a hell of a story," Dan continued. "Apparently, our boy here is in love, and he fought some kid for her honor."

"It didn't happen like that."

"Then what did happen?" Alex asked, smiling ear to ear.

None too happy to be the butt of their joke, Sean said, "I don't wanna talk about it."

"C'mon, man! What do you mean you don't—" Dan began to say.

"I don't want to fucking talk about it!" Sean shouted back.

"Whoa, buddy. Calm the fuck down. You don't have to talk about it," Alex said. He took a brief look around and asked, "Where are the other guys?"

Dan scanned the room and shrugged.

Sean chose not to respond at all, so Alex took it upon himself to search the rooms for Tim and Joey, neither of which he could find. "Nobody's here. We'd better look for them," he said.

"Can't we just stay here a little while longer and wait for them to come back?" Sean asked, still holding his head up with his hands.

"Checkout's in an hour, and I wanna get some breakfast. Besides, you look like you could use some Tylenol or something for that eye."

"Yeah, come on, you little bitch," Dan said. "It's his bachelor party, and if he says it's time to go, it's time to go."

Sean let out another moan and pried himself off the couch.

After they grabbed everything they'd need, at the door, Alex took another look at the suite. The couch cushions were scattered around the floor, along with empty liquor bottles and a tipped over ashtray. There was a bloodstain the size of a grapefruit on the wall near the entrance, and the entire place smelled like a combination of weed and cigarettes. He reached into his wallet and pulled out a fifty-dollar bill. He left it on the table by the door and found a random piece of paper on the floor. He took a pen from a nearby desk and wrote, "Sorry about the mess."

"What's taking so long?" Dan shouted from the hallway.

"Just leaving a tip," Alex answered. He threw the note on the table, but it fell off and floated back to the floor. As he bent over to pick it up, he noticed a note on the other side, written, in what was obvious to Alex, a girl's handwriting.

Sean,

Thank you for a great evening. I think we both needed this. I just got out of a God-awful relationship and am trying to get back on my feet. I'm sure you understand. Love you till the sun comes up…

Janice

Alex looked back over at Sean, who wasn't paying attention. He then placed the note back on the table and took another look at the room. The sun was up, casting its brilliance along every corner and seam, flooding the room with light, leaving not a single spot in darkness. It brought with it a comforting warmth, but for Sean, Alex thought, those rays had to be painful.

"Seriously, man, what's taking so long?" Sean asked, now all the way down the hall.

"Nothing!" Alex replied. He closed the door and met up with Dan and Sean by the elevator. "Let's just get the hell outta here."

"How are we going to find Tim and Joey?" Dan asked.

"I'll text them and tell them to meet us in the lobby. I hope their phones are still on and charged."

The three piled into the elevator as Alex sent the text. The elevator arrived at the lobby entrance, where only a little over eight hours earlier, pandemonium had ensued.

Tim walked up to them as soon as they stepped out of the elevator. "Hey, fellas!"

"Tim! Where were you last night, buddy?" Alex asked.

"Alex, man, I'm really sorry for missing most of your bachelor party. I was really hitting it off with Jenny, and then things sort of got crazy when those people got shot."

Alex, Dan, and Sean all looked at each other for answers.

"Wait…you guys haven't heard?"

"What the hell are you talking about?" Alex asked. "Who got shot?"

"I don't know—just some guys. I was waiting here for Jenny, like I said I would, and I heard gunshots outside. I ran toward them and found two dead guys lying on the ground in the garage in a puddle of blood."

"What!? Are you serious?" Dan asked.

"He's just fuckin' with us," Sean said, disinterested.

"I'm not! It's the truth. Jenny and Martin were there too. Martin stayed with the dead guys, and I brought Jenny back inside so we could call the police. I swear! The police have the whole section taped off now."

"Holy shit. Do they know what it was about?" Alex asked.

"I'm not sure. Maybe. After we talked to the police, Jenny took me to her room."

"Uh-oh! Tell us, man, did you throw it in her?" Dan asked.

Sean only smirked, pretending to be disinterested in Tim's possible sexual encounters when, in actuality, he was more than curious.

"Throw it in her? No, but we cuddled and talked for a while. We made plans for me to visit her next week. I'm really excited about her, man."

"That's great, Tim," Alex said, patting him on the back. "Fantastic news, buddy."

"Yeah, good job, man. Congrats," Dan added.

"Thanks, guys. Look! There's Joey."

Alex, Dan, and Sean all turned to watch Joey enter the lobby, his hand wrapped around the waste of Fernando, who was still wearing the hot pink mesh tank-top and cutoff blue jean shorts from before, but now sporting a black eye even uglier than Sean's.

"Hey, Joey! Over here!" Tim shouted.

Joey heard him and walked over with Fernando by his side. "Guys, it's so good to see you," Joey exclaimed. "All of you, this is Fernando."

"*Hola*," Fernando said, gripping Joey's side and sliding his hand over the left cheek of his ass.

"Hi. It's nice to meet you," Tim said, shaking Fernando's free hand.

Sean and Dan both looked at Alex.

Alex shrugged. "I think we already met."

"Oh my gosh! Of course you did," Joey said. "So, I guess I should just come out and say it." Joey pursed his lips, took a deep breath, and said, "I'm gay."

"Duh," said Sean. He shook his head and applied pressure to his black eye, which was still throbbing.

"You're gay?" Tim asked, the most confused.

"Yes. It took me a long time to realize, but I know it's true. I know who I am now, and I am not ashamed of it."

"That's great, Joey. I'm proud of you, man," Alex said.

Dan nodded in agreement.

"Thanks, Alex, and I promise I'll still be the best best man a groom can have. I can't thank you enough for our talk last night. You really opened my eyes."

Sean, Dan, and Tim all turned to Alex, who nodded his head and with a nervous smile said, "Don't mention it. Are you ready to head back?"

"You guys can go on without me. I'm gonna spend one more night with Fernando and head back to town tomorrow. I'll see you at the wedding!" With that, Joey and Fernando walked over to Miguel at the desk, Fernando's hand still lingering inside Joey's back left pocket.

"Wow," Alex said, breaking the short but awkward silence that followed Joey's departure.

"Indeed," Dan replied.

"I had no idea. Did any of you guys know?" Tim asked.

The other men looked at each other and shrugged. They remembered what they'd seen in Room 401, but no one thought it appropriate to talk about. They watched Joey talk to Miguel behind the desk and then slink away with Fernando, heading toward the courtyard.

"I guess that's our cue to leave," Alex said, heading toward the door.

"What about breakfast?" Dan asked

"There's a diner right before the exit onto the highway. I think there's a drugstore next to it. We can get food and some ibuprofen for Sean there."

"Yea, I wanted to ask, what happened to your eye, Sean?" asked Tim.

Sean cast Dan and Alex a glare before turning back to Tim and saying, "I got in a fight."

"Really? What happened?"

"It's a long story."

"Who were you in a fight with?" Tim asked.

"Janice."

"The waitress?"

"Janice."

"You were in a fight with Janice?"

"Janice!" Sean ran toward the front desk when he saw her there, grabbing some bags and throwing them over her shoulder.

"Uh-oh," said Dan as Sean ran away. "He's after his unicorn again."

"I'm still really confused," Tim said, scratching his head. "So Joey's gay, and Janice gave Sean a black eye?"

Dan laughed. "Something like that."

FORTY-ONE

10:23 a.m. – Fourth Floor, Hallway

Janice was in pain. The bandage on her arm was wrapped too loose but she couldn't get the knot taught enough using only one hand. Blood seeped through the gauze, and her head was throbbing from the bruise around her eye, even more so than when she had acquired it during her tumble the night before. Her legs were cramped and tired from spending the night on the floor, where she'd passed out, and her lower back ached from the heavy burden of her giant bag that was slung over her shoulder and weighing her down. She also had her purse clinging to the other side of her body, packed to the brim, making her lopsided. Behind her she dragged a small, wheeled suitcase, but one of the wheels stuck sometimes, causing it to jerk sideways at inopportune moments. Altogether, she was a mess. And she was in pain.

She pushed and pulled and carried her way through the hallway and toward the elevator. Piling everything in took some time, and she punched the elevator door as it tried to close on her prematurely. The punch caused her right hand to throb with pain, and it had been the only painless part of her body up until that moment. The door snapped back with a jerk, and then stayed open long enough to annoy Janice further, before finally closing so she could get down to the lobby.

There, Janice pulled everything out of the elevator and tripped over herself on the way. She landed on the floor, with half of her body in the elevator and the other half out. The door tried to close again, but she punched it again with her sore hand. The door jerked open, and she pulled herself up and crawled out of the way, dragging her baggage behind her. She sat on a nearby bench to catch her breath, grasping her aching fist.

After massaging her throbbing hand, she slung both bags around her body and dragged the one with the broken wheel over to Miguel who was still at his post behind the front desk. "Hey, I'm just gonna leave my stuff here for a minute, okay? I'll be right back for it," she said.

"Um, okay. You're leaving so soon? Aren't you on a fiver this week?"

"Yup," Janice said, her tone flat and emotionless. "I was originally." She walked away from the desk, still hurting but at least feeling lighter. Her bandaged arm twitched, shooting a cruel pain throughout her whole body. She held it close to her chest in an attempt to keep it from moving so much. By the time she reached Deluxe, she was using her good arm to prop up the other, just to keep it relaxed.

The front door was locked, so she sneaked through the stairwell. She paused for a moment at the spot she had marked with cigarette circles. She pondered a few bad memories, and then entered the kitchen through the back door.

Chef Nobles was already sitting in the office, looking over invoices from the previous week. He had heard the door open, but he didn't bother lifting his head to acknowledge his visitor. Instead, he just waited for them to say something first.

"No Balls," Janice blurted out.

Chef Nobles lifted his head up, glanced at Janice, and then dropped his head back toward his invoices.

Disheveled, dirty, bruised, and bleeding, she half-expected him to say something about her unkempt appearance, but wasn't surprised when he didn't. He hadn't noticed.

"Janice, how are you?"

"Pretty shitty, No Balls."

"Hmm."

"And guess what."

"What is it, Janice?"

"I quit! I quit, I quit, I quit!" Janice danced as she sang the words in a desperate attempt to live out the fantasy of this epic moment.

Chef Nobles looked up and straightened his glasses, then scanned Janice's face, as if to question her sincerity. Then he leaned back in his chair, still ignoring her awful appearance, her bleeding arm, and her black eye. "You quit?" he asked.

"That's right, you fucking arrogant shit. I quit. You'll have to find someone else to yell at, someone else to correct. Your shitty restaurant, shitty kitchen, and shitty cooks have no more control over me. I'm outta here, fucker!"

"Okay, Janice, slow down. What's wrong?"

"Nothing. For the first time since I walked into this dump, everything's right. You know, the moment after a hurricane is the best light in the world, when the sun finally shines through. You're my hurricane, and I think I'm the sun. You and your shit have passed, and now I have a chance to shine. So there it is. I quit."

"Why are you talking about hurricanes?"

"It's from a poem."

"A poem? You're quitting over a poem?" he asked, sounding more condescending than he ever had before.

"No, you idiot! The poem is to describe me or you or whatever. But that's not important."

"It clearly is if it's enough to make you want to quit."

"Forget the fucking hurricane poem! *You're* the reason I want to quit. Every time some dick at a table treated me like shit, you sided with him! Every time you told me about some shitty fucking special, I spieled it to a table perfectly, yet you yelled at me when customers complained. You are always kissing the customers' asses at your staff's expense! You're a narcissistic prick with an ego too big to fit inside this hotel. Maybe you thought you could be some big-time chef, with your own cookbook or show or some shit, but you're nothing but the head cook at some gaudy, trashy hotel, feeding gamblers your wannabe gourmet cuisine after they're too drunk and elated from their casino winnings to realize that the nasty shit on their plates comes from an even nastier piece of shit. You're a joke and an asshole, and I quit." With that, Janice turned around and walked back toward stairwell.

Chef Nobles jumped out of his chair to follow her, only to hit his knee on the desk in the process. He cursed, loud enough that Janice could hear it when she grabbed the door handle. "So that's it, huh?" he shouted in a rage. "You just quit? You've got no place to go, Janice! You've got no skills. Have you even thought about that? You're the joke, you mouthy bitch! This is your life, the best you're ever gonna do, and you can't just walk away and decide to do something else. You'll be crawling back here in two weeks, begging for your job back, but I won't even let you clean the toilets in this place! Do you hear me, Janice! You'll be begging me, and I'm just going to laugh in your face and send your uppity ass back into the streets!"

Janice stayed at the door with her hand resting on the handle. She straightened her posture, pulled her shoulders back, and puffed out her chest. She took a deep breath, then another, letting the chef's harsh words saturate her mind. With soft movements, she turned her head around to look him right in the eyes, and was pleased to find that his menacing stare brought her comfort. It always seemed like he was in control, like he had the power, because at Deluxe, he was king, but looking at him now, Janice only saw a defeated, desperate little man. It made her feel strong, big, and powerful. For the first time since the day she'd been hired, she flashed him a genuine smile, one that was for him to see but also for her to make. And with that as her weapon she held him in her gaze, eye to eye, and said in a powerful breath, "I'm counting on it."

She then twisted the door handle and disappeared into the stairwell, into the hole in the wall where she'd sat hours of her life away, smoking cigarettes, messing around on her cell phone, and hating everything—the same hole where she and Martin had shared a moment together as he'd whispered poetry meant for a woman he no longer knew, a poem Janice could now barely recite. Of all the memories of the time she'd spent in that hole, that memory of Martin would be the only one she would try to hang on to. She brushed her hand across the cigarette burns on the wall, and then walked away. Hearing the sounds of her footsteps echo back to her, she knew she would never step foot inside of that terrible stairwell ever again.

Back inside the lobby, she walked over to the desk where her bags were and tried to grab them without making much fuss.

"What's going on?" Miguel asked.

"I quit."

"You quit? Girl, why? Where will you go?"

"I don't know, Miguel. Back to town, I suppose, but beyond that, I've got no idea. I don't really care, as long as it's somewhere other than here."

Miguel's brow furrowed, and he turned away with a nervous quickness.

Janice wasn't sure why until she heard a familiar voice chime in from behind her.

"Janice? Janice! It's me, Sean."

She turned, looking for an escape, but there was none; she was trapped. "Sean," she said.

"Janice! I'm so happy I found you. I have something to tell you."

"You really don't."

"I really do."

"No, Sean. You—"

"Janice, I love you," he said, waving his arms in the air as the words came out. "And I know it's crazy, because I've only known you for a night, but goddamn it, I do! You've changed me somehow. All I could think about last night was you."

Janice noticed his swollen black eye and was about to say something about it but decided to wait until he said something about hers; there was no need to feign interest in a man who wouldn't take the time to feign interest in her. "Sean, you don't love me," she said. "You don't know anything about me. You're just…confused."

"I know you're great at sex," he replied with a smile.

And in one swoop Janice felt like a whore. She cringed and backed up, closer to her bags. "Sean—"

"What's with the bags? Are you leaving?"

"Yes. Last night was my last night…for everything. I'm done here."

"Then come with me."

"What?"

"I'm not kidding. Come with me right now. I own my own business about two hours south of here. I could hire you—"

Janice shook her head, cutting him off without even moving her lips.

"I'll take care of you," he continued. "We could grow together, maybe get married one day."

"Stop, Sean."

"I can save you, Janice. You're my unicorn. I'll take care of you."

"Your what?"

"My unicorn—beautiful, mysterious, and insatiable. I love you, Janice. I'm downright infatuated with you. You're everything I've ever wanted in a woman."

"Oh yeah? And what's that?"

"Beauty, confidence, and wit," he said after a little hesitation.

Janice smiled and shook her head. Her unnoticed black eye started to throb. "Sean, I'm not anybody's fucking unicorn."

"You're mine."

"No I'm not."

"You are to me. You're beautiful, and I want you."

"I'm not who you think I am. I'm just some girl you banged last night, and you're ego took a hit when you came back and I was gone. That's it. I'm not a fucking unicorn, okay? Honestly, that's some of the gayest shit I've ever heard a man say to me. Why are you talking about unicorns?"

"But you're beautiful and mysterious and truly magnificent and—"

"Look, I appreciate the compliments, but you're wrong. That's not me. I'm not some mythical beast out of a fairytale. If anything, I'm much closer to being an old, beat-up horse with a dildo sticking out of it."

"What?" Sean asked, deflated.

"Listen, you're a healthy, heterosexual guy, right?"

"We both know I am," he said, winking.

"Right, so naturally, you want every girl."

"I'm not sure I follow—"

She held up her hand to stop him from interrupting. "Don't feel ashamed about it. It's just who you are, part of your DNA. You want me because you can't have me, but the thing is, you've already had me, Sean. You've had me, and now you can move on to the next one."

"I want all of you, Janice."

"I won't give that to you."

"I can give you everything you've ever wanted."

"How? You don't even know what I want."

"I can take you away from here, give you a good job with nice pay, a place, a car, and a life of your own. It doesn't matter if you believe I love you. All that matters is that you're happy. We can go on vacations to places with palm trees and oceans and swim-up bars. You can go back to school if you want or learn a new skill, like basket-weaving."

"Basket-weaving?"

"I know I sound crazy. It's just that…well, I think we could start over, both of us. I know this isn't what you expected out of life, but me neither. I want to be who I was before. I want to write poetry again."

Janice turned away. Just the thought of poetry made her think of Martin, and that made her want to cry.

Sean grabbed her hands and held them in his. "We can do it, Janice, you and me. We can do anything we want. We can go skydiving, power-sailing, and bungee-jumping. We can buy a house with a fenced back yard and get a dog. We can take tango lessons and visit Broadway, maybe drink wine in a gazebo as we watch the sunset. I promise to be there for you and to love you always."

Janice's bad eye started to tear up, and she lacked the strength to stop it. She squeezed her eyes closed, but the salty tear escaped, running down the side of her cheek, past her nose, around her lips, and then dropping down to the floor by her feet.

"Leave with me, Janice, and I'll give you everything you've ever wanted."

FORTY-TWO

10:23 a.m. – Front Desk

"So then what happened?" Miguel asked.

"It's kind of embarrassing actually," Noah said, blushing a little and turning away.

"Embarrassing? Sounds juicy."

"I punched him in the face."

"What!?"

"Yep. He kept pushing me, so I threw him down and punched him in his eye."

"Oh my God! Noah, I've never known you to be a fighter."

"I'm not. It was probably the most awkward punch ever thrown, but I landed it hard."

Miguel laughed. "Oh no! Why'd you do it?"

"I just didn't like the way he was talking to Mary. I was also kind of winded from running around. Maybe there was no blood pumping to my brain."

"What did he do?"

"He just sort of left. Mary talked to Janice through the door for another minute, but when she wouldn't open the door, we left too."

"I heard her screaming from her room," Miguel said.

"Well that's good, I guess."

"It is?"

"It's better than hearing nothing at all. Mare was really worried about her."

Miguel sensed what Noah was talking about and nodded his head in agreement.

Noah moved his stool inside the coat closet and leaned against the wall, then yawned.

"Tired?" Miguel asked.

"Exhausted. I can't believe I have to deal with another six-hour shift after all that, but at least I don't have to do it with Rachel."

Miguel smiled, knowing he was Noah's favorite concierge. He hated Rachel, too, and that only made it better.

"What happened down here?" Noah asked from inside the coat closet. "Everybody's talking, but nobody seems to really know,"

"Well, let's see. Where do I begin? First, the casino was robbed."

"Robbed!?"

"Yup," he said, sounding as pleased as if her were talking about a party. "Apparently, that was what the blackout was all about, although I don't know any of the details. Henry came up to me, frantic and spewing a bunch of stuff about how we can't give away any comps or anything. That's why the casino's closed. It'll probably stay closed until the insurance kicks in."

"No shit?"

"Way shit, but that's not even the half of it."

"What's the other half?" Noah asked.

Miguel walked over to the coat closet so his voice wouldn't travel too far to any prying ears. "Two men were murdered in the parking garage last night."

"What!? Miguel, that's crazy!"

"Shh! I know!"

"How? Why? When?"

"Shortly after the lights came back on. I walked up to my room to check on Fernando. He's missing, by the way, but that's a whole other story."

"Missing?"

"Yeah. I haven't talked to him since last night. I hope he's all right."

"I'm sure he's fine, but what happened in the garage?"

"Well, after I realized Fernando wasn't upstairs, I walked down the hall to come down here. That was when I heard Janice screaming. When I got to the lobby, Henry told me about the robbery and said he needed me to stay behind the desk and not to give out any comps or credits, no matter what."

"And?"

"Do you remember that nice woman who came here in tears yesterday because her boyfriend had blown everything in the casino?"

"Jenny? Yea, I saw her with some guy in the courtyard when I proposed to Mary."

"Right! Well, she and that guy ran in here saying two men had been shot in the garage."

"That guy wasn't her boyfriend, right?" Noah asked. "The one who had lost everything?"

"No. That was somebody else. I'm pretty sure he was the one she had walked away with when all of the lights turned back on."

"Gotcha. So then what happened?"

"I called 9-1-1, and the police came. They questioned all of us. I don't know what happened after that. I hear it's all taped off down there, but I haven't been able to leave the desk since last night."

"Wow. And to think you said nothing exciting ever happens at The Reverie."

"I know! Shame on me. Uh-oh," he said, tempering the giddiness in his voice. "Look who's coming."

"Who?"

"Janice."

"Ugh. I don't wanna deal with that," Noah said, huddling behind some hanging coats, out of view. "I'm not here."

"Hey, I'm just gonna leave my stuff here for a minute, okay? I'll be right back for it," Janice said, letting her bags fall off her body and onto the floor.

"Um, okay. You're leaving so soon? Aren't you on a fiver this week?"

"Yup," she replied with an unnatural quickness before turning away and mumbling. "I was originally."

Miguel watched her leave. When she was out of sight, he whispered over to Noah, "All clear, hon'."

"Whew. What was that about?" Noah asked, still hiding behind the coats.

"I don't know, but she looks horrible. Talk about needing a makeover."

"You mean, like a train wreck?"

"You could say that."

"Finally, her looks match her personality."

"Stop! That's mean."

"Whatever. She's a crazy bitch."

"Yeah, well, she's also your fiancée's best friend, so you'd better start being friends with her too."

"As true as that is, I'd rather just hide in the coat closet for the rest of my life."

Miguel smiled and tapped away at the keyboard, checking the reservations and the empty room list for the day. His focus was broken when he looked up and saw a beautiful woman standing in front of him, wearing a familiar smile. "Jenny."

"Miguel."

"How was your stay at The Hotel Reverie?" he asked with extreme professionalism.

Jenny walked around the desk and hugged all the air out of him. "I can't thank you enough, Miguel…for everything."

"Oh, sweetie, stop! It's my job. If you want, you can pay me in information."

"Huh?"

"I heard through the grapevine that you were getting it on with some handsome fellow in the courtyard."

"The grapevine?" she asked.

Miguel nodded toward the coatroom, and Noah stuck his hand out and performed a meek wave in her direction, still partially hidden behind the coats.

She recognized him from the courtyard and blushed. "Oh! The grapevine. Yes, well, we weren't getting it on, so to speak, but he's a very nice man, and I'm sure this won't be the last I see of him."

"That's wonderful! I'm so happy you ended up having a good time."

"Thank you again for everything," she said, giving him one last hug. Then she peered into the coat closet. "And congratulations to you. She's a very lucky lady."

"Thanks. I'll tell her that!" Noah said with a laugh.

After Noah and Miguel waved goodbye, Jenny turned around and walked back toward Tim, who was standing on the other side of the lobby, waiting for her. They tapped their lips together for a brief kiss before she walked out the door and out of sight.

Tim watched her leave and stared long after she was gone.

"I'm so happy for her, for both of them. They'll be good together, don't you think?"

Noah didn't respond, because he was too busy texting away on his phone.

Miguel just shook his head, and then reached underneath the desk to grab some glass cleaner to touch up the mirror behind him. He was searching for it behind the sponges when another voice he recognized called his name.

"Hello, Miguel."

He looked up and saw Joey, only a different version of the man he'd met just the day before. This one looked cleaner, sober, and confident. "Joey!" Miguel ran around the desk to give him a hug but discovered a smaller man standing behind him.

Fernando was wearing a sinister smile on his face, telling Miguel what had happened without having to use words. "Hi, sweetie!" Fernando said with his hand down the backside of Joey's pants.

"Oh."

"Miguel, I want to thank you for opening my eyes," Joey said endearingly. "If you hadn't taken the time to, uh…well, teach me, I never would have come to accept myself for who I am. You mean the world to me."

"I see."

"I'm staying an extra day, and I hope the three of us can spend some time together."

"You know, Joey, I can do a lot more than Fernando."

"What was that, bitch?" Fernando asked.

"Please, honey. You're just a whore," Miguel said, swatting with his hand as if Fernando was just a troublesome fly that he wanted to shoo away. "Joey, baby, I'm a man. If we were together, you'd never have to worry about being alone or confused ever again. Trust me, there's plenty more I could teach you, puppy." Miguel then wrapped his arms around Joey and pulled him close, pushing Fernando away in a simultaneous action.

Joey kissed him but stopped, pulling back. "Thanks for the offer, Miguel, but now that I've discovered myself, so to speak, I'd like to date around for a while, to find out what type of men I really like. I'm sure you understand. I can't thank you enough for everything though. Call Fernando when you get off work, and we can have dinner together…or something." Joey smiled and walked with Fernando out of the lobby.

Miguel could only stare at them in shock. He turned toward Noah, who was attempting to hide his laughter but failing. "Unbelievable," Miguel said, walking back behind the desk. "What a little faggot."

"I'm sorry, man," Noah said, still laughing through his words.

"After all that work, he runs off with Fernando. Of all people, a coke-addicted, sex-craving man-whore. My God. I'll never find anybody."

"You will, Miguel. I believe there's somebody for everybody. Besides, it's not like he was that pretty or anything."

Miguel smiled, knowing how uncomfortable it was for Noah to scrutinize a man in such a way. "Thank you, Noah. And you're right. I can do better." Miguel placed himself back behind the desk in enough time to see Janice coming through the stairwell door and sprinting across the room. "Uh-oh. Here comes trouble. You better hide," he said to Noah.

Noah crammed his body back against the wall of the coatroom as Janice came stomping back for her bags.

"What's going on?" Miguel asked.

"I quit."

"You quit? Girl, why? Where will you go?"

"I don't know, Miguel. Back to town, I suppose, but beyond that, I've got no idea. I don't really care, as long as it's somewhere other than here."

Miguel saw one of the men from the bachelor group run up behind her, his left eye puffy and swollen. He thought this was probably the man Noah had punched in the face, and he moved away to give them both space, as well as to, with a sly hand gesture, warn Noah to stay put.

Noah couldn't understand Miguel's hand gestures until the man began to speak.

"Janice? Janice! It's me, Sean."

When Noah recognized the man's voice, he stuffed himself even tighter against the wall, trying hard not to be seen.

Miguel walked to the other side of the desk, until he was almost out of earshot. He didn't want to eavesdrop. He knew Noah would be able to tell him everything later. So he attempted to look busy at his computer for several minutes while they conversed.

After a short while, the man picked up Janice's bags, and she walked with him out of the lobby.

FORTY-THREE

10:39 a.m. – Casino Floor

There were thousands of books, possibly millions, stacked in giant pillars, reaching all the way up to touch the hundred-foot ceilings, everything from leather-bound volumes to travel guides. Some were organized on shelves in a precise arrangement, while others were thrown about recklessly, their pages flapping and blowing in an unnatural wind. The aisles went on for miles in every direction. Martin stumbled past the shelves, tripping over the discarded works on the floor. Random pages flew around in the air, as if they'd fallen from the sky. *Raining words.* He was looking for a certain book but couldn't find it. At least he thought he was, but he couldn't remember.

The covers began to blend together, and there was no longer any distinction between the tomes. Everything seemed fluid, as if it were changing with the wind. In one moment, the book Martin was holding was a deep sea blue, then hunter green, and then cranberry red. The words were gibberish, moving around on the page like ants on a picnic blanket. Martin tossed several books aside, flinging them over his shoulder as he searched for the perfect volume.

He turned down another aisle but was blinded by a light. He raced back to where he'd been before, but the light followed him there, and he still couldn't see a thing. He felt warm, but not in a comforting way.

Martin awoke in a stained slot machine chair on the far side of the closed casino. There was a lone window, one he hadn't noticed at night, and sunlight was beaming down on him like a spotlight from above. The rest of the casino was lit up with unnatural fluorescent light, gleaming over the empty tables and abandoned slot machines. It was a gambler's graveyard.

He steadied himself on the chair and looked around in a daze. He could hear voices, but he didn't see any faces. A television hung from the ceiling in front of him, obviously the source of the voices. Martin stood up, taking in an undesired whiff of his own body odor, then stretched out as best as he could. His pants were moist, having soaked up the sweat from his legs, and his pits reeked. He walked over to the television where the *Price Is Right* gambling had taken place, and checked the time. It was 10:39, just minutes before checkout time.

He went to the bathroom and, for whatever reason, was surprised to find himself looking back at him when he glanced in the mirror. He wasn't sure who he was expecting to see, but the reflection provided no answers. He threw some water on his face before sticking his head under the faucet for a drink. The water felt good on his skin, and he used more of it to straighten up his hair as he processed the reality around him.

"Need a towel?"

Martin shot around to find a young boy manning the attendant's station. He took the towel, a little embarrassed that he hadn't seen him standing there before. "Thanks," he muttered. Then he patted the water droplets from his neck and threw the towel in a linen basket in the corner. "Would you mind if a grabbed a mint?" Martin asked.

"Go right ahead."

Martin plucked two from a can and moved them around in his mouth. He then grabbed two more and dropped them into his pocket. "No cigarettes?" he asked, noticing that there were none on the stand.

"Sorry, sir. Fresh out," the attendant replied. "There were three packs here last night, but someone jacked them when I wasn't around."

Martin remembered when he had snatched one of those packs. He felt his pockets and pulled it out. The edges were worn, but half of the cigarettes were still there. He placed one behind his ear before tossing the pack over to the attendant. "Take mine," he said.

"You sure?"

"Yep. I don't have any money to tip you, and I don't really feel like smoking anymore anyway."

"Thanks, mister. That's nice of ya."

"No worries."

Martin walked out of the bathroom, through the casino, and into the lobby. The lobby was so bright in comparison that it took a moment for his eyes to adjust. He walked over to the front desk, where Miguel, the hotel's "incredibly gay concierge," as Janice had put it, was talking to somebody in the coat closet. They didn't notice Martin as he approached.

"So what'd she say?" Miguel asked.

"She laughed at him for calling her a unicorn," the voice from the coat closet answered, "and then he told her she should move down South with him."

"Oh my God! Is she going with him?"

"Excuse me," Martin interjected. "I have to check out."

"Oh. Sorry about that, sir. We usually just charge whatever credit card you make the reservation with and—"

"I know, but that card will be declined."

"Oh."

"I was in Room 302. The name's Martin."

"I see." Miguel tapped on the keyboard. "I can print out an itemized invoice for you if you would prefer."

"No need. Just tell me how much."

"The total is $242.95."

"After the shit I put this dick through, I think he deserves a comp," Janice said, sneaking up behind him. She was wearing a weak smile, which she tried to hide the second Martin looked at her; he, on the other hand, didn't make any attempt to hide his.

"Henry said no comps," Miguel said to Janice.

Janice slammed her hands down on the counter and berated Miguel. "You mean to tell me that of all the shitty fucking comps you douche bags hand out, you can't hand out one fucking more!?"

"Janice, I'm sorry, but—"

"That's bullshit, Miguel. It just takes a couple clicks of a button."

"It's my job!"

"It's okay," Martin said. "I have the money."

Janice and Miguel both looked dumbfounded as Martin pulled out a wad of cash from his pockets.

"Remember when you went into the hallway to talk to Mary last night?" Martin said.

"Yeah."

"Well, Fernando had sorta woken up, and he kept calling me a weird name and screaming at me to take the money and leave. Just to get him to shut up, I took it, and I forgot I had it in my pocket till early this morning. This oughtta cover the room," Martin said, then handed the $250 to Miguel.

Miguel smiled and took it, more than ecstatic to allow Fernando to pay for Martin's room.

"Won't you need that money?" Janice asked.

"Probably, but I don't care. I'm starting anew, and part of that is not creating new debts."

"Wow. What spawned that?" she asked.

"A promise I made."

"Hold on one moment, sir, and I'll get your change," Miguel said from behind the counter.

Martin didn't hear him. Instead, he touched Janice's wrist with a gentle inspection of where the bandage was falling off. He unraveled it with care and rewound it for a more secure fit. "So what made you chicken out?" he asked.

Janice let out a small laugh. "The same," she said. "A promise I made."

Martin moved her around, looking at all of her bumps and bruises, lightly brushing his thumb by each one as if that told the severity. "We're a mess," he said.

She couldn't help it anymore. It was too much work to force herself not to smile.

"Here's your change and your receipt." Miguel slid the change across the desk.

Martin shoved it into his pocket.

"Where are you going?" Janice asked. "That's not gonna get you very far."

"I don't know," he said. "How long are you going to wait for Admiral Prince Charming to sweep you off your feet?"

"I'm not. Prince Charming can fuck off. I don't need him. This damsel can rescue herself from distress."

"Glad to hear it."

There was a pause. A conversation exchanged with flashes from the eyes and the subtle movements of lips, where words would only clutter the moment. She leaned in slightly and he stepped toward her.

"So…" Martin said, putting his arm around her waist and pulling her close. "Where are you going?"

"North," she said with conviction.

"North?"

"North."

"Mind if I tag along?" he asked. "I've got eight bucks for bus fare…and a couple mints for dinner."

Janice nodded and grinned at him. "What more could a girl ask for?"

Martin held her hand and gave it a light squeeze.

"If you're going north, maybe you can use these." Noah popped out of the coat closet and rummaged through a box under the desk.

Janice thought she should have been angry learning that he was hiding back there, but she wasn't when she thought about how it might be the last time she saw the twerp.

"Some guys were fighting when the lights came on last night. They ran away, but they left these in the elevator. I haven't seen them since, so I don't think they'll be back." He pulled out two large men's coats and handed one to Martin and one to Janice.

"Wow. A men's trench coat. Just what I always wanted," Janice said, taking the coat from Noah.

"If it's not your style, I can put it back in lost and found," Noah said.

"No, seriously. Thank you."

"Yeah, no worries," he said back.

"And congratulations," she said, softer. "I know I haven't said anything to you about it, but I'm happy for you and Mary. You make her smile, and she's very lucky to have you."

"Nah," he said, shaking his head and smiling. "I'm lucky to have her. You'll be back for the wedding, won't you?"

Janice smiled as she pulled the coat over her body and threw her arms into the sleeves. It was about five sizes too big, but it covered almost every bruise and blemish. "We shall see."

"So you're really not coming back?" Miguel asked.

Janice nodded, and Miguel started to cry. "No! Miguel stop!" she said.

"I can't! I'm gonna miss you!" Miguel ran around the desk and gave Janice a hug.

Martin put on his coat and thanked Noah with a silent nod.

Janice pulled away and gave Miguel a kiss on his cheek before she and Martin walked, hand in hand, toward the door.

"What should I tell Mary?" Noah asked as they walked away.

"Tell her I'll write her…and that she hasn't heard the last of crazy old Janice!"

They walked through the front doors and outside where the sun was baking the earth with a rejuvenating warmth, and then over to a stack of bags sitting on the curb.

"All yours?" Martin joked.

"Hey, it takes a lot to look this good." Janice pulled out a pack of cigarettes and cursed when she saw that her last one was crushed.

Martin pulled the one from his ear and handed it to her. "I don't have a light though."

"Hmm. Maybe there's one in here," Janice said, rummaging through the inside and outside coat pockets. "This thing smells like a smoker wore it."

Martin decided to check his pockets too. In the first one, he found a shiny car key. "What's this?"

Janice grabbed it from him and pressed the red unlock button, causing a horn to honk and lights to flash inside the garage. She looked back at Martin. "I guess, we should probably return the key, right?" she asked.

Martin smiled. "I don't know. That kid did say these guys aren't coming back."

"And I hate the fucking bus."

"Technically, it would mean we're stealing a car."

Janice held the key in her hand and fell into Martin's chest, wrapping her arms around his torso and pulling him close. "How romantic," she said.

Martin picked up her bags, and they hustled over to the garage. Janice pressed the button over and over, until they tracked down the black Lincoln Town Car. They loaded all of her bags into the trunk before Martin took the wheel and Janice hopped in beside him.

Martin felt a bulge in one of the pockets and reached into the outer pockets to feel it.

"What is it?" she asked.

"I feel…something else." He reached into his inner pocket and pulled out a hefty wad of cash, most of it hundreds, and both of them sat staring in awe for a couple of seconds.

"Holy shit," Janice said. "Who were these guys?"

Martin motioned over to the portion of the garage that was sectioned off by yellow police tape. Detectives were taking pictures of the white outlines of the two dead bodies. "Maybe it was those poor bastards," Martin said.

Janice followed his eyes to the scene before she felt the wad of cash land in her lap.

"You hold it," he said to her.

"Why? You already promised not to gamble it."

"I still trust you with it more."

She opened the glove compartment and placed it inside, then locked it up and handed him the key. "Shall we?"

Martin started the car and drove away. In his commitment of not forming any new debts, he slid a five-dollar bill into the automatic gate by the exit and watched as the remaining stubby wooden shard angled upward. As they pulled out of the garage, Martin watched the faces of the people entering. He wondered what stories went along with those faces. He wondered where those people were going, and with whom. He wondered how happy or miserable their lives were. He then looked over at Janice.

She had her window down; the wind was blowing her hair around, and the sun was warming her skin with a gorgeous glow. Her smile stretched from ear to ear and her happiness radiated throughout the car.

Nothing compares to the sunlight that shines through after the hurricane has passed, Martin thought, and he smiled from ear to ear as well.

End

ABOUT THE AUTHOR

Jason Shprintz grew up in a household of avid readers and book enthusiasts, so it only made sense for him to take the next step and become a writer. THE REVERIE is his debut novel. He currently resides in Philadelphia where he slings drinks behind a bar and types away at his next manuscript.

Visit www.jasonshprintz.com for more information.

ACKNOWLEDGEMENTS

The exact moment when I came up with the idea for *The Reverie* can be traced down to mid January 2012. There was a contest at the restaurant where I worked on New Year's Eve. The contest was who could sell the most bottles of expensive champagne. I sold one bottle, and therefore won. The prize was a complimentary stay at a prestigious hotel in (beautiful) downtown Philadelphia.

Not having much use for a hotel room in a city I already lived in, I decided the best course of action would be to use the room as a setting for a late-night poker game. I invited friends from work and elsewhere, and had a grand ole time.

I wasn't about to let the whole day's worth of a free hotel go to waste by only utilizing it at night, so I arrived in the early afternoon and took advantage of the hotel's many amenities. I exercised at the gym, swam in the pool, sweated in the steam room, drank at the bar, and ate at the restaurant. While doing all of this, I started to recognize familiar faces I had seen earlier. I ran into the same couple twice and the same family three times. I began to daydream (as all great writers do) and soon I was thinking of what these people were doing behind closed doors. Before the poker game ever started I was mapping out ideas in my mind for a novel, which eventually turned into *The Reverie.*

At this point, Chapter One was already written. I had written it as a stand-alone short story after a terrible night of gambling. I lost $500 dollars playing craps when I didn't have $500 to lose. I felt awful and decided the only thing that would make me feel better after losing $500 was to hear a story about a guy who lost $5,000. I couldn't find that story, so I wrote it.

I decided to use this story as a jumping off point for the novel and the rest (as they say) wrote itself. There were many people who helped and inspired me along the way and I would like to take this opportunity to thank them all.

Thank you Patricia Shprintz, Bradley Shprintz, and Jennifer Shprintz for all your love and support. We're the best family ever.

Thank you everybody who worked with me at Union Trust Steakhouse but specifically Ian Pratt-Young, Frank Terranova, Marcel Fisher, and Kristen Stang.

Thank you everybody who worked with me at Tiffin Bistro but specifically Roman Chepenko, Maria Colasanti, Shaun Cerborino, Kelsey Dale, Anthony Reznick, Grace Mitchell- Dimicco, Cassandra Norman, Jade Wilson, Lindsey Cleckner, Angelica Borda, and Brad Lang.

Thank you everybody in Peter's writing group but specifically Peter Ott, Kyle Albasi, and Tim Flood.

Thank you everybody who read the earlier drafts and offered insight and edits but specifically Stephanie Funk, Autumn Conley, Sarah Birl, Samantha Gordon, Emily Vartanian, Priya Madhok, and Andrew (tiny) Shattuck.

Thank you to Dominic Davi for designing the best cover ever, and a second thank you to Emily Vartanian for designing the best logo ever.

Thank you to the fantastic online community of writers and editors but specifically David Gaughran, Joel Friedlander, Stephanie Funk (again), Nathan Bransford, and all those who actively post on Bransford Forums and Kboards.

Thank you to my close friends for their support but specifically Ian Pratt-Young (again), Frank Terranova (again), Andrew Shattuck (again), Dennis Angeline, Emily Vartanian (a third time) and Mike Elnick.

Most importantly, thank you for reading my debut novel. I hope you enjoyed it.

-Jason Shprintz May 5, 2014

www.ingramcontent.com/pod-product-compliance
Lightning Source LLC
LaVergne TN
LVHW010640110826
845149LV00014B/2908

* 9 7 8 0 9 9 0 3 8 0 3 1 3 *